RUTHLESS

ALSO BY CHRISTINE BESZE

Destined Trinity

REVENGE SERIES

Revenge

Redemption

RUTHLESS

REVENGE
BOOK THREE

CHRISTINE BESZE

Love N. Books Press
An Imprint of Wolfpack Publishing
1707 E. Diana Street
Tampa, FL 33610

www.lovenbookspress.com

Cover design by Rachel Chaya Design
Edited by My Brother's Editor

Ruthless was originally self-published in 2022 by Christine Besze.

Paperback ISBN 979-8-89567-649-3
Ebook ISBN 979-8-89567-648-6
LCCN 2026931375

This book is for you, the reader. Thank you for falling in love with this family and these characters like I have.

AUTHOR'S NOTE/TRIGGER WARNINGS

First, I'd like to thank you for reading Zane's story. This book was an emotional roller coaster for me. I had to step outside of my comfort zone and write about some difficult topics. From the beginning of the series, I knew he would be the character that would challenge me the most, and he didn't disappoint. Having said that, please read these trigger warnings and decide if this is a journey that you would like to go on.

There is subject matter contained within this book that is both graphic and could be triggering to anyone who has dealt with sexual assault of any kind. There is also graphic violence. So, please bear that in mind before you begin reading this book. With that being said, happy reading, and I hope you enjoy the conclusion of the Savage family.

PLAYLIST

1. Don't Fear the Reaper by The Spiritual Machines
2. Monsters by brother Sundance featuring Ella Boh
3. Salt And The Sea by The Lumineers
4. I Can't Go on Without You by KALEO
5. The Sound of Silence by Disturbed
6. Someone You Loved by Lewis Capaldi
7. Far From Home (The Raven) by Sam Tinnez
8. Under Your Scars by Godsmack
9. Break In by Halestorm
10. With Or Without You by 2 Cellos
11. The Wish by Madohm
12. Undead by Hollywood Undead
13. Highway of Heroes by The Trews (The Epilogue)
14. Listen To Your Heart by Through Fire
15. I Don't Care Anymore by HELLYEAH
16. Numb (Acoustic) by The Veer Union
17. Dead Man Walking by Jelly Roll
18. Scars by James Bay
19. Into The Fire by Asking Alexandria
20. Control by Zoe Wees
21. Everybody Wants To Rule The World by Lorde
22. Zombie (Acoustic) by Bad Wolves
23. Wrong Side of Heaven (Acoustic) by Five Finger Death Punch

"Out of suffering have emerged the strongest souls; the most massive characters are seared with scars."

— KAHLIL GIBRAN

RUTHLESS

PROLOGUE
KENNEDY

From the time we leave the club to the time we make it to my tiny apartment is all one big blur. Since the second we stumbled into each other outside of the bathroom at Orphic, my body's been riding a high of anticipation.

We barely make it to my door with our clothes still on. That all changes the moment we step inside. He slams the door shut behind him and has me thrown up against the nearest wall before I can blink.

His mouth swallows my gasp as he wraps my legs around his waist. The spikes of my heels dig into his ass as he presses his body into mine, letting me feel all of him. Every single inch of him is firm, but it's the hardness of his massive dick digging into my center that has me humming out a low moan. His tongue takes advantage of my open mouth, slipping inside and tangling with mine. The kiss is hard and demanding as he takes control.

Fingers dance along the side of my hips, up my rib cage, squeezing my breast through my dress. His thumb moves in small circles until my nipple hardens. I am so glad I opted to go without a bra tonight. Every touch is magnified against the silk material. He gives my nipple another firm pinch before moving on and does the same thing to my other one.

I let out another moan that resonates deep in my throat, and I grind my core deeper into his. The friction of our two bodies rubbing together through the thin material of our clothes is hitting my sweet spot and causing the throbbing between my thighs to intensify. He's not even out of his clothes yet, but I can feel every mouthwatering inch of him against me. This mystery man is much bigger than anyone I've ever been with before, and the thought of having all of that inside me is equally terrifying and exciting all at the same time.

I ache to see all of him.

My hands clench the sides of his shirt, ripping it open, sending buttons flying everywhere, and peeling it off his shoulders. I throw it on my floor behind us but never break eye contact. "I've always wanted to do that." A small laugh leaves me, but it's quickly silenced by the image before me.

Tattoos decorate a rock-hard wall of muscle, making my mouth water at the sight. The silver barbells on both of his nipples only add to the temptation before me. I want to trace every single image with my tongue to see if this stranger tastes as good as he looks.

His lips twitch as he rains kisses down the side of my face. "What else do you want to do?" he whispers in the shell of my ear. The fine hairs of his beard tickle the sensitive flesh as his lips move. The deep rumble of his voice sends a wave of liquid heat through me that I feel down to my toes.

I hum in pleasure as I grab his head and force him to look me in the eye. "I want to be bad. I'm so tired of being good."

The Jameson is coursing through my veins, making me braver than I usually am. Liquid courage is the only explanation for my sudden lack of filter. I might regret this in the morning, but I'm living in the moment right now. Living for me. Not my family. Nor the heavy weight our name carries. Just me and this moment of pleasure with this hot-as-fuck stranger.

Intense blue eyes burn into mine as he opens his mouth to say something, but his mouth crashes back against my lips before I can ask what. He breaks away from the wall, and my legs tighten around his waist to keep from falling as he walks us down the darkened hallway of my apartment.

He breaks our kiss just long enough to ask, "Which way is your room?"

"First door on the left."

Our heavy breathing fills the room as his mouth dives back down on mine, but his steps never falter. The muscles of his arms flex with the firm grip he keeps on me. His tongue plays mine like a symphony as he continues to move us. I barely register the flash of light when he hits the switch. It isn't until I feel the softness of my mattress hit my back and his hard body comes down on top of mine that I come up for air. All thoughts of sanity leave me as I get lost in him and his fuckable body.

My fingernails scratch along the muscles of his abdomen and back up his chest, causing him to suck in a deep breath and shudder against me.

"Harder," he growls.

Knowing he likes this, I continue tracing over his body hard enough to leave a small indent of my nails behind, but not hard enough to draw blood. After a while, his skin becomes red and irritated, so I pull away. The last thing I want to do is hurt him, but he grabs my hands and places them back on his chest.

"Hurt me." He applies more pressure to my nails and drags them down his chest until I feel the wetness of his blood coat my fingers. A hiss escapes him while his body trembles, but he never stops. "Yes. Just like that."

Blood trails down his chest, but the tiny flicker of pain behind his eyes has me losing my breath. My hands jerk against his to pull back, but in a flash, everything changes. Gone is the torment I saw on his face moments ago, and in its place is something much deeper, much darker than that—hunger. Liquid heat pools between my legs the longer those deep blue eyes penetrate mine.

Then desire takes over, and he's moving on me in seconds. His hand slides up my thigh, hooking into the side of my underwear. With one quick tug, he's ripped the scrap of satin off me and tossed it aside. Two fingers slip inside me, hitting so deep that my toes curl against my shoes.

"You're so fucking wet." His breathing comes out in short, erratic pants, much like my own, but his fingers never stop working me. "Are you ready for me, Hummingbird?"

"Hummingbird?"

"You're tiny as fuck and hum every time I touch you." His lips brush against the side of my neck with each word as the short hairs of his beard tickle along my oversensitized skin.

My teeth dig into my bottom lip, fighting the smile that wants to break free. I've always hated how small I am compared to my brothers. It's almost like I've never quite measured up to the rest of them because of my size, but I feel the opposite in this man's hands—like something to be treasured, even if it's just for tonight.

With a shaky hand, I pull a condom out from inside the bodice of my dress and dangle it between two fingers in front of him. "Here." I may be feeling reckless, but I haven't completely lost my mind.

He takes it and tears open the packet with his teeth before undoing his pants and putting it on. My eyes widen when I get my first look at all of him. What I felt through his clothes is nothing compared to the pierced monster he was hiding underneath.

He glances up and must see the look on my face because he cups my cheek and whispers, "I'll go slow. I promise I won't break you." The soft tone in his voice has me nodding my head while I swallow the lump in my throat.

The heat of our bodies causes the temperature in the room to go up and fog over the lens of my glasses. Without a word, he slides them down my nose and places them on my nightstand before grabbing my ankles and digging the tips of my heels into him.

"I can't see much without those, you know." My fingers slide through the mess of hair on top of his head, but he grabs my wrists before I can dig them in and pins my hands above by the side of my head.

"You don't need to see, Hummingbird. All you need to do is hold on to me and enjoy the ride." His teeth dig into the sensitive place where my shoulder meets my neck so hard I'm sure I'll have a mark to cover up later.

He slowly eases inside of me, inch by agonizing inch, until he's all the way inside of me. A sharp breath escapes him as he braces on his elbows and stares down at me, watching my face for clues.

"Holy shit." A blissful mixture of pleasure and pain fills my body as I let out a small gasp and become accustomed to his size.

He stills and watches me. "Did I hurt you?"

"No, it's fine. Just give me a minute." I suck in a few breaths until the muscles in my body relax against him. Once I'm sure I can take more, my hips move, encouraging him without words to keep going.

His grunts fill the room as he slides out and back inside me several more times. "You feel so fucking good." He presses into me so hard the headboard rattles against the wall. With each thrust, I'm pressed deeper into the mattress.

An ache forms deep within my belly as he hits my sweet spot. I dig the heels of my shoes deeper into the cheeks of his ass, causing a throaty groan to escape him. The pain sets him off, and he thrusts into me faster and faster until I can barely breathe.

He takes control with every thrust of his hips, owning my body from the inside out. It isn't long before my thighs tremble, and I come apart in his hands.

He lets out a deep grunt as I squeeze down on him. "Oh fuck." A few more deep-seated thrusts have him following me over the edge seconds later.

We stay there like that until our heartbeats slow back to normal, but he isn't through with me yet. Still, inside me, he hardens once more, and we lose ourselves in each other a few more times during the night.

The following day, I wake up to an empty bed, but the scent of tobacco and sandalwood lingers on my sheets. A pleasant ache between my thighs has a smile spreading across my face as thoughts of last night replay in my head.

It was quick and dirty. There were no niceties. No names. No strings attached. We lived under the veil of anonymity for the night, just the way I wanted it. Too bad some secrets don't stay hidden as they should.

1

ZANE

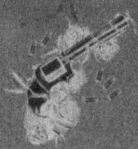

The cold metal of the silver band bites into my finger as I twist it around in circles with my thumb—a reminder of what I've just done, what we've just done. It feels as foreign against my skin as I have felt in it these past twenty-four hours. The heaviness in my gut hasn't settled since we boarded the plane. Things will be fucked the second we land in Atlanta, but as I glance at the tiny brunette to my right, I know it's all fucking worth it. The only thing that might be saving me from my new father-in-law stringing me up by my nuts and gutting me is that I managed to make sure we were married by a Catholic priest.

I can't say this is how I thought my weekend would go, but that all changed the second Connor punched me in the face, and I showed up at her place to find her in tears.

"Ken!"

My fist pounds on her apartment door as blood still drips down my lip onto my beard, but adrenaline courses through me, and I don't feel shit. Connor's lucky I deserved the hit, or else I would have knocked him the fuck out, but getting out of there and finding her was more important. I left Axel to deal with her brothers and their bullshit since he likes to run his mouth. It'll be a fucking miracle if he doesn't create more of a shit show for me to deal with later.

A few seconds pass, and I'm greeted with silence. It only fuels the fire burning in my chest because I know damn well she's in there. Her Honda Accord is in the parking lot, and it's cold, meaning she hasn't been anywhere in quite some time. I slam my fist against the door, hard enough to rattle its hinges.

"Open this fucking door, right now!" I'm trying to keep my shit together, but I can't breathe until I see her for myself.

Muffled footsteps echo from the other side of the door seconds before it cracks open, revealing the petite brunette who's turned my world upside down. Her watery blue eyes are red and puffy as they meet mine through the foggy lenses of her glasses. It hits me like a punch in the gut seeing her like this, but I need to hear it from her, not her brothers.

I step inside as she steps back away from the door, allowing me entry. My feet don't stop until I reach the far wall across the front door, which doesn't take me long. The apartment is small and warm, like her. I lean back against the wall and watch her close the door. She twists the lock into place and turns to face me but makes no move to come closer.

Silence hangs between us like a dead weight as I stroke the end of my beard and continue staring back at her, but I make no move to break it just yet. I need a breather before I say something that'll have me putting my foot in my mouth. Instead, I take her in. Her dark hair is thrown up in a messy knot much like my own, but it's her lack of clothing that has all the blood leaving my body and heading south. Wearing short shorts and a tight camisole has her looking like a gift ready to be unwrapped, but it's the points of her nipples poking through the thin fabric that have my dick aching against my jeans.

I cross my arms over my chest and continue playing with the tip of my beard to keep from slamming her up against that door and fucking her senseless. It's been weeks since I've been inside of her or heard her hum out my name like it was the answer to her prayers—something I've been thinking about nonstop ever since. We only had one night, but it has been running on a constant loop in my mind. It's easy to get lost in those blue eyes and forget all the shit of my past.

I shake out of my thoughts, shifting my focus back on why I'm here. "Is it true?"

Her gaze fixates on my bloody nose, and her mouth drops open. She shakes her head as her tiny nose wrinkles, causing her glasses to slide farther down her nose. "Which one of my idiot brothers did that?"

"It doesn't matter." Nothing else matters but hearing the truth from her lips alone. "Is. It. True?" I can't contain the demand in my tone.

She shoves off the door and moves closer into the room until she's near her kitchenette. She leans her hip against the counter, crossing her arms over her chest, mimicking my stance. Her blue eyes were burning into mine from behind her glasses the entire time. She's stalling, but little does she know I can wait her out all night if I have to. Years of training have taught me that patience brings the prey to you.

"What do you care?"

"Answer the question, Kennedy."

I expected her hostility. She's been pissed off at me ever since she walked into her father's office and found my brothers and me inside discussing business. The hurt etched on her face is something that still haunts me. I've been waiting for the right time to approach her now that Axel's shit is handled. I just never thought it would be under these circumstances.

"Yes, it's true. I'm pregnant." *She hangs her head and stares down at the floor like it holds the answers to the universe as her purple-painted toes stab at an imaginary speck of dust on the tile floor.*

Everything inside me stills, hearing her confirm it. Numbness takes over as my world spins on its axis. She's just thrown me into chaos, and I don't know what the fuck to do, but then her next words stop me cold.

"My dad also knows and said no grandchild of his will be raised by a single mother. He's making me marry one of his business partners' sons up in Boston. Says he's a good Catholic boy that'll make me happy."

My blood boils at the thought of some other prick thinking they can come in and take them from me. I push off from the wall and close the distance between us until I can feel the heat of her body against my own. I lean down, cupping her heart-shaped face in my large hands, forcing her to meet my eyes. Watery blue ones stare back at me, causing an ache to splinter across my chest.

"That's not happening. I won't let it."

"How?" *She wipes at the tears that have fallen down her cheeks and sniffles.* "Nobody goes against the great Finnegan Donnelly. He says jump, and they do it. No questions asked. You know that."

I do. Which means we're both fucked, and not in a good way. Different scenarios run through my mind for a way out of this, but I keep coming back to the only one that makes sense.

"Marry me." The words fall out of my mouth without a second thought.

"What? No way. I can't do that." Her head is shaking before I can even finish, but I'm not letting her stubborn ass off the hook that easily.

"You have a better idea?" I cock an eyebrow at her, waiting for her to come to the same conclusion that I have. There isn't one.

Her mouth opens and closes a few times as all of her reasons filter through her mind, and she realizes the inevitable.

"Pack your shit. We're leaving for Vegas."

Movement next to me pulls me out of my memories. Kennedy keeps shifting in her seat as she chews on her purple-painted fingernail, lost in thought. She hasn't said a word since we said, "I do," and boarded the flight back home.

I put a hand on her bouncing knee, halting the movement, and give it a gentle squeeze. "You okay?"

"I'm fine." The slight hitch in her breath belies her words. There's also the fact that she keeps her gaze pointed out the plane's tiny window, refusing to look at me. I'm not an expert on women, but I know her tells. They're slight and hard to pick up on, but I imagine that comes from being brought up in the Donnelly house. When your father is the head of the Irish mob in Atlanta, I can only imagine what she's seen.

Not many people would notice how her calves flex against her leggings as she stretches out her toes in her Vans to keep from fidgeting in her seat, but most people aren't me. I'm trained to pick up on any inconsistency.

I lean down in her space until my lips brush against the

shell of her ear. The scent of lemon floods me. It's light and mouthwatering, like her. I have to force my dick to behave and focus on her. "I can always tell when you're lying, Ken."

Her body trembles when the hairs of my beard tickle the sensitive flesh as the words leave my mouth, proving she's still just as affected by me as I am by her. At least I'm not alone in this. Whatever the fuck *this* is.

"Fine. I'm not okay at all. I'm terrified, all right? My dad is going to be beyond pissed when he finds out. Not to mention my brothers..." Her blue eyes glance up to my nose as she lets her words trail off. We both know what they'll do, but too bad. It's done, and she's mine. They both are.

I twist the diamond ring on her finger until the diamond is back in place and give her hand one last squeeze. "You are my wife"—my chin dips down to her flat stomach—"and that's my baby growing in there. No one is gonna fuck with either one of you, or they'll answer to me. And that includes your family. We're in this together. For better or worse. Got it?"

She pushes her glasses up the bridge of her nose with her free hand and meets my stare head-on. "Yeah, I got you."

"Good." I lean down and press a kiss on her forehead. "Get some sleep. We're gonna need it."

My head rests against the vinyl seat as I stare at the reading light above my head. Sleep isn't something I've had much of in eight years and not something that'll come anytime soon. Especially now that we're married, we'll deal with whatever bullshit comes our way together—as husband and wife.

The drive from the airport to our property is filled with just as much tension as the plane. I chomp down on my gum and let it settle my nerves as I watch the sunrise. I've been itching for a cigarette ever since we hit the road a half-hour ago, but this pack of Juicy Fruit I bought at one of the airport's gift shops is holding me over. It would be easy to light one up right now, but I'll be damned if I do that with Kennedy in the car next to me.

It's about an hour outside of Atlanta to our property, but it's far enough away from the bullshit of a crowded city that I can breathe easily. Fresh air and trees are all around our land. My body won't settle until we're back there.

Kennedy grips the door handle of my truck tighter the closer we get, and I can only imagine what must be going through her head right now. I'm not sure what to expect from my brothers, but I know the girls will help her feel more at home.

Her phone rings again for the hundredth time since we landed, and my fingers itch to throw the fucker out the window, but something tells me that wouldn't go over real well. She glances down at the caller ID and chews on her lip.

"You gonna answer it this time?"

"Nope." She shuts her phone off and tosses it inside the center console. The lid snaps shut with a resounding click that resonates through the cab as she leans back in her seat and sighs.

"Fair enough." I shift my attention back on the road and relax a bit. The truth is, I'm in no hurry to deal with her family either. Mine is plenty enough right now.

I feel her eyes on me. When I glance away from the road, I find her gaze on the snake tattoo that peeks out from the sleeve of my T-shirt.

Her head tilts to the side as her eyes trail over the artwork that decorates my right bicep. She's dissecting every single detail, trying to figure out its significance. "You must really like snakes."

I grind my teeth together, biting down on the gum, as the thought of those fucking copperheads Asher messed with a couple of years ago fills my head. "I fucking hate them."

"Then why get it tattooed on your skin where you'll see it every day?" Her dark eyebrows pinch together as she keeps staring at my skin.

"To remind me that I can't be controlled by my fear."

My confession causes her to sit up straighter in her seat as she fidgets with the diamond on her ring. What I've said must have struck something inside of her because when I glance over to see her wide-eyed expression, there's a flicker of light in her eyes, like my answer holds the key to something more.

"Does it work?"

My gaze shifts back to the road, and I let out a deep exhale at her question. "Don't know yet."

"Right." She nods, and we both grow quiet once more, getting lost in our thoughts.

When I pull up the dirt drive a short time later, I find the new cameras Asher installed, clocking our every move. If my brothers didn't know we were here before, they do now. So much for sneaking in under the radar. I shake my head and lift my left hand to give the nearest one my middle finger, knowing damn well Axel is talking shit.

Thick Georgia Pines line the way as I pass by Asher's place and all of the baby toys that litter the front yard to park directly in front of the bigger two-story cabin. Two heads are pressed against the glass of the windows that align the front wall, watching us pull up. A stone fire-place separates them, but it's the two assholes staring at me from the rocking chairs on the front porch that have my fingers digging into the steering wheel.

I kill the engine and twist to the side to face Kennedy, who has gone stiff as a board. "Are you ready for this?"

"I thought I was, but is it too late to back out?" Her bright blue eyes glisten behind her glasses as she sighs. She looks so lost right now, like an injured bird stuck inside a gilded cage, and damn if I ever want her to feel like her wings have been clipped.

I reach over and squeeze her hand. "It'll be okay. I promise. Wait here a sec." I get out and walk around the truck's cab to get our bag and the door for her. She climbs out, takes my free hand, and together we walk toward my brothers.

Axel strolls down the steps with Asher right behind him, wearing a shit-eating grin that I want to smack off his face until they meet us halfway.

"Well, look what the dog shit out."

2

KENNEDY

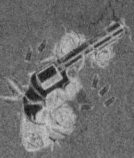

The palm of my hand sweats as I squeeze my grip tighter around Zane's. He returns the gesture, causing my heart's pounding to settle down some, but not enough to stop the flow of blood from reaching my face.

I've only seen his brothers once in my dad's office, and I was so overcome with emotion that day that I can't even recall paying much attention to them. My gaze was focused solely on Zane with a mixture of wonder and betrayal for anything else to matter at the time. I did spend several hours looking them up online afterward. Other than knowing Asher spent time in prison for falsely being accused of murdering his pregnant wife eight years ago and that Zane and his other brother Axel have military pasts, I only found enough information to tell them apart. Now seeing them all together, I can see the familial similarities. From the same deep shade of blue eyes to the dark brown hair, down to the same stubborn square jaw, there's no denying that they're family. Even their muscular build is similar.

All three of the Savage brothers are well over six feet and tower over my five-foot-two frame, making me feel small and insignificant. I dig the heels of my Vans into the dark Georgia clay and do my best to remain calm. I'm not sure what the hell I was thinking running away with Zane to get married, but it's better than the alternative.

Not that there's anything wrong with Aidan. He's always been nice to me, and not just because he's best friends with my brother Connor or the fact that my brothers would kill him if he made me cry, but he doesn't make my pulse race at the sight of him or make my heart feel like it's going to explode out of my chest from just one touch.

My thoughts fall back to the bearded giant next to me that's covered in tattoos, and my body shivers. Our one night together is something I replay in my head often. I've only slept with two other people besides him, and they in no way compare to what we did that night. I'm not sure where we go from here, but we are having a baby together, and that's more than enough for right now.

"Fuck off, Ax," Zane growls out through his clenched jaw.

Axel laughs, flashing a pair of deep-set dimples on either side of his cheeks. He's not bothered by his brother's hostility one bit. If anything, he looks like this is a regular occurrence. He pushes them to the brink, and they snap back.

"Your fucking phone broken, Z?" Asher crosses his arms over his chest and glares.

There's an edge to him that would have most people wanting to turn around and run the other way. It's a good thing I'm not most people. I've been raised by four overbearing brothers and my equally protective father with the same roughness, and it's not something I can't handle. He's not as easygoing as Axel, and in a weird way, he reminds me of my brother, Connor. Both are hardened by the obstacles life has thrown their way.

My stomach plummets at the thought of my oldest brother. Having to face him and the rest of my family isn't going to be easy. Nerves overtake me and have me ready to throw up on the spot.

Axel must sense that I'm ready to bolt because while Asher and Zane are locked in a stare down, he shoots me a wink and steps closer to us.

"Nope. Works just fine." Zane pushes his shoulders back as he clenches his jaw, making him seem taller and pose more of a threat. The two of them don't say a word for what feels like an eternity as they continue to glare at each other. The silence is deafening. A lump forms in my throat the longer I watch this go on. Both are still as statues, looking pissed off at the world.

I tug on the edge of my blue tunic and attempt to make myself invisible as the warm August air hits my arms. There's no way I want to be in the middle of whatever silent battle they're involved in.

"Do her brothers know she's staying with us?" Axel cuts through the silence as his mouth splits into a lopsided grin that causes his dimples to appear even more profound, and he shakes the bag in his hand.

Asher's face is blank, giving nothing away as he glances down at our joined hands. "Fucking Vegas? Seriously?"

"I should have known you'd track my fucking

phone." Zane runs his free hand over the messy knot on top of his head, showing off the muscles of his bicep before he starts playing with his beard. I've realized he does this whenever he is either nervous or trying to calm himself.

"If you think her dad isn't doing the same with her" —Asher points a tatted finger in my direction but still doesn't acknowledge me—"or knows the second you two left Atlanta and got back, then you're a fucking dumbass."

"Fuck off." Zane drops my hand and shoves Asher back a step, getting in his face. The sunlight reflects against the ring on his finger as he does, outing our secret for both brothers to see. I'm sure they already knew, but this is evidence of what we've done in their face.

I brace, waiting for him to yell, but Asher is too focused on Zane to notice. He grinds his teeth together and clenches his fists, but before the two of them can come to blows, Axel laughs, causing all heads to swing in his direction.

"I told y'all he married the sexy librarian." His eyes go straight to the diamond on my left hand, confirming his suspicions. He drops our bag onto the ground, lifts me in a hug, and spins me in a circle. The motion causes my glasses to shift sideways, knocking things out of focus, but he's too excited to notice. Every jerky motion causes my stomach to turn on itself as I feel my nausea creeping back up. I have to suck in a deep breath to keep from throwing up all over him.

"Put her down." Zane punches him in the shoulder. "She's pregnant, dickhead."

"Shit, I forgot." Axel sets me down but doesn't let go until I've gained my balance and am steady on my feet. "Sorry about that." He wraps an arm around my shoulder and gives me a one-armed hug while I readjust my glasses. His grinning face comes back into view as I do. He's so much like my younger brother Keegan, it's scary.

Asher's gaze finally swings to mine at Zane's words as if he's forgotten I'm even standing there until now. "Connor called me after you turned your phone off. He's pissed, but I managed to buy the two of you some time."

"Thanks." Zane nods, giving him gratitude for both of us.

"Don't thank me. Any of this shit blows up and lands on my doorstep, or any of the girls get hurt, I'm holding you responsible. You got me?" The lines of Asher's face harden.

"I got you, Ash. But, that ain't gonna happen." Zane's nostrils flare as he remains focused on his brother.

Asher sucks in a deep breath and nods, but when he doesn't make a move to step out of our way, I know he has more to say to his brother and doesn't want to do it in front of me.

Zane must pick up on it, too, because he grabs our bag from the ground and shoves it back against Axel's chest. "Take Kennedy into the house for me and get her settled in."

"Do I look like an errand bitch to you?" Axel arches a dark eyebrow at him as his fingers dig into the black canvas until the knuckles of his fingers turn white.

"Just do it." Zane sighs and shakes his head. The movement causes him to shift a smidgen closer to his younger brother.

Axel isn't intimidated by Zane's actions as he leans in and sniffs Zane's breath. "Is that Juicy Fruit?" His nose wrinkles at the thought.

Ignoring the question, Zane shoves Axel out of his face. "Just take her into the fucking house."

"Damn, man. You'd think marriage would have chilled your ass out some." Axel doesn't pay Zane's attitude any attention and continues to goad him.

"Ax." Zane grinds his teeth together and shoots his brother a death glare.

"We're going." Axel waves him off and flashes me a smile. "Come on, Short Stack." He takes my hand and tosses the bag over his shoulder as he moves to lead me into the house, but before he can take a step, I spare Zane one last glance.

He must see the unease written on my face because he kisses me on the top of the head and nudges with his chin for me to follow Axel. "I'll be there in a minute."

I nod at his answer, suck in a deep breath, and let Axel lead me inside the house and into my new life.

When we walk through the door, I do a quick glance of the giant living room, but it's the two women standing in front of us wearing huge smiles that have my heart stuttering in my chest. They're making no effort to hide that they were looking at us through the large front window. The one closest to me is only a few inches taller and has long dark hair, olive skin, and bright green eyes. A small mirror image of her bounces on her hip with a tiny fist shoved inside her petite mouth.

The taller one next to her has curly red hair, fair skin dusted with a few freckles, and blue eyes similar in color to mine. My eyes study her the longest, looking for any other familial similarities, but other than her eye color, that's where they end.

She stares back at me with a funny expression on her face while she twists her hands out in front of her. I'm guessing she's struggling with how to approach me, much like I am her. We only recently learned of the other's existence, and it's still taking some time to get used to. We were the closest of cousins when we were little, but I have no memory of it or her, and I hate it.

We haven't had much time to talk since the murder of her mother and the disappearance of her father, the former governor of Georgia. Rumor has it that he embezzled funds and left the country to start a new life, but I'm not naive and know better. This has my father written all over it.

Axel drops my hand and points to the two women. "I'm gonna take this into her room. Y'all keep her company." He slaps the redhead on the butt as he walks past, leaving me with yet another set of strangers.

The dark-haired one, holding the baby, waves her hand out to me as her green eyes brighten. "I'm Charlee, and this is Lily."

I clear my throat and plaster a smile on my face. "Kennedy."

"And I'm Kelsey, as I'm sure you already know." She bites her bottom lip and hesitates for a brief second. Just when I think she's going to give in to the urge and hug me, she stops herself. Instead, I'm given a small wave of the hand. I'm not sure whether I'm relieved or disappointed at that.

"Nice to meet you." I press my lips together in a thin line and dip my chin. It's formal and cold, but my nerves are shot, and I have no clue how to act around her.

Someone who was once a close relative is now a complete stranger to me.

Charlee opens her mouth to say something else, but Axel walks back into the living room, ensuring that all eyes are on him. He wraps an arm around Kelsey and pulls her into his side.

"Your cousin packs much lighter than you do, Wildcat." He presses a kiss against the side of her head and laughs.

My body tenses at his choice of words as our eyes grow wide. Hearing him call her my cousin still seems so foreign to me, but he just blurts it out like it's no big deal.

Kelsey elbows him in the side. "Way to go on not making things awkward, Ax."

"What'd I say that was awkward? It's true. She's blood to you." He glances down at my diamond ring again and jerks his chin out, drawing their attention. "And now she's family to us all."

"Oh my god!" Charlee screams, causing Lily to struggle in her mom's arms.

The baby reaches out toward Axel with a slight grunt.

"You want your Uncle Ax?" Axel holds his hands out, takes the excited baby from her mom, and blows a raspberry on her cheek, causing her to let out a high-pitched giggle.

Both Charlee and Kelsey rush over to inspect my ring and bombard me with questions. It's a bit unnerving. I've been raised in a house full of men, and I'm not used to being around so much estrogen in my life. It was hard to make any friends growing up. They were either scared of my family or using me to get in my dad's good graces. I learned to stick to myself early on and became somewhat of a loner in that aspect of my life. The only close friend I have is Fiona, and she's moved up to Boston.

"Let's leave these crazy women to do their thing and go see what your dad and Uncle Z are up to, Wild-flower." Axel bounces Lily against his hip as he heads toward the door but doesn't even make it a couple of steps before Charlee stops him.

"Don't you dare use my baby girl as a buffer, Axel Savage." She storms after him, but he stops halfway to the door and flashes her a smile that could drop panties everywhere.

"Look at this face, Hellcat." He lightly pinches one of Lily's chubby cheeks between his tattooed fingers. It causes her to smile, showing dimples that rival her uncle's in cuteness. "There's no way anyone could throw punches with her around."

"Fine, but be careful with her." Charlee sighs and lets it go.

"As if any of us would let anything happen to Wild-flower." Axel shakes his head at the same time Lily wiggles in his arms and lets out another excited giggle. "That's right. Tell your mama, baby girl. Uncle Ax is always right." He waves a hand over his shoulder to us and whistles as the two of them walk out the door.

Charlee watches them go and then turns her attention to me. "I bet you're tired. I remember those first few months of my pregnancy. I wanted to live in my bed and sleep the day away. Let's show you to your room, and you can get some rest. We can catch up later." She spins on her heel, and I follow close behind, rubbing my hands together the entire time.

Kelsey hangs back next to me, looking as lost as I feel on how to act around each other. I don't blame her at all. I'm sure we'll talk later, but fatigue is starting to set in now that I'm out of the truck.

They lead me off to the left of the living room and down a small hallway into the first open doorway we find. The room is so big that my tiny apartment could fit inside it. Black wooden furniture rests on the dark wood flooring and slate gray walls. There's a bay window that has a built-in seated bench with black curtains draped on the side of it. In the center is a king-size bed with a plain charcoal gray comforter and enough pillows to get lost in. A small nightstand is on either side of that. Off to the right side of the bed is an open doorway leading to what I'm presuming is an en suite bathroom. A couple of big dressers align the wall that is opposite it. Everything is neat, nothing out of place. There's no over-the-top decor either. It's all so simple and dark—much like the angry bearded man I now call my husband.

"We'll leave you to get settled. Let us know if you need anything. You and I will catch up later once you're rested." Kelsey smiles and shuts the door behind her. The resounding click echoes like a hammer slamming down on my uncertain future.

Ready for this day to be over with, I lie back and slump down on the bed and let the mountain of pillows swallow me whole. My hand goes to my stomach as I let out a long sigh and think of the little life growing inside me. It's been a crazy minute since I've had time to myself or been able to breathe since Zane burst through my door and asked me to marry him. Now that the dust is settling, chaos fills my head.

Am I doing the right thing? Did I make a mistake?

I wish my mom were still alive so I could ask her what the hell I'm supposed to do now. The unknown has me in knots. I'm lost at sea and drowning with no rescue in sight. The only thing I know for sure is that it's done, and there's no going back. I'm a Savage now. Until death do us part.

3
ZANE

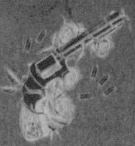

I watch the back of Kennedy's head until she's tucked away inside the house, away from us and all of our bullshit. The last thing I want is for her to hear Asher ream my ass out even more. Sometimes he's like a dog with a damn bone that won't let up until he sinks his teeth in deep and leaves a trail of blood behind. Too bad I'm not in the mood to let him and set him straight before he can.

"I don't want to hear any more about it. What's done is done. She's a Savage now, and that's all there is to it." My fingers flex at my sides as I stand up taller and hold his stare, daring him to argue.

His gaze holds mine as a muscle in his cheek jerks. When he sees that I'm not backing down, he dips his chin, letting it go. My brother isn't stupid. He knows when to push and when to back down, but something about this feels too easy. He's typically not one to let shit go this quick.

"Follow me."

"Fine."

I trail after him toward his house, grinding my teeth against the gum I've been chewing on the entire way here. It's stale and has lost its flavor, but at least it's keeping my mind off my smokes for a bit longer.

Without a word, Asher leads me inside his space, which is a smaller version of the big house. When Charlee was pregnant with Lily, we had this house built not too far from the main one to give them their own space. Axel and I stay in the main house, where Kennedy and our baby will be. I may have to rethink that and look at building us a home of our own soon because the last thing I want to do is live with my kid and Axel.

Charlee's shit is scattered around, turning it from a simple house to a home. We walk through the decent-sized living room and into the kitchen, where he leans his hip against a nearby counter and crosses his arms over his chest while he stares me down. He doesn't say anything, but neither do I. We're both more comfortable with the silence. It's Axel who prefers the noise.

And speak of the devil. Axel walks inside with a wild Lily wiggling in his arms. He swings his gaze from me to Asher and shakes his head. "Damn. I thought you two would have come to blows by now. I guess I didn't need to bring out the big guns." He holds Lily up in his arms to emphasize his point. "Looks like we missed all the fun, Wildflower." He tosses her up in the air and catches her just as fast. She lets out a giggle that has drool falling down her chubby cheeks. How she misses getting any on Axel's face is beyond me, but I wish she would. I know that if Charlee caught Axel throwing her up like that, she'd castrate him. The thought does have some merit the more I think about it.

Rather than say anything and have Asher punch me for swearing in front of Lily, I extend Axel my middle finger.

He laughs but isn't done. "I didn't want to scare your new wife, but you do realize that Finn is gonna string you up by your teeth and make a piñata out of your nuts? Not to mention she has four bloodthirsty brothers that will want their pound of flesh." Axel slaps me on the back as his gaze snaps to my nose. The same one Connor punched that night in the bar. "But, hey, congrats, man."

I ignore him and spit the old piece of gum in the trash before replacing it with a fresh stick. The sweetness floods my mouth as I get lost in the taste, forgetting for a brief moment how fucked things have gotten in the last seventy-two hours.

Of course, I also forgot that it's Axel I'm dealing with. He's like a toddler and doesn't miss a damn thing when you want him to. "And when the hell did you start chewing gum?"

"I'm trying to quit smoking." I shrug and cross my arms over my chest, like Asher.

Axel throws his head back and laughs, causing Lily to mimic him. When he sees I'm not joking, his face falls, and his eyes narrow. "Wait, you're serious?"

"I am. It's not good for the baby." I run a hand through my beard, ignoring the shit-eating grin on his face. "And if I catch you lighting up anywhere near Ken, I will break your fingers."

"All right, man. I hear you on that loud and clear, Z." He holds his free hand out to me, but I know my little brother and can tell when he's bullshitting me.

"Ax." There's no missing the warning in my voice because I'm losing my patience with him.

"I won't even pull a smoke out in front of her." He holds his pinkie out to me. "Want to pinkie swear on it?"

"Axel." Jet lag is starting to set in, and I want this day to be over already. I've been going nonstop since Kennedy and I eloped to Vegas. Add in dealing with Axel, and it's a lethal combination.

"Uncle Z is grumpier than usual since he found out he's gonna be a dad." Axel talks to Lily in a high-pitched voice like she's a pet, and she, in turn, wipes a slobbery hand on his cheek. He leans back and wipes at the streak of drool left behind, making her laugh some more. "Not cool, Wildflower."

"Give it a rest, Ax." Asher shakes his head and uncrosses his arms, extending them to Lily. "And give me my kid."

"Sorry, kiddo. I have to give you to your smelly dad." He sighs and hands her over.

Asher takes her from Axel and kisses the top of her dark head with a softness he reserves only for the girls. She's got her mother's looks, but her temper is a Savage all the way. Watching him with her has my thoughts drifting to what my future holds. Having a mini version of myself running around with Kennedy's looks and my temper has a heaviness settling deep in my bones.

"Traitor." Axel points a finger at her, but Lily knows she has us all wrapped around her damn finger even at seven months old. She claps her small hands together and laughs.

Asher ignores Axel, pulls a manila envelope out from a stack of papers on the counter behind him, and tosses it to me. "Here."

I catch it with one hand and rip it open. The photo I pull out has me damn near choking on my gum. "What the fu—"

"Not in front of Lily," Axel cuts me off, wearing a smirk, and waves a finger at me. "You're gonna be a daddy now, and daddies use *safe* words."

I shoot him a look and tighten my grip on the photo to keep from swinging my fist into my brother's face. Something tells me that would be much worse than dropping a simple "fuck." I go back to staring at the black-and-white photo. It's a little grainy, and it's been eight years, but I'd know Isaac anywhere. It's his eyes that give him away. People age or change their hair color, but their eyes are the one thing that will always remain the same. That's something both Asher and I can agree on.

My eyebrows pinch together. The longer I stare at this, the more my gut tells me something isn't right. Asher wouldn't make a big deal out of this without reason. "You had me stay behind so that we could rehash the shit from my past?"

"Just look through the rest of it." Asher rubs his hand against Lily's back as he shoots me a hard look.

I do as he says and shuffle through the papers until one word jumps out at me. "A fucking traitor? Canton?"

"Yup." Asher nods, letting me have the time I need to come to terms with the bomb he's just dropped in my lap. Otherwise, he'd punch me in the face for swearing in front of Lily. "He's our next job. Word is he's been selling secrets to the Armenians for years, and they want him brought in alive."

"No way. That's a mistake." Every muscle in my body tightens the longer I stare at Isaac's picture. As a flash of heat spreads across my chest, and a knot coils in my stomach. I puff out my chest and glare at my older brother. My fingers tingle with the urge to punch a hole in the nearest wall. "It *has* to be a fucking mistake."

Asher isn't surprised by my reaction. I think he planned for it, hence why we're hiding out in his living room away from the girls. "There's no mistake. That's our next job."

I don't back down as I hold Asher's stare. "The guy was in my unit for years. You walk through hell with someone, and you know exactly who they are. I'm telling you, there's no way he's selling us out. He went through the same bullshit as me. He's a good man and an even better soldier. The last thing he would ever do is turn his back on our country and start feeding intel to the enemy."

"You know how this works, man. It doesn't matter what we think, only what they can prove. They want him brought in, and if it isn't us, it'll be somebody else. Somebody who doesn't care who he is." Asher's direct and to the point, as always. "What I want to know is will you be able to handle it when the time comes to do the job and bring him in? Or will we have to leave you behind?"

My gaze shifts from him to Axel, not liking any of this one fucking bit, but I don't have any other choice. At least if I'm there, I can control some of the situation to keep it from turning into a shit show. "When do we leave?"

"A few days. A week max. We need time to plan the job and bring him in without a fight. Like you said, he won't come quietly. The more intel I can gather, the smoother it will all go. I hacked into his bank account, but there are no large deposits that would raise any red flags. Tonight, I'm gonna hack the feed on the cameras around his house and the places he frequents to nail down his routine and find our window of opportunity." Asher shifts Lily higher in his arms and jerks his chin toward my little brother.

Axel hands me another folder that's much thicker than the previous one. This time there's nothing but a bunch of photos inside. Some are of a beach house, and the rest are of Isaac and a woman. The couple is shown at a restaurant, a club, and walking along the shore while holding hands.

"These were taken the other day in Key West. Your boy's been living it up down there with that hot piece." His chin dips to the photos I'm holding.

"Where the hell is he getting all of this money?" I toss the envelope on the counter as my mind struggles to connect the dots.

"That's the million-dollar question, isn't it, brother? As far as anyone else can tell, he's living on his disability." Asher tilts his head to the side and cocks an eyebrow at me.

I play with the tip of my beard as I absorb all of this. This keeps getting worse with the more information they shove at me. With all this evidence stacked against him, it's impossible to deny what's right in front of me. My gut tells me there's more to it, and we're missing a bigger piece of this puzzle.

Lily fusses in Asher's arms, signaling she's as done with this bullshit of a conversation as I am. He attempts to bounce her, but it only makes things worse. Her cries become louder as tears spill down her cheeks and her tiny face turns red.

"I'm out. I need to find Charlee." Asher pushes off the counter and heads for the front door but stops halfway to face me again with one hand rubbing over Lily's back. His eyes dart to the floor before coming back up to me, and the pain I see there is one I haven't seen in two years, since he was released from prison and found Charlee. "I am happy for you, brother. Just be smart about it, is all I'm saying." He jerks his chin my way before disappearing out the door, leaving me wondering if I just imagined it.

"You ready for all of that?" Axel cocks his head in the direction Asher just left as he leans against the counter next to me and crosses his arms across his chest.

"Ready for what?" I know he's got a point to this conversation, but my brain is preoccupied with other shit right now, so he'll need to spell it out for me.

"You know." He shrugs and kicks at a spot on the wooden floor. "Changing diapers and all the other shit that comes with it?"

I let his words sink in and, for the first time, I voice what I've been thinking since I found out Kennedy was pregnant. "No, I'm not. But it doesn't matter. It's done, and ready or not, I'll deal with it."

"You'll deal with it?" He arches an eyebrow as the corners of his eyes crease. "You realize we're talking about your kid, who will probably scream and make noise? It's not some puppy that you can return and say *sorry, it didn't work out.*"

"I know that, dickhead." I rub the tips of my fingers together and focus on my breathing. It almost pisses me off how well my little brother knows me, but I'm not gonna give his concerns any credit. That'll make it real, and I'm not ready to face it.

"Just checking, big brother." Axel punches me in the shoulder as his face loses all humor. "In all seriousness, you know that we have your back—with everything?"

"Yeah, man. I do, and thanks."

I knew my brothers would come around to all of this eventually, but hearing them both say it settles down the small part of me that wasn't so sure.

He nods and rubs his thumb along his bottom lip. That's his biggest tell that he's about to say something I'm not gonna like. "And at some point, you'll need to fill Ash in on *all* of it."

"He knows enough." There's no doubt that my brother used his computer skills to hack into my file and find out what he could about my past. Most of it will be blacked out, but there's just enough to give him a slight clue what happened.

"Be better if he heard it all from you and not have to search for it behind your back. Besides, you and I both know that he won't find any of the important details by searching. It has to come from you."

"He has enough going on. He doesn't need to add any of my past shit onto his plate."

The last thing I want to do is burden my brother with my demons. Asher harbors enough guilt about being locked up and refusing to let us visit him in prison. No good will come from sharing things he had no control over. That shit is gonna stay dead and buried where it belongs.

"I just think he'd get his head out of his ass more if he knew everything." Axel presses his point. But I'm not ready and not sure I want my brother to know that about me.

"Get off my back, Ax," I snap at him as the veins in my neck throb. The thought of Asher looking at me like the piece of shit I feel I am most days is enough to push me over the edge. He'd never let me around Lily ever again. "You only know what happened because the hospital called you, and I was too drugged out of my mind to keep my mouth shut."

"I know that, but Z—" He shakes his head at me.

"Leave it." My words slice into the air—final and deadly.

"Fine." His jaw clenches as he sucks in a deep breath. He's not happy about my decision, but as he exhales, I see the tension fade away just as quickly as it appeared. He's letting it go and moving on. "Savages till the end and all that shit." He nods and then points a finger at me. "Just don't ask me to change a shitty diaper or clean up any puke. That's where I draw the line." He pulls out his pack of cigarettes and goes to light one up, but I jerk the whole pack out of his hand before he can even take one out and throw them in the sink behind him.

His jaw drops as his head jerks from the sink and back to me. "What the fuck? Kennedy ain't even here."

I reach into my back pocket and then shove a pack of Juicy Fruit into the palm of his hand. "Here. Take this instead."

He swipes it out of my palm and throws his hands up in the air. "Aw, come on, man. That was a brand new pack."

"It'll be good practice for you." I shrug.

"Asshole." Axel groans as he shoves half the pack in

his mouth and stomps off out the door, leaving me alone for the first time in days.

Everything around me is quiet—too quiet. Most people prefer it this way. I fucking hate it. There's a reason I let the others talk as I fade into the background. They drown everything out, making it easier to forget the hell that replays in my head every night. Sleep never comes easy for me, no matter how hard I try. Or at least it didn't until I met a tiny Irish brunette.

I've been so wrapped up in our shit for the last two days that I haven't thought of anything else, but what happens when the dust settles and things go quiet again? In the silence is when all of my demons come out to play. I just hope they don't end up killing us both.

4

ZANE

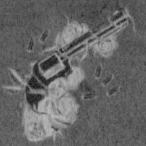

The heat from the block wall seeps into my back as I burrow against it and keep watch. Sweat drips down my face, but I keep my eyes open and ready for anything. I'm not worried about what I can see. It's what lies in the darkness if you peel back the layers and look deep enough that should.

"You see anything?" I whisper to the back of Isaac's dark head as I glance back and do another perimeter check. We're shrouded in darkness, but it's the deathly silence that can scream the loudest back at us.

"No movement on the north end." He sets down his night vision scope and speaks into his mouthpiece. "Our end is clear. What's your six?"

A small burst of static floods my ears, followed by Isaac's voice. "South end is all clear and secure."

"Roger that. Let's move out," Isaac whispers back.

The soles of my boots scrape against the sand as I crouch down and follow behind him. Two shadowy figures on the left mimic our movement as Grady and Nelson do the same and join us once we reach the outhouses.

"Ugh, that fucking stinks." Nelson cringes and buries his nose into his shoulder.

"It's not as bad as that carpet viper den Savage stumbled across last time." Isaac shakes his head at Nelson and scans the area.

"Yeah, fuck that." My pulse pounds in my neck at flashes of running into one of those fucking carpet vipers hit me, and I shiver at the thought. Thank fuck we're out in the dead of night when they're asleep.

"Suck it up, Staten." Grady flips him the finger, showing off the wolf tattoo on his middle finger. It's just the head, and we've been teasing him for years because he was too much of a pussy to get the whole thing.

"Eat shit, Rodriguez," Nelson fires back.

Grady rolls his eyes and cranes his neck in the direction of the main building, focusing on why we're here.

Besides the outhouses, a few mud huts line up along the farthest side of the main building. Other than that, it's desert for as far as the eye can see.

We crouch down, guns at the ready, moving as stealthily as we can from the outhouses until we're pressed up against the side of the building. Chunks of concrete are chipped away from the sides of it. There are a few lights on in some of the windows. The ones without glass have been boarded up.

Our backs slide across the side of the building, the rough-ness of the blocks snagging on the fibers of my uniform as we round the corner and near the front door. The rusty metal glares back at us—a taunting menace of the horrors that are hidden behind it.

Isaac mouths his orders and goes to open the door but stops when we see movement. A small figure is hunched in the shadows at the foot of the door. The closer we get, the more he comes into view. It's a young boy, who appears to be no more than twelve, huddled up in a corner. The dirty rags he's swimming in are a poor excuse for clothes, and his feet are bare.

When he lifts his head and sees us, I put a finger up to my mouth, signaling for him not to make a sound. His dark eyes hold mine for a brief second, and then he gives me a slight nod of his head, letting me know that he's understood me.

I hold my hand out to him and motion with my fingers for the boy to come to me while Nelson comes closer to me. The boy hesitates briefly before crawling on his hands and knees to where I'm crouched down in the dirt.

Grady and Isaac shift toward the door, ready to open it, but my focus remains on the boy and getting him away from the shit show that's about to commence.

I pull the boy into my side and glance at Nelson, letting him know that I'm good and that he can go on ahead. That was my first mistake. The second was assuming there is such a thing as innocence in the devil's playground.

Pain explodes along the back of my head as everything around comes crashing down. Gunfire rings out as chaos erupts all around us. Nelson and Isaac shout at Grady, but their words are lost to me—nothing but white noise against my ringing ears as the world fades to black and I succumb to the darkness pulling me under.

The metallic tang of blood fills the air as my own coats my tongue and drips into the back of my throat, making it hard as fuck to breathe the second I come to. I'm not sure how long *they've left us strung up like a fucking piñata this time, but it's long enough that I can't feel my arms. The heaviness of my limbs is nothing compared to the fire that's licking up the open wounds on my naked back. The balls of my bare feet barely keep me upright as my body is stretched beyond its limits.*

The clanking of chains off to my side has my eyes peeling open. It takes a good minute before the dark spots in my vision subside, and I can focus on my surroundings. Nelson is strung up next to me, and he isn't any better off than I am. One of his eyes is swollen shut, and his bottom lip is split wide open.

I have no clue where Isaac or Grady is. They taunted us with their screams, but I haven't set eyes on them myself since we've been dragged into hell. I hope they're better off than we are, but I'm not holding out much hope. They've starved and beaten us for so long that the days and nights have bled together into one giant clusterfuck.

The creak of the door opening draws my attention in time to see the fuck with no teeth smiling our way. He gestures with his chin and says something in Pashto that we can't understand to the other two dipshits behind him, but it doesn't take long to put two and two together. The bald fucker that had the whip earlier undoes Nelson's chain and ties his wrists behind his back with some rope before dragging him into the center of the room.

"Fuck you. You cock-sucking pricks!" Nelson fights against their hold as best he can, but it's no use. With no water or food for days, he's no match for these assholes. It's a wonder he's even still coherent. They went at him the hardest because they thought he'd be the first to break since he's the smallest one in our unit. Little do they know he's the toughest fucker of us all.

The toothless prick shoves Nelson onto his knees, facing us, and stands behind him. Holding a machete against Nelson's throat, he glares in our direction. "Who sent you?" he asks in broken English.

I swallow down the pain shooting through my body and focus on keeping my breathing steady and even as I watch him. My mind runs through different scenarios, weighing our options, but there's no other outcome. We're fucked. There's no way I'm getting out of here alive, but Nelson might have a chance if I can manage to distract them long enough.

He must read the expression on my face because the muscle in his cheek jerks, and he draws their attention back to him. "Don't tell him shit!" A sheen of sweat drips down the side of his pale face. His chest caves in and out with every breath he takes, but he never breaks.

Toothless grips Nelson by the hair and pulls his head back so far that the tendons in his neck are stretched to their limits and straining from the pressure. He holds the blade tighter against Nelson's throat until a thin trail of blood trickles down. "Who sent you?"

"Nelson—" I force out the side of my mouth, ignoring the sting of my busted lip, and hold my friend's stare. He knows what I'm about to say, but he cuts me off.

"No. If I die, then I die my way. You will not cower to them. Do you hear me?" His hazel eyes burn brighter as he takes a shallow breath. "De Oppresso Liber."

My eyes are glued to Nelson. This is my brother in arms. My best friend. The one who's always had my back, even when Asher was locked up and Axel was off causing trouble. I shake my head, refusing to believe that this is it. The end of the road for us. It can't be. I refuse to believe it.

"Say it, Zane." Nelson's body trembles as he grunts from the blade's pressure against his throat.

I glance at the fucker behind him with the corner of his mouth curled up and growl. "No."

Toothless shouts and jerks his hand against Nelson's throat, repositioning the machete. "Last chance."

"Goddammit, Z!" Hearing Nelson's voice rise an octave is my undoing. He's never used the nickname my brothers gave me unless he was serious, and reality sinks in. This is it. The end of our journey together, but he's going out on his terms. And not a traitor.

"Until Valhalla." My throat's so dry that it feels like I'm swallowing broken glass, but I hold my brother's stare and vow to myself to take these fuckers out the first chance I get. Even if I have to wait for them to join me in hell, I'll make sure of it.

No sooner do the words leave my mouth do I see the change in Nelson's demeanor. He sucks in one last breath and closes his eyes, accepting his fate with open arms.

Toothless curls the corner of his mouth as he moves the machete against Nelson's neck in slow back-and-forth motions, tearing into his flesh. The crimson liquid drips down his neck, a stark contrast to his pale skin, pooling into a sea of crimson that coats the skull tattoo on his naked chest. His gargled screams pierce the air like a dagger straight through my fucking heart.

"Fuck you, you motherfucking bastards." My body thrashes and jerks against the chains, ignoring the burn of my skin ripping along my wrists. Blood drips down my arms, but it's a small price I'm willing to pay to wrap my hands around this bastard's throat and snuff the light from his eyes. The cold cement digs into my bare feet, but it's not enough *traction. If I could, I'd break my arms to get free and rip that motherfucker apart—limb from limb.*

Every sound of the machete slicing through muscle and bone tears at my frayed nerves—sending me deeper and deeper over the edge. The sliver of sanity I'm grasping onto hangs on by a mere thread that's ready to snap at any moment. I fight against the metal, hearing the chains buckle under the pressure, but it's still not enough to set me free.

Nelson's head rolls to the ground, stopping at my feet as his lifeless body falls to the wayside. His vacant stare glares back at me, making my stomach turn. I grit my teeth until my jaw aches from the pressure. Each shaky breath I take adds to the trembling in my body. The stiffness of my muscles is pushing past the point of no return, and I shut my brain off to it. They won't see me break. I'll rip out my own throat and die before that happens.

A shrill scream fills the air, causing the hackles at the back of my neck to stand on end. Toothless cranes his head to the side, his eyes watching my every move as a flash of blond hair appears. She's shoved onto her knees against the hard cement until she's right in front of me. The stained T-shirt she's wearing hangs to her knees. Dirt and blood coat the pale skin of her hollow cheeks.

One of the guys behind her grabs a fistful of hair and forces her face up to meet mine. Blue eyes glisten with tears as she takes me in, and her tiny body trembles with each breath. Since the picture was taken, she's lost so much weight, making her appear much younger than eighteen, but there's no doubt it's her—Admiral Wallace's daughter. Her blond hair is covered in dirt, and there's a tattoo of a paw on the side of her neck. The black ink looks fresh.

"What are you doing?" I push past the fatigue that's wanting to pull me under and jerk up harder on my chains.

They creak and groan under my weight, giving more, but it's not enough.

"Quiet." The one holding her hair tightens his grip until she cries out in pain. He laughs the second she does.

"Let her go, asshole. She's just a fucking kid." My blood pounds in my ears as I struggle for air.

"No! Let me go!" She screams and fights against them with as much effort as she can, but her tiny body is no match for the two of them. The bald one closes his fist and hits her across the face to silence her, while the short one laughs. Her head jerks back, but it doesn't deter her from attempting to fight them off.

The short one that I haven't seen before rips her T-shirt off, exposing her naked body, and tosses it aside. She cries out, trying to cover herself, but it's no use. Two of them hold her down, and one stands behind her. Bile fills my stomach as he pulls down his pants, and the reality of what they're about to do sinks in. I'm helpless to stop it.

Toothless holds my stare, not saying a word, but jerks his head, and the prick behind her shoves his hips forward into her tiny body.

Her screams are like razor blades slicing into my open wounds deeper and deeper each time they violate her. "Help me, please!"

My eyes shoot open, and I jerk up to a sitting position on the couch. Sweat drips down my face, but it might as well be her blood I'm painted in. Sucking in deep gusts of air reminds me that I'm here—I'm still alive—but it doesn't help. It never does.

Every night it's the same dream, the same damn ending. No matter what I do, I can't change the outcome. That's the day I realized the devil comes in many forms. Images of those few days trapped in purgatory are permanently etched onto my skin—buried deep within my bones, and there's no escaping them— no escaping my failure.

I rub away the tightness in my chest and eye the pack of gum on the coffee table but shake my head and grab the pack of cigarettes next to it that I stole from Axel instead. The hum of energy flowing through me is relentless. Every noise has my body on high alert. I want to shove my demons back into their box and bolt it shut, but once they're out, it's damn near impossible. There are only two ways to work this off, and neither is an option right now. My brothers are with their families, and I won't bother them with my shit.

The other is...my eyes flick to the darkened hall where Kennedy is no doubt sound asleep in my bed alone. Thoughts of slipping inside her and forgetting all about that night tempt me, but I'm not gonna burden her with the fucked-up shit that runs through my head.

There's no going back to sleep after this. There never is, so I head outside. The fresh air will help clear the clusterfuck of emotions running through my head. I light up a smoke as I sit down on the bottom step of the front porch and run my fingers through my beard.

Everything is brighter, clearer this far out in the country, away from all the crowded bullshit of the bigger cities. Cicadas are the only thing keeping me company as the night air clings to my skin. It brings a strange sense of peace, like the calm before the storm.

A cloud of smoke leaves me as I stare out into the darkness. It's a typical humid August night in Georgia, but at least it's home. Nothing like the heat in Afghanistan, and thank fuck for that. Trees line our property as far as the eye can see, and that's the way my brothers and I prefer it. It keeps others out while ensuring what we treasure most stays protected and safe inside.

Tightness in my chest builds until I can't ignore it. My body itches with the need to purge the only way I know how. I take one last drag off my cigarette before dropping it to the ground and stubbing it out with my bare foot—the slight sting of the flame igniting the craving for more.

I walk up to the nearest tree and clench my fists up in front of me. The second my knuckles make contact with the trunk, a tremor of pain rocks up my arm, and I relish it. Pain is the only thing that dulls the chaos inside my head. It fuels the need to erase the memories. I continue to pound away. The roughness of the bark scrapes at my skin, but I never let up. Blood drips between my fingers, and I clench my fists tighter until they crack.

Their screams fill my ears, coaxing me on further until their voices melt into a sea of white noise. Every burn, every sting of pain, heats my blood. The rush of endorphins coursing through me fills the void in my chest, and yet it's not enough. It's never enough. It becomes an addiction—a high I crave more of.

Bits of bark fly off as I keep attacking the tree. The trunk morphs into faces—the guys, those pricks that tortured us, that little boy's, hers, and eventually settling on mine. I slam my fist into it harder and harder, not stopping. My eyes sting, but I never lose focus. I need this.

Sweat drips down my chest, but I keep going. I have to. It isn't until my hands are on fire and numbness washes over me that the tightness in my bones settles into a dull ache. I tilt my head back and shout up at the moon until I'm hoarse.

If Nelson could see me now, he'd be laughing his ass off, call me a pussy, and tell me to get over it. But he can't. The dead don't talk back.

The wood creaking from the porch alerts me that I'm not alone. When I glance over my shoulder, I find Kennedy leaning against the railing with her hands crossed over her chest. The porch light glows like a halo behind her, outlining her petite frame.

She takes the remaining steps that separate us until she's standing right in front of me. Her blue eyes watch my every move from behind the lens of her glasses. "Everything okay?"

Now that she's closer, I take in the rest of her. She's wearing one of my T-shirts that hangs just below her knees. Her dark brown hair is thrown up in a messy knot on top of her head, and she's gnawing on her plump top lip.

"I'm fine." I clear my throat and suck in a deep breath.

The scent of lemons fills me, and I have to bite back a groan. It's fresh and clean, just like her. And I don't want to taint her with the dirt of my past.

Her eyes bounce from my face to my bloody knuckles and back again. If she's frightened by what she sees, she plays it off well, but her father is Finnegan Donnelly. Chances are she's seen much worse shit than this. "You want to talk about it?"

"No." Every muscle in my face tightens the longer she stands here observing me.

"Are you sure? I'm a good listener." She moves to step closer, seeking to close the small distance between us while I take one back. The last thing I want is for her to witness me like this.

"I said I'm fine. Drop it," I snap, and the second she flinches, I feel like a huge dick, but it's for the best. I'm not in the right frame of mind to be around her right now.

Her body tightens at the harshness in my tone, and I want to take the words back, but it's for the best. Without another word, she spins on her heels and closes the door behind her with a soft click.

I ignore the sinking feeling in my stomach at what I've just done and stare back out into the darkness. The clouded thoughts from earlier resurfaces, and Axel's voice ricochets in my head. Maybe I am too mentally fucked up to be around my kid. Still, I'm not letting Kennedy or our baby out of my sight. I want them here where I know they'll be safe and protected.

I failed them. I failed *her*, but I won't fail my kid. Even if that means I have to protect them from me.

5

KENNEDY

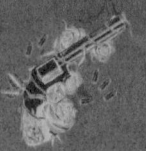

My heart pounds against my chest as I grip the handle of my bag tighter in my right hand and power walk. The Georgia clay crunches under the soles of my shoes the closer I get to the edge of the property, but my steps never falter. The faster I make it out of here, the better for me. Moonlight is my only guide for where I'm going, and I'm thankful that it's extra bright tonight, or else I'd end up walking face-first into one of the many Georgia Pines that line this property.

A knot twists in my stomach the farther away from the house I get, but I bury it deep down someplace I'll think about much later, when I'm alone and have time to think. I'm not quite ready to deal with it just yet. I'm not one to run from my problems, which seems to be all I've been doing lately. My hand goes to my flat stomach as a deep sigh leaves me. Putting the baby's needs first will always be my number one priority. And so far, I'm failing miserably at it.

Trees give way to the deserted country road ahead of me, the closer I get to the end of the driveway. The frogs croaking all around me are my only company, but I keep my focus straight ahead until I'm at the edge of the property. Connor should be pulling down the road any minute. I clutch my phone in my left hand and keep double-checking the screen for a text that he's close by, only to find a blank screen. When I called my brother earlier, he was ready to rip me a new one until he heard me sniffle into the phone, then his demeanor completely changed. My eyes are still puffy from crying, which only pisses me off more. I'm usually not a big crier, but these damn pregnancy hormones have me feeling extra sensitive over the slightest thing, and it's driving me nuts.

A twig snaps behind me, and I jump so high that I almost drop my phone. I whip around to find Axel coming out through the shadow of the trees. "Going somewhere, Short Stack?"

My fingers dig deeper into the leather strap of my bag as I suck in a deep breath, trying to calm my racing heart. Thoughts of ignoring him and power walking to the end of the road to wait for Connor cross my mind, but I'm sure he'd catch me before I could make it even a step.

Left with no other choice, I roll my shoulders back and straighten my spine as I attempt to meet the gaze of the youngest Savage brother. All three brothers are well over six feet tall and tower over my five-foot-two frame. I have to tilt my head back to be at eye level with him, but I don't let that intimidate me. I may be short, but I'm scrappy. The frame of my glasses slide up the bridge of my nose, smashing the ends of my lashes against the lenses as they do. I'd fix them, but my hands are full between my bag and my phone.

The glow from Axel's cigarette illuminates his face, showing off the strong lines of his jaw. His eyes dip down to the bag in my hand and back up to meet mine. He arches his eyebrows at me in silent question, waiting out my silence. If he's anything like my brothers, then he won't back down until I answer him.

I clear my throat a couple of times and wipe any remaining tears with my wrist before caving and answering him. The last thing I ever want to do is look weak, but it's too late to save face with that, so I don't draw attention to it.

"I am."

Axel blows a cloud of smoke out the side of his mouth and cocks his head to the side as he stares at me. He still doesn't utter a word, but I can see him working something out in his mind. I shift my weight from side to side and let out a deep breath while he continues to watch me, wishing like hell my brother would hurry up and get here already.

Something must click into place for him because the next thing I know, he's bending at the waist, reaching his hand out toward my bag. "Let me hold this for you, Short Stack."

"Oh, I got it. It's no trouble." I readjust my grip, but it slips from my fingers before I can even finish that sentence. He grabs it and tosses it over his shoulder one-handed as he plants himself next to me, sending a slight scent of tobacco mixed with a hint of cedarwood through the air when he does. They're both bold, smoky smells that seem to fit his persona perfectly.

"My mama would come back from the grave and

kick my ass if I didn't." He pinches his cigarette between his lips and winks at me. Unsure of what to say, I just nod my head.

We stand at the side of the road in a contented quiet. Like he's come to accept my decision to leave and is supporting it. Neither of us speaks, but it isn't awkward like it was seconds ago. Moments later, my brother's truck pulls up right next to where we're standing, and all tension leaves my body, but that momentary bliss only lasts a fraction of a second.

As soon as it's in park, Rory hops out of the passenger side and walks over to us. I should have known that Connor wouldn't come alone. All of my brothers are close, but Rory and Connor are the two oldest and have always been thick as thieves.

"Country." Rory jerks his chin in Axel's direction, his voice hard like granite.

My brother matches Axel in both height and muscle and is equally as intimidating. The only difference is that Rory has gotten more tattoos in the last few months. The full sleeves of art that cover both his arms extend all the way up to his neck, stopping just underneath his jaw. A fact my father wasn't too pleased with, but my brother—the rebel—always does what he wants.

"Irish." Axel takes the cigarette out of his mouth to return my brother's greeting. "Here." He slaps my bag into the middle of my brother's chest harder than necessary, causing his weight to shift back, but he stops himself from stumbling back up against the truck.

Rory's tatted fingers fist my bag until his knuckles turn white. He clenches his jaw but doesn't make a sound otherwise.

My eyes bounce between the two of them, watching, waiting. This is the first time they're seeing each other since Connor punched Zane in the face, and we eloped. I'm not sure what to expect because they're both hotheads that prefer to hash things out with their fists, and there's no way I can pull them apart before they attempt to kill each other. That doesn't mean I'm going to just stand by and watch either.

"Ror, just get in the truck." My heart pounds against my chest as he continues to stand there. I know he won't take a swing if it risks hitting me in the process, so I push my way in between them and put my hands on his chest. "Please, big brother."

Rory darts his blue gaze down to me for a brief second before it swings back to Axel, but he doesn't budge otherwise. The tic in his jaw is his only tell that he's holding himself back. I'm pretty sure that if I weren't standing in his way, Axel would be bleeding and on the ground right now.

My fingers dig into his broad chest in one last-ditch effort to get through to him until I feel his skin fold under the pressure. The muscles of his chest tense from underneath my touch, but he refuses to listen. I'm debating on another option when Connor hits his horn, knocking them out of their stare down. I let out a breath I didn't know I was holding as Rory backs away toward Connor's truck without a word.

My feet stay rooted to the spot next to Axel as I watch and make sure he doesn't backtrack this way to sucker punch him. Only when he's done tossing my bag in the back seat and planted in the passenger seat with the door shut do I make a move, but Axel once again stops me with his words.

"This is gonna be fun." Axel smiles to himself, causing his dimples to appear. Before I can question what he means by that, he asks, "Just do me a favor, will you?"

"What's that?" My eyebrows pinch together.

"Give him hell for me, Short Stack." Axel holds his cigarette up and waves it in front of me. "And let's keep this between us." He winks and disappears into the darkness.

I rub my forehead and adjust the frame of my glasses as I stare at the space he left behind, letting his words replay in my head.

"Let's go, Ken." Rory smacks the side of Connor's truck, knocking me out of my thoughts.

I jump, but it's enough to get me moving. "Coming." Without another thought to Axel's cryptic favor, I slip into the passenger side of the truck and shut the door.

Before the interior light shuts off, Connor takes one look at my puffy face and narrows his eyes. "That fecker hit you?" His slight Irish accent is nowhere near as thick as our dad's, but like all of us siblings, it comes out more the angrier he gets.

"What? I'm going to fecking kick his ass." Rory moves to get out of the truck, but I put a hand on his shoulder, stopping him before he can. I just want to get out of here and have some time to think.

"No, he didn't hurt me. I'm fine, Con. Can we just go, please?" I shake my head, collapse into the leather of my seat, and sigh. The last few days have been beyond stressful for me, but tonight caught me off guard, and for the first time in a long time, I'm second-guessing my life choices. My hand absently rubs my flat belly as I wonder if I'm already failing as a mother.

My brothers must sense that I'm not in the mood to talk because they leave me alone with my thoughts. For that, I'm grateful. The last thing I want right now is to be forced into any conversation. I know all four of my brothers will give me an earful later, but at least right now, I'm being given a reprieve.

I stare out the window and try not to let my thoughts drift back to Zane and what happened earlier tonight, but that's an epic fail. His haunted face plays on a constant loop in my head. The way blood dripped down his knuckles as he continued to punch the trunk of the tree, mindless to the pain. I can't help but wonder if he was always teetering on the edge, and I was the catalyst to finally push him over the edge.

A part of me is wondering if I should have sucked it up and stayed. Fought harder to get him to talk to me. But, for three nights, I was alone in his bed, wondering why all of a sudden he became distant. It was like a switch flipped inside of him, and he just shut me out and left his family to deal with me.

We don't know each other well, and maybe that's why it was easier to shut me out, but I need some time away to think about things. To be around my own stuff again, instead of feeling like an outsider looking in.

The closer we get to my apartment complex, the bigger the knot in my stomach. It's only about a ten-minute drive from my father's place, but it's the only sign of independence I have from under his shadow. It's also as far away as my father will allow me to live from him. He likes us all close by in case of an emergency. It's not a penthouse or anything like that, but it's home. I'll just be thankful to have my own space again.

Thoughts of sinking into my tub have me itching to

get out of this truck, and before I know it, Connor is pulling into my parking lot. He pulls up to the glass front doors of my apartment complex and puts the truck in park.

I'm reaching for my bag, anxious to get out of here and inside my own space. Rory rolls down his window when I shut the door, and I know I'm not getting away completely unscathed.

Connor has one arm resting on the steering wheel, and his head is turned in my direction. "Dad wants to talk to you, but I figured you've had enough for tonight. Be warned. If you don't talk to him soon, he'll be coming to you. So, do us all a favor and don't wait much longer. You miss another Sunday Mass, and he's going to lose his shit."

"Thanks for the warning." I push my glasses up the bridge of my nose and let out a deep sigh. "I won't. I promise."

"Night, Ken." Rory flicks his wrist in a small wave as Connor pulls away and into traffic.

I stand there watching until their taillights disappear, taking a moment to collect myself. The parking lot is empty and dark, but I can't help the feeling that I'm being watched. It sends shivers up my spine. There's nothing but darkness surrounding me, so I spin on the heel of my Vans and make my way through the glass doors and into the elevator as fast as I can. I'm not taking any chances. When it stops on the third floor, I practically jump out, anxious to put this night behind me.

My apartment is the last one at the end of the hall, which is a huge perk for me. I have the only balcony that overlooks the city. I'm almost to my door when a small ball of white fur runs straight for my legs. He rushes up to my feet and starts barking.

I kneel and scratch behind his ears like I know he likes, as he leans into my body. "Hey boy, how's my favorite little thug?" He lives up to that nickname because he gets out any chance he gets and always manages to cause some sort of trouble in the apartment complex. Nobody ever complains because he's just too cute to get mad at.

"Thor?" I glance to the open door off to my left and find my neighbor standing in her doorway. Her gray eyebrows pinch together as she glances down at her Maltese and then back up to me. "Oh no. He got out again?" She shakes her head, causing the gray bun on top to wiggle with the movement.

"Evening, Mrs. Baker." I smile and continue to rub behind Thor's ears. His head tilts to the side as he leans into my touch, enjoying every bit of it.

"Haven't seen you in a few days." She closes the front of her robe and crosses her arms over her chest.

"Yeah, I was out of town." No way am I telling her the real reason. The entire building will know my business before I can blink. Mrs. Baker is a great neighbor, but she's also lonely and talks to whoever will listen.

"I've kept my eye on things just in case. You never can be too careful." The wrinkles in her cheeks deepen as she smiles.

"Thank you. I appreciate that." I give Thor one last rub before standing to my feet.

He wags his tail and then rushes back toward Mrs. Baker. She picks him up with her slender arms and holds him against her side as he licks the side of her face.

"Well, good night." She rubs the side of Thor's head and smiles once more.

"Night." I dip my head as she shuts her door and disappears into her apartment.

I sigh and do the same. After setting my bag down on the floor and locking the door behind me, I lean against it and look around my small space. Everything is just as I left it. Frozen in time. But it's also quiet. It's the silence that amplifies my emotions.

The humming of my fridge is the only sound that greets me as I stare at my black leather couch and debate on hanging out here, getting lost in one of my favorite movies, but it's late. I had to wait until after dark when I knew Zane was either asleep or down in the basement working out so that I could slip away undetected. Just thinking his name has my spirits plummeting once more.

With a heaviness that I feel down to my bones, I walk into my bedroom and change into a clean pair of pajamas. My head is spinning in several directions, but I'm hoping that sleeping in my own bed tonight will at least quiet the noise. I slip off my glasses and place them on the nightstand next to my bed before sliding underneath my covers, letting the coolness of the maroon bamboo sheets soothe my aching body. Everything around me feels familiar and foreign all at the same time. At least when I wake up in the morning, I won't be disappointed to find the other side empty.

I lie on my back with my arms resting on my stomach as I stare up at my ceiling, my mind going a mile a minute. My body's wound up so tight with emotions that I can't relax. Even my box breathing isn't helping to calm the storm raging inside of me. Sleep won't be happening unless I alleviate some of this pent-up energy.

Letting out a deep breath, I slide my hands down into the front of my pajama shorts and underneath the waistband into my underwear. My clit throbs in anticipation, and I need to take the damn edge off. I let my knees fall to the side, spreading myself open with my left hand as two fingers of my right hand stroke my clit in slow circles.

The second the tips of my fingers make contact with my warm flesh, my hips buck up off the bed. A grip of sensations floods through me. Since I've gotten pregnant, everything has been heightened. Every touch intensified, practically pushing me over the edge from the slightest breeze. Even my sense of smell has become stronger, and it's wreaking havoc on my insides.

My core clenches as liquid heat pools low in my belly and spreads farther down my legs and into the tips of my toes. The coolness from the bamboo sheets rubbing against my skin has every nerve ending coming to life—the friction sending liquid heat coursing through me.

I tilt my head back and close my eyes as I get lost in the high I'm feeling. Small mewls of pleasure leave me as the sound of my wetness fills the room, making my muscles tighten. I curl two fingers and slip them inside my pussy. My thumb continues to stroke my clit as I thrust them in and out.

Flashes of Zane creep their way into my mind, and my heart races, remembering how good it felt when he was buried deep inside of me. How he hit every hidden spot I didn't know I had with such skilled precision. How the ends of his beard teased my nipples as I fisted his long hair and sucked on his tongue while begging him to fuck me harder.

Beads of sweat drip down my chest the faster my pulse races along the side of my neck, but I don't slow my pace. I thrust my fingers in and out of my wetness in a steady rhythm. The first hint of orgasm hits, and I flick my clit with the tip of my thumb, sending myself tumbling over the edge of ecstasy. Everything inside me clenches so tight that my hips begin to cramp from the pressure. I clamp down on my fingers and continue to milk every last bit of my orgasm from me. Never stopping until I'm wrung out and completely sated.

I slip my fingers out of my pussy and lie there panting for breath. I'm sated and relaxed. All of my earlier troubles have faded to the back burner and can wait until morning. It takes a couple of minutes for my breathing to return to normal, but once it does, my body sinks deeper into the mattress. The storm that was raging inside of me earlier has been tamed. Everything seems calm for now.

With a final exhale, I roll over onto my side and relax further into my mattress as I shut my eyes. Tomorrow is a new day and a promise of good things to come. Sleep pulls me under, and I float off into a cloud of darkness that's filled with sweet dreams.

6

ZANE

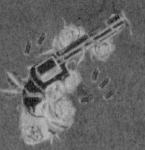

The smell of grease popping has me shooting up off the couch. I'd been trying to stay awake as much as possible the last few days, but it looks like my body finally gave in and crashed last night. One minute I was lying in the dark, counting the cracks in the ceiling to stay awake, ignoring the burning in my scabbed-over knuckles, and the next thing I knew, I'm waking up to the daylight shining through the window. I rub a hand over my face and try to ignore the protesting of my aching muscles, but it's damn near impossible when every inch of me is cramping up. For the past three nights, I've worked my body out past the point of exhaustion, hoping like hell it would stop the nightmares from coming. It didn't do shit. The only thing it left me with was more scabs on my knuckles. At least not until last night.

I glance down the hall like I have every morning, and an ache splinters across my chest. The distance I've put between us is killing me, but I can't risk her getting too close. The last thing I want to do is hurt her or our baby.

My body itches with the need to move and get this clusterfuck of a day started. A growl leaves me when I plant my feet down onto the wooden floor and stand up. Fuck, do my muscles hurt. I slip into the gray sweatpants that I tossed over the back of the couch after my shower last night. Showering at night helps me relax. Listening to the sound of running water always helps me get lost in my head and let go of whatever is bothering me. My hair is still wet and pulled up, but at least it's out of my face. I make a step to head into the kitchen, but when I hear Lily's giggles, I stop and toss on an old black T-shirt. The last thing I want to do is scare the girls with the horrors that mar my back.

My stomach grumbles the closer to the kitchen I get. I haven't eaten much the last few days, and it's starting to catch up to me. Maybe having a full stomach will help me better figure out this clusterfuck of a situation.

Kelsey sits at the counter when I walk in with an excited Lily bouncing in her lap as they watch Axel flip pancakes like he does that shit for a living. Asher and Charlee are nowhere to be seen, but it doesn't take a fucking genius to know why, and it means I'm not heading over there to talk to Asher anytime soon.

My eyes continue glancing around the room and come up one person short.

"Kennedy still asleep?" I ask them both, not wanting her to miss out on food. She needs to eat more since she's eating for two now.

Kelsey jumps and lifts her head at the sound of my voice, but she won't meet my eyes, which has the hair on the back of my neck prickling. Her fingers flinch against

Lily's back, and that's the second clue I get that something isn't right.

Axel turns around, takes one look at me, and I know exactly what he sees. Hell, I can feel the bags underneath my eyes at this point. "You look like shit."

"Ax." I'm not in the mood to deal with his shit this early in the morning. I have more serious issues I need to handle, and his little bitch fit isn't anywhere near the top of that list.

He continues to stare me down, and I can already tell what kind of morning it will be. He's in a real fucking mood. "Morning to you too."

"Axel." This time, Kelsey snaps a warning at him, but my brother is hell-bent on being a dickhead and ignores her. He doesn't break our stare down as he grins at me, but it's the gleam in his eyes that leaves me feeling unsettled.

Something is fucking off around here.

My eyes harden as I repeat my question, much slower this time, in case he's having trouble hearing this morning. "Is Kennedy still sleeping?"

Axel crosses his arms over his chest and leans his side against the corner of the counter, but his face stays the same. I have a feeling that I'm not gonna like whatever it is he has to say just by his body language alone. "She left."

"What the fuck do you mean, she left?" Tightness grips my chest as my hands ball into fists, splitting open the wounds on my knuckles, but I ignore the bite of pain and focus on what he's just said. He has to be fucking with me.

Axel gauges my body's reaction and sees the vein that I can feel throbbing on the side of my neck but doesn't give a shit and keeps on going, reminding me of my epic fuck-up. "While you were busy beating the shit out of the bag again instead of spending time with your *wife*, her brothers came and picked her up."

The tightness in my chest spreads farther down, settling deep into the pit of my stomach. I should have expected this with how fucked up I've been acting. It doesn't mean I like it. Axel continues to narrow his eyes at me, which only pisses me off more. He doesn't understand why I'm acting like this. And thank fuck he never will.

Then my mind plays catch-up and figures out what he hasn't been saying. "Why did you let her leave?" I grind out through my clenched jaw.

He cocks his head to the side, still wearing that fucking smirk that I'm tempted to knock off his face with my fist. "I didn't realize she was a prisoner."

"She's not. You know what I mean." I run my hand through my beard to keep from acting on the urge to knock him on his ass.

"Nope." Axel shrugs. "Can't say that I do, big brother."

"Ax," Kelsey whispers again, but it falls on deaf ears.

Axel's got his dick in a twist, and he isn't gonna stop until he has everything he wants to say off his chest.

"Go ahead. Lay it on me, *little* brother. Tell me how I'm the big bad fuck-up, and you're perfect." I lean against the side of the counter across from him and cross my arms over my chest, mirroring the little shit's stance.

"Don't put words in my mouth, Z." He cocks his head to the side as he continues to watch me. "You've been so fucked up in your head that you haven't seen how miserable she's been."

His words hit me straight in the chest. It's one thing to know I've been a dick; it's another to hear it aloud. Turns out he's not done reaming my ass out, though.

"Maybe you should have just let her be married off to that prick from Boston instead of being alone and miserable here."

"What the hell did you just say?" A muscle jerks in my cheek as I suck in a deep breath and do my best not to lose my shit. I'm in no mood for his bullshit right now. I'm feeling shitty enough all on my own. Not to mention the thought of her with anyone else has me ready to commit murder.

"You fucking heard me." He pushes off the counter and closes the distance between us, getting up in my face. He's only an inch shorter than me, but that doesn't mean dick. He gives as good as he gets. Asher and I made damn sure of that growing up. It doesn't mean I still can't take his ass down a notch.

"Back the fuck up, Ax." I drop my arms and press my shoulders back, meeting his gaze head-on.

"No." He shoves me in the chest so hard that I fall back a step. "Make me."

"Goddammit, Ax. I'm warning you." My jaw clenches as I focus on keeping my breathing steady and not beating the shit out of my brother.

"I bet Finn is flying that fucker down from Boston and marrying her off as we speak. You'll never see them again. He's gonna be raising your kid and fucking your woman."

His words are my breaking point.

"That's it, asshole." I bend down and tackle him at

the waist. We crash onto the floor, wedged inside the small space between the sink and the breakfast nook. Kelsey starts screaming, but whatever she says is drowned out by the noise of us slamming each other against the wooden floor.

Axel manages to land on top and gets a few swings in. He nails me in the side of the head, but I'm too far gone for the pain to register. "If it mattered so much to you, you wouldn't have been such a pussy about it."

I put my hands up and block the right hook he tries to sneak in. "Shut the fuck up, Ax."

"Make me, asshole." He grips the collar of my shirt tighter and attempts to swing at me again, but I jerk my head out of the way before he can.

I plant my foot against the small space between the edge of the cabinets and the floor for leverage and flip us over, reversing our position. I straddle him and swing my fist, nailing him right in the mouth.

"That all you got? Lily hits harder than that." He laughs and continues to taunt me as blood drips out of the side of his mouth.

"Fuck you." My fist is cocked back and ready to punch the little shit in the side of the head when I'm ripped off of him and thrown across the room. I stand up, prepared to charge at him again, but Asher jumps in between us. He has one hand pressed up against the center of my chest and the other digging into Axel's.

"What the fuck are you two dipshits doing?"

"We're fine." Axel takes a minute to catch his breath as he wipes away the blood that's dripping from his bottom lip and smirks at me. "Just helping Z get his shit worked out is all."

My chest heaves up and down while I do my best to

calm my nerves. Everything inside of me is amped up and ready to explode. I should have known what Axel was doing the moment he started in on me. It's his MO. He'll continue to push you until you feel backed into a corner and have no choice but to react.

Asher stays right where he is and continues to watch me until I feel my heart rate slowly start to come back to normal. "You good?"

"I'm fine." I nod and wipe away the blood I feel running down my nose. He must have snuck that hit in when I was flipping us over.

"You want to tell me why I shouldn't shoot both your asses for fighting in front of my fucking kid?" Asher whips his head back and forth between us, looking ready to rip us apart.

"He started it." Axel points the finger at me, and it's like I'm ten years old all over again. Some things never change.

"Grow up, Ax. You're twenty-seven years old. Start acting like it." Asher shakes his head at our little brother's stupidity.

"Me?" Axel points to himself and then to me. "What about him? He's almost thirty and gonna be a daddy. Daddies don't fight. They use their words."

"You're a fucking idiot." I shake my head at him as I work my jaw back and forth until it no longer aches.

Axel shrugs. "Don't be a sore loser 'cause I kicked your ass."

"You got lucky." Fuck, but does he hit much harder than he used to when we were kids.

"Whatever you need to tell yourself to feel better, big brother." Axel laughs, and just like that, any earlier tension between us dissolves, fading into the distance.

"Guys are so dumb." Kelsey rolls her eyes as Charlee shakes her head and bounces a giggling Lily against her hip. Up until now, I forgot there was anyone else in the room except for my brothers and me.

"No, Wildcat. We just work through shit quicker." Axel winks, but Asher and I share a look because he's digging himself into a hole, and we're gonna let him bury himself alive when she murders his dumb ass. I have more important shit to do anyhow.

I grab my truck keys off the hook and head toward the front door, but Asher steps into my path, blocking my way.

"Where do you think you're going?" he asks.

"I'm gonna go get my wife." The keys dig into my palm as flashes of her leaving hit me. I'm hoping she doesn't slam the door in my face, but I wouldn't blame her if she did.

"It'll have to wait." Asher crosses his arms over his chest and shakes his head before I can even finish talking.

"I'm not fucking waiting." My blood boils at the thought of waiting a second longer.

"You're gonna have to. The call came in. They want Canton brought in ASAP. I have everything ready to roll. We leave for Florida in twenty minutes."

"Goddammit!" I slam the keys onto the counter and fight the urge to punch a hole through the wall, but I'm pretty sure Axel and I have already tested Asher's patience beyond its limits with our breakfast brawl, so I don't. Plus, I'm not sure my battered knuckles can take much more.

"Let me get my shit." I'm letting Kennedy go for now,

but at least I know her family will watch out for her until I come to claim what is mine.

The flight from Atlanta to Key West didn't take us long. As soon as we landed, the three of us packed inside a blacked-out Suburban that Asher rented and headed toward our destination. The motel we found is a total shithole, but it's serving its purpose while we hide out until nightfall.

Asher has all the files open and spread out across the bed as we strategize and make sure our plan is rock solid. He grabs his laptop and pulls up an exterior shot of a house on the screen. It's a sky-blue two-story house with white shutters, white trim, and a white balcony that goes all the way around the second floor. It's definitely not something Isaac could afford off his disability income.

The quicker we get this shit done, the quicker I can get back to Kennedy. I'm not happy that I had to leave things unsettled between us, but the girls promised to swing by and check up on her for me.

"That's where he's staying?" Axel shakes his head, bringing me out of my head and back to the present.

I glance over at the image of the house on the laptop and have to agree with him. It's suspicious as fuck that Isaac can afford something as nice as that. Then again, with the offshore bank account Asher found, it explains how he could afford it. It still doesn't explain where it all came from, though. Despite what my brothers think, I know Isaac. He wouldn't sell out his country. A country we both bled and nearly died to protect.

Asher ignores Axel and pulls out the blueprints of the house. "It's on a dead-end street that'll raise suspicions if we park too close"—he points to the document—"but also secluded enough that we won't have to worry about waking the neighbors if shit goes sideways."

"Secluded how?" Axel asks from his spot on the bed.

"Both the house across the street and the ones a block over are rental properties that are currently vacant." He switches back to the screen on his laptop and points to the right side of the house. "Through this grassy field here is our best option of where he might exit if he sees us coming."

I sit back in the chair and stroke my beard, taking in everything my brother says. "So, we make sure he doesn't see us coming."

Asher nods. "I've also hacked the feed on his security cameras and set a timer for them to go offline right when we get there to keep the element of surprise on our side. With someone like him, catching him off guard is our best chance of making this a clean and quick catch."

"Great." Axel claps his hands and stands to his feet. "I'm gonna go hit up the vending machine. Y'all want anything?"

"I'm good." Asher shrugs him off and goes back to his laptop. He won't eat or drink once he's in the zone until we have our shit handled. We're alike in that sense.

"What about you, Z?" Axel stops at the door and twists to face me, his cut lip scabbed over. I should feel bad, but my sore nose reminds me that he gives as good as he gets.

"Nothing for me." There's no way I could stomach anything right now, even if I wanted to.

"So, just more of that shitty gum for you and munchies for me. Got it." He smirks, showing off his dimples and reminding me of our niece. The only difference is that Lily is a fuck of a lot cuter than my dipshit brother.

"Ax." It's one word, but he knows enough by now to take that as the warning it is, or else he'll end up with my foot up his ass this time.

"Fine." He waves me off and heads outside.

I lean back against the headboard and attempt to pick apart the plan piece by piece, making sure I'm as ready as I can be for what is sure to be one of our most demanding jobs, but Asher has other ideas.

"You want to talk about that shit show I walked into at breakfast this morning?" he asks, never looking up from the monitor.

"What about it?" I toy with the end of my beard and lean farther back against the headboard.

Asher stops typing, closes his laptop, and shoots me a look. "I'm not Axel. I won't push you until you take a swing at me, but just know that I've been where you are, and when you're ready to talk about it, I'll listen."

This is as close tp a heart-to-heart as my older brother and I have come to in years, but we're more alike in the sense that we don't need to fill the silence with words. Sometimes it's what we don't say that's more important.

"Thanks."

He nods and lets the subject drop. Asher knows he's

made his point, and if or when I'm ready, I'll come to him. That's enough for now.

I tilt my head back against the headboard and shut my eyes, trying to clear my mind. It's pointless. A petite brunette with black-rimmed glasses and deep blue eyes fills my vision. I twist my wedding band around my finger and make plans for when I return. She can run, but she can't hide from me.

7
KENNEDY

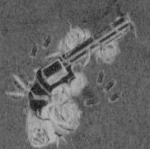

My phone vibrating against my wooden nightstand explodes through my bedroom, knocking me out of a dead sleep. I tuck the ends of my pillow up over my ears to muffle the obnoxious noise. It's too early to people. Not to mention, I tossed and turned most of the night because my brain wouldn't shut off. My thoughts were consumed by a certain silent, brooding, bearded man. Even pleasuring myself to images of him wasn't enough to curb my appetite, but it will have to be because he's a stubborn ass that I am currently mad at.

My phone rumbles again, reminding me why I'm even awake this early, to begin with. I contemplate letting it go to voicemail, but if it's my dad, he'll show up here, and that's the last thing I want. With a sigh, I reach over and grab it. When I glance at the caller ID, butterflies assault my stomach. Now I feel like an even bigger ass. I haven't just been avoiding my father, but my best friend, and I know she isn't going to take it easy on me.

The second I answer, I brace for impact. "I'm alive. I swear, Fiona."

"That's not good enough. I have been going out of my mind with worry, Ken." Her voice raises an octave, and I can picture her hazel eyes burning holes through me from the other side of the phone.

"I know, and I'm sorry. I didn't mean to make you worry. It's just that things happened so fast and I didn't have time to call you. One minute he was banging on my apartment door, and the next, we were married." I roll flat on my back and stare up at what I think are water spots on my ceiling. I'm not wearing my glasses, so anything past three inches from my face is blurry.

"Let me tell you something, Kennedy Shannon Donnelly, the next time you do something as crazy as eloping to Vegas without your best friend, you call said friend pronto. You don't let a full week pass by and make her have to track your ass down." Her voice rings out loud and clear in my ear.

"I will. You have my word. The next time I get married, I'll make sure my best friend is there." My lips twitch as I imagine her rolling her eyes at me.

"You better." She pauses for a brief second and then backtracks. "Wait, does this mean that things aren't all good with you?"

I sigh into the phone and toy with the edge of my maroon comforter. Admitting how messed up every-thing is out loud will make it real, and I'm not sure I'm ready for the truth bomb she'll lay on me. I know I need to talk to someone before I lose my mind. "Yes. No. I don't know."

"I'm afraid I'm going to need more than that to go on

before I decide if I need to fly down from Boston and castrate your new husband or not."

"And I can't give you more than that right now. I'm sorry, Fi. Maybe I jumped the gun on all of this." Saying the words out loud leaves a bitter taste in my mouth, but there's no denying the doubt that's been festering inside me ever since Zane decided to shut me out.

"You did the right thing. Your dad forcing you to marry my turd of a brother is ridiculous and, not to mention, archaic. I mean, seriously, who does that?" She huffs into the phone as her temper grows.

I don't answer her because we know the truth—both of our fathers would do that. Instead, I choose to focus on what she's not saying. "Have you spoken to your brother?"

"No." Rustling from her end fills the phone, and I've known her long enough to know what she's doing. "Everything has been oddly quiet around here. I've been doing my best to avoid him and the great Patrick Kelly because I'm not in the mood for another lecture."

Heat fills my cheeks at hearing that. I am a terrible friend, leaving her calls unanswered for so long. "Is everything okay?"

"It's fine. I'm a big girl. I can handle it." Her breathing turns heavy as an image of her rummaging through her closet fills my head.

"Check the top shelf of your closet next to your favorite band shirts." I picture her scrunched-up face as her end goes silent.

It isn't long before she shouts into the phone. "Yes! That's where I put my damn camera. It's scary how well you know me."

"Isn't it too early to go out by yourself?" A sudden

wave of nausea hits me, so I sit up and suck in a few deep breaths while focusing on a spot on my silver oak wooden floor. There's a small dust bunny that is holding my attention, and if I didn't feel like death all of a sudden, I'd be sweeping it up.

"The best photos happen early in the morning. Besides, if I don't get out of here and have some fresh air, you might see me on the news." Fiona's voice knocks me out of my head.

"Why? Your dad in another one of his moods?" I rub a hand against my stomach and slowly put the pieces together. While my father isn't as tough on me, hers rules the house like he does the streets of Boston, with no mercy. "You know you can always come here."

"He is, but I'll be fine. He knows me better than that. There's no way in hell I'm going to be a good little doormat while he barks orders and expects me to fall in line." There's no missing the smile in her voice, and the turning in my stomach intensifies. My friend always did love to play with fire. I'm just scared that eventually, she'll get burned.

"Just be careful." Something about her father has always made me feel on edge. I can't put my finger on what, but I've made sure that I always kept my distance or had one of my brothers with me whenever he was near.

"I'll be fine. Sooner or later, he'll realize that I'm not a little kid anymore. I'm a twenty-two-year-old woman who wants to live her own life and not be forced to settle down and pop out kids. If I have to listen to him casually mention my 'child-rearing hips' one more time, I'll stab him with my fork."

"Thanks a lot." I let out a deep sigh as her words hit too close to home.

"Sorry, Ken." Once she realizes what she's said, she backtracks. "I didn't mean anything by it."

"Apology accepted." I wave it off as the turning in my stomach creeps its way up my throat.

"Besides, you're a mature twenty-two-year-old with a banging bod. I'm the short, plump friend with a giant ass."

"One, telling me that I act old is not any better, Fi. And two, stop deflecting. You are one of the most beautiful people I've met, inside and out. Now, stop deflecting because you know that's going to blow up in your face."

"Don't worry about me. I can handle my punishment." Her resolve hardens on that last word.

I nod my head even though she can't see me, and in true Fiona form, she continues talking like nothing happened.

"So, when is your due date?" Things clunk on a counter as she starts to have a funny echo behind her words. She must have made her way into the bathroom.

"I don't know, but I am going to see Dr. Rourke for my first appointment this Thursday." A lightness fills my chest at the thought. I took the test and know that I'm pregnant, but the idea of going to the doctor and having him confirm it scares the hell out of me.

"You better call me the second you're done. I want to know everything." She squeals into the phone, and I can practically hear her bouncing around her room in excitement.

"You have my word." Sweat beads along my forehead as I feel my nausea settling into the back of my throat.

"Good." She claps so loud it echoes through the phone. "I'm out of here before my dad can catch me. Go have fun climbing your new man like a tree, and I'll call you later."

I don't wait for her to hang up before I rush to the bathroom. I toss my phone onto the counter and kneel in front of the toilet. My head barely manages to make it inside the bowl before I lose the contents of my stomach, which isn't much at this point. I haven't had much of an appetite lately.

After about ten minutes of reliving the only time Fiona and I got into my dad's whiskey, I can lift my head out of the toilet for good. I wipe at my mouth and fall on my butt, the cold tile an unwelcome surprise against my bare legs. It takes me a good minute before I can finally stand and not feel like the room is spinning. There is no way I can drive feeling like crap, so I text Connor and ask him to swing by and pick me up on his way to the gym.

Ten minutes later, I've showered, brushed my teeth, and sat in the passenger seat of Connor's truck. Neither one of us makes an effort to strike up a conversation, and for that, I'm thankful. My brother knows when to leave me be. He pulls into the first spot he finds, and I'm out before he turns the ignition off.

My stomach turns when I see our dad's black Bentley in the parking lot. I let out a sigh, and Connor comes to stand beside me and gives me a light squeeze on the shoulder.

"You'll be fine, Ken. He won't even be mad at you.

You're everyone's favorite. You know that." There's no malice in his tone, only teasing.

"I am not." I roll my eyes and ignore his laughter behind me as I open the door to Morrigan's and mentally prepare for this conversation.

"Just bat those eyelashes at him and promise you'll come to Sunday lunch after Mass, and all will be forgiven," he whispers against the side of my head to get the last word in.

The sound of "Hells Bells" by AC/DC blares through the speakers as soon as we enter. That tells me all I need to know about who has been in charge of the music in my absence. I walk up to the front desk where one of my younger brothers, Keegan, is sitting, and try not to have a heart attack at the sight before me.

A black fedora with a red feather sits in the corner of the front desk, on top of a mound of paperwork—paperwork I had spent many hours on weekends and late nights organizing. In just a matter of days, he's managed to make it a complete mess. He's scribbling on a piece of paper, but the second he looks up and sees it's me, his blue eyes light up. Morrigan's is imprinted in bold white lettering in the center of his black T-shirt, just like the one I currently have on, and he's wearing a pair of ripped skinny jeans with his favorite wallet chain hanging off the side.

He rushes around the side of the counter and wraps me up in a hug. "Where the feck have you been?"

"Keegan." There's no missing Connor's warning in that one word.

Keegan sighs and apologizes into my ear, but he doesn't let me go.

I laugh and step back, taking in the mess of papers

over his shoulder, and wrinkle my nose. "What have you done to my desk, Keegan?"

"That's all Teegan's mess. I don't do paperwork." His slight Irish accent becomes thicker the more he talks. All five of us have the same slight Irish lilt mixed with our American accent when we speak, but mine is nowhere near as thick as my brothers'. "This face is too pretty to be stuck doing that shit." He points at his baby face and smirks. He's barely twenty and acts like it too.

"Everything was labeled on where it should go. How can it be that hard?" I throw my hands up in the air and put them on my hips to keep from strangling him.

"About that." He rubs the top of his dark, buzzed head and spears me a look. "Teegan reorganized it."

"He did what?" My eyes widen as I push my glasses up the bridge of my nose.

The smile on Keegan's face grows at seeing the expression on mine, and I know he's said it to get a rise out of me. And it worked. Teegan is a dead man.

"Where is he? I'm going to kick his ass."

"He's in Dad's office," he offers as the phone starts to ring. "Hold up. I want to watch this."

"You're an idiot." I shake my head at him, but he isn't done getting under my skin.

He slides over the counter to answer the phone, knocking all the papers to the floor and making an even bigger mess. "What?" he snaps into the receiver.

"Keegan! That's not how you answer the phone." I throw my hands up at him and ignore Connor's laughter from behind me. He's enjoying this too much, and I'm going to pay them back for this later. If I weren't feeling queasy, I'd hop over that counter and start with Keegan.

"It's fine. Nothing's broken." He brushes me off and goes back to talking on the phone like he didn't make a huge fucking mess.

"I'll deal with this later." One problem at a time. "I'm going to go talk to Dad."

My feet are moving before I have time to think better of it or what I'm even going to say, for that matter. I've never openly defied my father before, and I'm not sure what to expect from him now.

Connor follows behind me as I pass through the rows of machinery, ignoring my tired reflection on the wall of mirrors, and around the corner, past the boxing area, to the door of my dad's office. I square my shoulders, suck in a deep breath, hold my hand up, and do the last thing I want to do—knock.

"Come in." My dad's firm baritone voice reverberates from behind the door.

The second I twist the knob and walk in, my eyes do a quick scan of the room. At least my brothers managed not to destroy anything in here. It's an average-sized office. Nothing as upscale as my dad's home office, but his taste is still littered throughout it. A couple of dark green chairs line the wall closest to me. The walls are plain white except for a few black-and-white pictures of old boxers. Rory sits in a green chair next to my dad with his legs stretched out. Teegan is seated in the other one opposite the desk, near the wall. They are dressed in their Morrigan's shirts and jeans, looking like they'd rather be anywhere else than in here.

Then I take in my dad. He's dressed from head to toe in a black pinstripe suit. There's a snuffed-out cigar in an ashtray next to his right. My friends always said he reminded them more of a 1920s gangster than anything else.

He's on the phone, but the moment he sees me, the tight lines around his face soften into a smile. One that he only reserves for me. "I'll have to call ye back, Patrick."

My spine stiffens at the mention of Fiona's dad, and the urge to kick Teegan's ass fades. At the same time, Connor grunts behind me, and when I glance over my shoulder at him, a muscle jerks in his cheek, and his fists clench at his sides. I want to ask him about it, but he gives me a slight shake of his head before I can. I'm pretty sure that if we weren't in the room, he'd be having it out with our dad.

"There's me, *a stóirín*." Hearing my dad call me "daughter" has my attention shifting back to him and why I'm here. When I turn back around, he's watching me.

"Are we interrupting?" My voice cracks. Since we left for Vegas, this is the first time that I've felt the full consequences of what I've done. No matter what, being in my dad's presence always makes me feel like a small child.

"Never." His lips press into a thin smile that doesn't reach his eyes. I have a feeling that we did interrupt something, but he's not going to admit to it. At least not in front of us.

My dad tilts his head to the side, takes in my stance,

and then his eyes narrow. "Come here, *a stóirín*." He gestures with his head for me to go to him as he rises to his feet.

On a sigh, I cross the room to meet him halfway, and he wraps me up in his arms the second I'm within reach. My body relaxes into his familiar warmth, and just for a split second, I'm a little girl all over again. I wasn't expecting him to be so calm about this.

He eases back, doing a head-to-toe scan of my appearance, and I have to bite my tongue so hard I feel blood fill my mouth. "Are ye okay?"

"I was a little sick earlier, but I'm better now." I nod and plaster a smile on my face as my hand rests on my lower stomach. It seems just the mention of being nauseous is enough for the feelings to return.

My dad's dark eyebrows pinch together the longer he studies me. It wasn't easy for him to raise the five of us as a single parent, but he's never made us feel like he didn't have time for us. Next to his business, the family has always been the most important thing to Finn Donnelly. After our mother was murdered, he made it his mission to be there for us in every way.

"But ye're all better now?"

"So far." I offer him an even bigger smile.

Satisfied with that, his gaze drops from my face to where my hand rests. A muscle jerks in his cheek, and I realize what he's glaring at—my wedding ring. The diamond suddenly feels like an anchor weighing me down into a bed of quicksand. It's the only sign he shows of what he thinks of this situation.

"Where's yer new *husband*?" My dad's voice drops on that last word, and there's no missing the discontent he feels for Zane.

"He's at home doing family stuff. I told him I needed to come in and catch up on my work here." At least that's the story I'm going to stick with because if he hears any different, my child will be fatherless.

"And thank fuck for that," Teegan chimes in, reminding me of the other reason I came in here—to bust his ass.

"Speaking of." I turn to face my younger brother and plant my hands on my hips. "What the hell did you do to all of my paperwork?"

"Me? That was all Keegan." Teegan shakes his head, and I want to scream at him. I should have known better. The two of them are constantly blaming the other to avoid any of us kicking their asses.

"Do you have any idea how long that took me to do?"

"Enough." My dad puts an end to our conversation with one firm word. "Yer sister is back now. Go help her clean up yer mess."

"Fine." Teegan sulks as he stands and walks out the door. I follow behind him, and so does Connor, but my dad stops him.

"Connor, a word."

My big brother's jaw clenches, but he nods as Teegan and I make our way back up front and out of the line of fire, but then my dad speaks, and my hope dies a small, fiery death.

"I'll see ye both at Sunday Mass, Kennedy."

8

ZANE

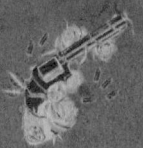

The three of us stay holed up inside the motel and rest up the rest of the day until it's time. There's no way I'm chancing having another nightmare, so I stay awake the entire time. I go over all of the notes Asher has and run through the game plan until I know it like the back of my hand. Time drags ass, but I don't stop until it's time. None of us call to check in on the girls because it'll only be a distraction, and when we're on a job, we need to keep our heads in the game. One fuck-up, no matter how small, could end up getting one of us killed.

Hours later, night falls, giving me a reprieve from my fucked-up head, and we're back in the Suburban with Asher behind the wheel. I'm letting him drive this time because the rock in my stomach has become a fucking boulder. Something about this whole fucked-up situation still isn't sitting right with me. I hope that Isaac won't fight us and come clean with the truth once we catch him. Everything in me knows that he won't go quietly. We've been trained to fight to the death.

"How's this gonna go? We don't have any weapons or shit with us?" Axel asks from the back seat, rubbing his thumb along his bottom lip. That's the only tell he has that his nerves are getting to him. We've hunted down others before Isaac, but none have ever been our equal. And that's fucking with my little brother's head.

Asher lights up a cigarette and offers me one before answering him. "Check the very back seat. There should be a black duffel bag with everything we need inside."

Axel doesn't say another word as he twists around and reaches between the other bucket seat. He slides out the black duffel bag, unzips it, and lets out a low whistle. "Christmas fucking came early." He uses the moonlight to rummage through the bag, pulling out a handful of black zip ties, some burner phones, and a Glock 19. Then he digs deeper inside and cradles an MP5 rifle like it's his new favorite toy.

"That's military issued." My eyebrows pinch together as I wonder how the fuck my brother got ahold of this shit. Sure, we're doing an off-the-books job for the US government, but even they wouldn't supply us with all of this. "Where did you get all this shit?"

"I know a guy." Asher shrugs, but I catch his fingers tightening against the steering wheel.

"Do I want to know how you know a guy like that?" Axel never takes his eyes off the rifle as he continues to caress it with his hand like it's foreplay for him. One thing my little brother loves more than getting laid is firepower.

"Prison," is all Asher says, but it's plenty. None of us like to remember the shit that happened those six years he was locked up. He goes back to watching the road while I do my best not to get lost in my head. I need to keep focused. Otherwise, this shit will go sideways real fucking fast.

We park a block over, in front of one of the rental houses that's currently empty. Hiding in plain sight will keep us under the radar just enough to get the job done. As soon as Asher kills the ignition and the lights, Axel hands out the MP5s.

The moment we step out of the truck, the slight breeze in the air sets my insides ablaze with life. Shit is about to get crazy, real fucking fast. I slip on the same gloves Axel and Asher are wearing and wait for them to meet me on this side of the Suburban.

We're dressed in black from head to toe as we blend in with the night. The three of us creep up the driveway of the carport of the vacant house, keeping our rifles raised and at the ready. Our heads constantly scan our surroundings, ensuring no surprises await us along the way. Each one of our senses is on high alert. No matter how small, every noise is amplified and processed for a perceivable threat. My pulse ticks in my neck like a time bomb waiting to explode the closer we get to Isaac's house.

We press our backs against the wall and take slow, steady breaths to keep focused. Isaac's house is pitch black, making it appear that no one is home. It could be legit that we've missed him, or it could be a trap. Either way, we're not taking any chances. Asher holds out his hand to stop us and jerks his chin. A camera faces the side of the house. He pulls out one of the burner phones that was in the duffel bag and disables the cameras.

"Got about thirty seconds before his firewall senses mine. We need to hurry." Asher waves us forward.

We climb over the four-foot fence and suction our backs to the wall. We slide along the vinyl siding, keeping our bodies pressed close to the house to blend in among the shadows. Our feet are silent against the concrete the closer to the back door we get. Once there, Axel kneels to pick the lock, but something catches my eye. I tug on his shirt to get his attention and jerk him back next to me.

"Wait."

Axel glances at me over his shoulder and opens his mouth to ask me why but snaps it shut the second he gets a look at my face. When we're on a job, we all know to listen to each other without question. That's how we keep our asses alive.

"There's a scuff mark." I jerk my chin at the smudge on the bottom left corner of the door. It'd be easy to miss if you weren't paying attention. That's not the only issue I'm having with this whole situation.

Asher closes rank behind me and tenses up, sensing the same thing I am. Things are quiet. Too fucking quiet. Nothing about this feels right.

"The lock is busted up, too." Axel lightly taps on the door, and it gives way. "Fucking hell! What's that smell?" He gags and covers his nose. The ominous feeling in my gut intensifies.

Asher and I share a look. We both know what that odor is. Decomposition has a unique stench. It's not one you ever forget, either.

"Fuck," Asher grits out. His jaw clenches, and his whole demeanor changes. He's picked up on the same thing I have. Someone beat us here.

"How do you want to play this?" Axel stays put and waits for an answer.

The three of us have been running jobs together for the last two years and run like a well-oiled machine, so he knows what we're thinking. Plans have changed. This job is no longer a snatch and go. It's become a recovery instead. Still, we have to be smart. If we rush in, we risk setting off any traps that may be hidden inside.

"Follow my lead." Asher moves to the front and is the first to breach the threshold. He keeps his rifle out in front of him and sweeps the front room. "All clear in here."

Axel gags and lifts his shirt over his nose and mouth. "Ugh. I think I'm going to be sick."

"Suck it up, Ax. Don't be a pussy." Asher shakes his head and continues deeper into the house.

"You gonna suck it up? Or you gonna be a little bitch and stay out here?" My patience is running thinner than usual with him.

"Fuck off. I'll be fine. Just give me a second." He heaves a couple of times, but I'm not waiting around. Asher's in the house already, and I don't like that he's in there alone.

"I'll be inside when you manage to find your balls."

"Whatever," Axel growls behind me as I step through the door and into what I'm presuming is the formal living room. At least that's what the blueprints we studied earlier said it is.

Asher's long gone, but I still mimic his earlier movements with my MP5 out. He's already cleared the room, but it never hurts to double-check and cover our asses. I grab the TAC light from my back pocket with my free hand and tense at what I find the second it lights up the room. The place is trashed. Empty of any personal belongings, but trashed nonetheless. Whoever beat us here caught up to Isaac and his woman before they could take the last of their shit.

"Aw, man." Axel sighs from behind me. He recovered faster than I thought he would if he's already surveying the room.

"What is it?" I spin around and find him staring at the fish tank, his lips pressed into a tight line.

"Fuckers even killed the goldfish." He shakes his head as a muscle in his jaw tics.

"Ax." It takes everything in me not to lose my shit on my little brother. He has the attention span of a fucking gnat.

"What?" He cocks an eyebrow, unaware of how close I am to strangling him.

"Go that way and check out the front rooms." I jerk my chin toward the front of the house.

"Fine." He rolls his eyes and ignores my harsh tone as he steps to the side and heads off in the direction of the open doorway.

I scan the formal living room, making sure that I don't miss a thing. Isaac's a smart fucker, and the biggest clues can be hidden in the smallest places. Nothing of significant importance stands out, so I make my way through the kitchen.

The house is unusually silent. There's no humming from a refrigerator or anything. Even the fish tank was unplugged. I've lost track of where Asher's at. Since I don't see him anywhere nearby, I'm assuming he made his way up to the house's second floor. Axel is clearing the kitchen and the left side of the house.

I keep walking forward through what turns out to be

a small hallway. The stench gets more potent, which means I'm heading in the right direction. I'm only a partial way down the small space when a trail of red catches my attention.

"I got blood," I say into my earpiece. I follow it, careful where I step. The last thing I want to do is leave any evidence behind connecting me to this shit. My feet step sideways along the wall as I continue on the path to see where it leads me.

A few pictures line the wall of Isaac and who I'm presuming is Carly. At least her description matches the images Asher managed to find of her—blond hair, green eyes, tan skin, and petite. They're both smiling with their arms around each other like they don't have a care in the world. It only adds to the sinister feeling that's shrouding this entire house.

The trail leads me to a door at the end of the hall. It's only partially closed, but the smell is so strong it's making my eyes burn. I'm definitely in the right place. I nudge it with the barrel of my rifle, but it doesn't budge. Something or someone is blocking it. I lean the side of my body into the door and push it with a bit more of my weight, keeping my rifle up and at the ready as I do. It's enough for the door to give, allowing me access into the room. The second it's open, my suspicions are confirmed.

"I've got a body," I say into my earpiece and creep farther into the room.

"Carly?" Asher asks.

My eyes take in the bloody, matted-up mess of blond hair and sigh. "Yup. It's her." I squat down and shine my TAC light over her body. She's covered in bruises and scrapes. Her dress is shoved up above her waist, and her ripped underwear is on the other side of the room. It's pretty clear why they're that far from her when I glance down and find a small amount of blood between her legs. One of her arms bends at an awkward angle, and the other is barely visible. Pink fingernails are all that poke out from underneath her lifeless form. A few are cracked, and one is completely gone. I find it on the other side of the room by her underwear. Whatever horror happened here, she put up one hell of a fucking fight. I make a silent vow to her right then and there that these pricks won't get away with this.

"Shit." Axel comes to stand next to me and squats down to get a better look at her body. His eyes take in every detail that I've already filed away in my head for later. They harden when he gets the pool of blood between her legs. "They—"

"Raped her." I grit my teeth together so hard I feel my molars crack.

"Fucking pieces of shit," Axel spits out as a muscle in his cheek jerks.

"Yeah." My voice comes out rough like sandpaper as I do my best not to lose my shit.

"We'll find whoever did this, and we'll make them pay." Axel's staring down at Carly's body and voicing the same exact promise I made to her seconds ago in my head.

My eyes take in the room, looking for any clues or signs I might have missed. Nothing sticks out. Then I glance up to the far wall, and what I find has me seeing red. Kennedy's picture sticks to the wall. Judging by the clothes, it's a fairly recent one. Holding it in place is a very familiar knife—the kind we're given at graduation —an Ontario MK 3.

"We need to get the fuck out of here and get back home now." I shove Axel toward the front door. There's no time for a stealthy exit.

Isaac just declared war with that stunt. And now it's open season on his ass.

9
KENNEDY

I'm shuffling through the mess of papers on top of the counter. Since yesterday, I've been working on them, trying to figure a way out of going to church this weekend. Short of death, there's no other option. You never tell my father no.

A small fit of giggles breaks into my concentration, and when I look up, Lily is sitting in Keegan's lap in the back corner of the gym. Charlee and Kelsey popped by to visit and check out the gym. Both of my little brothers wasted no time offering to give them a tour.

Both Keegan and Teegan are giving Lily their undivided attention, but she's more focused on the red feather on Keegan's fedora. She clenches it in her tiny fist and tries to bring it to her mouth, but Keegan stops her before she can. Her face pinches into a frown that's close to the same one her father and her Uncle Zane make. She's worming her way into my family as if she were our own flesh and blood. My hand goes to my stomach as images of my brothers spoiling my child hit me. Things certainly will change, and I'm hoping for the better.

Unable to concentrate any longer, I head to the back of the gym where the boxing ring is. Kelsey and Charlee are sitting in chairs off to the side, watching as my oldest brother, Connor, and my father's prodigy, Dalian, are practicing.

Dalian is a few inches shorter than Connor's six foot three, but what he lacks in height, he makes up for in skill. Ever since he immigrated from Cuba seven years ago, he's been training here like clockwork. Sweat glistens off his tan skin as he continues to hold his own against my brother.

I slip into the empty seat next to Kelsey and take everything in. Teegan and Keegan are still playing with Lily on the floor. Rory is off with my dad doing other business stuff, and the only reason my dad is okay with that is because I'm here to properly run things again.

"This place is amazing." Charlee bounces in her seat, but her gaze fixates on the two sweaty bodies inside the ring.

"It really is. We might have to just come with you to work every day." Kelsey winks at me as she twirls one of her red curls around her finger and stares at Dalian.

I laugh at what she's implying. "That's nothing. My brothers had me in that same ring as soon as I could walk."

"Really?" Charlee's whole face lights up at the mention of that, and she sits up straighter in her chair.

"Yup. They wanted to make sure I could take care of myself if anything ever happened to them." I run a hand through my hair as my gaze goes back to Connor and

Dalian. Dalian is a southpaw, but his form is damn near perfect, according to Rory.

"Asher's showed me a few basic moves, but not much else." Charlee twists her lips to the side and crosses her arms over her chest. She's itching to get in the ring.

"Well, I feel cheated. The only moves Axel has shown me take place in the bedroom." Kelsey shakes her head before arching her auburn eyebrows in my direction. "Think they'll show us?"

"I don't see why not." I shrug, happy that I have found some type of common ground with them. I'm not sure if it was the phone call with Fiona that put me more at ease or if it's being back in one of my favorite places, but I'm starting to feel more like the old me again. And if the three of us can bond by kicking ass, that works for me.

We watch Connor and Dalian go at it for a few more rounds before they call it quits. Dalian greets me with a jerk of his chin but stays off to the side as he takes off all of his padding.

Connor climbs out through the ropes and walks over to where the three of us are sitting. His gaze does a quick assessment from head to toe of me before he grabs a nearby towel and wipes at the sheen of sweat beading along his forehead.

"You feeling okay today, Ken?" He cocks his head to the side, studying me.

"I'm good right now." I nod, hating that the men in my family keep treating me like I'm a piece of glass that's going to shatter at any moment.

His dark eyebrows pinch together as he works something out in his head. "You three stand up and follow me." He jerks his head in the direction of the side of the ring.

"What? Why?" My eyes narrow, wondering where he's going with this.

"What have I always told you, Ken? Dad and the rest of us may not always be around to protect you, and you need to take care of yourself as best you can from any feckers who try to hurt you."

"I don't think that's a good idea." Thoughts of all three Savage brothers finding their women in the ring flash through my mind, and it looks an awful lot like World War Three I don't have to voice that out loud because Connor already knows why.

"Have I ever given a feck about that?" He crosses his arms over his chest and holds my stare, daring me to argue further. The tattoos that go up the sides of his arms stretch with the movement, making him look even more intimidating than I know he is. At least with me, he's not like that.

"No." I sigh, knowing it's pointless to disagree with him. He's as stubborn as I am when he gets an idea in his head. "You haven't."

"Exactly." He motions with his hand for Kelsey and Charlee to move to the side of the ring where some mats are. "Come on. Let's go." His hand reaches out to grip my arm, and he pulls me to my feet. Before I can move to follow the girls, he bends down and whispers in my ear, "Don't worry. I'll be extra careful and take it easy on you, *deirfiúr*." He purposely uses one of the few words in Gaelic that he does know to convince me, and it works.

"Yes! Let's do this." Kelsey claps her hands together and jumps to her feet, skipping the entire way. There's no hiding her excitement.

Charlee is at least a bit more subtle about her feelings on this as she walks right behind her with slow, steady steps. The two of them are as thick as thieves in everything they do.

Connor trails after them but stops to kneel and pick up some gauze and gloves before stepping onto the mats. I stare after them for a few beats before my legs carry me off in the same direction. Once I'm standing directly in front of my brother, he dangles some gauze between his fingers and the pair of red gloves he picked up in his other hand.

"You remember how to wrap your hands, right?" He's testing me, and it's starting to piss me off.

"Yes. Would you like me to refresh your memory of how good my right hook is?" I put my hands on my hips, daring him to deny it.

"There she is." He clucks his tongue against the roof of his mouth, flashing me a quick smirk. "I was worried we lost you to all of this bullshit for a minute. Good to know that you're still more Donnelly than Savage." His eyes glance down at my left hand. "And lose the ring. It'll do more damage than good."

"Give me that." I roll my eyes and snatch the wad of gauze and gloves out of his hands before he can say anything else that will annoy me. Staring down at my wedding ring, I hem and haw for a split second before taking it off and placing it on the chair I was sitting in. I hold the end of the gauze with my thumb and start wrapping my hands, making sure most of it goes over my knuckles.

Unbothered by my slight attitude, he goes over to where Dalian is wrapping Charlee's hands and starts helping Kelsey with hers. He hasn't said it in so many words, but I know the fact that Kelsey is our cousin is another reason for today's lesson. Charlee is also becoming close like family, which only adds to his reasoning. He wants to make sure that all the women in his life are prepared and given the same chance that our mother wasn't.

I don't let Connor's taunts get inside my head and focus on finishing up wrapping my hands. Today is the first day in a while that my nausea has felt somewhat manageable, but that doesn't mean it can't change soon. I plan on taking full advantage of this reprieve out on my brother. I might also be picturing a certain bearded bastard as I do.

Once my gloves are on and we're ready, Connor has us all stand in a line. He positions Kelsey directly across from him and motions for Charlee to stand next to her with a few inches of distance between them.

Dalian stands off to my right, ready to assist my brother as needed. He's wearing loose shorts and a black tank top that reveals the tattoos covering his arms and gives a peek at the rose over his heart. His tan skin is covered in sweat from going several rounds with Connor. When he catches me looking his way, he dips his head in greeting.

"Que bolá, pequeña?"

"Hey, Dal. It's going. What's new with you?" I smile, missing our conversations that are always in Spanglish.

"Busy training for my next match." His accent isn't as thick as it used to be, but it's still heavy enough to hear in his words. "No sickness today?"

"You heard about that?" Of course, my brothers would run their big mouths to everyone.

His lips twitch as he fights off a smile. "The twins

told me." Dalian laughs, causing his black eyes to light up. "Though, I am sorry I missed watching you lose it on *tu hermano*."

I roll my eyes at that but let out a small laugh. He's practically family to us, making him just as obnoxious as my brothers.

Whistling from off to the side snags our attention. I glance over to find the twins have now occupied the chairs we were sitting in and are now watching every second. Keegan has a bag of popcorn and is shoveling it in his mouth by the handful. Teegan has Lily in his lap and gently bounces her as she gnaws on her tiny fist. Her green eyes are focused on where Charlee is standing. It looks like this is going to become a family show.

I shrug it off and focus back on what Connor is doing. He's instructing Kelsey on her stance. She puts her right foot forward, raises her arms until they are level with her chest, and presses her shoulders down. Her face is blank as she takes in everything he tells her. She's all into this.

Connor takes one look at her stance, and I know what he's going to do the second he lifts his hand. "Are you right- or left-handed?"

Kelsey clears her throat before answering him. "Right."

"Then switch your feet and put your left one in front and the other behind you." He taps her thigh to emphasize his point, but he's not done assessing her form. "Always protect your face." He taps at her fist, showing her why. That's one thing about Connor. He takes self-defense seriously and won't hold back just because we're girls. It's something I've always respected about my brother.

Charlee mimics Kelsey's stance, minus the weak form. Her thumbs rest on the outside of her fists, and Connor gives her a nod of approval. Asher has at least shown her how to do that much.

Connor motions Dalian forward until he's standing in front of me. "Show them how to throw a proper punch, Ken."

Dalian gets into his fighting stance and waits for me to do the same. "Hands up, *pequeña*. Remember, I want to have *niños* someday." He winks as his lips spread into a wide grin.

"Sure thing," I tease as I plant my left foot in front of me and slightly bend my knees to ensure my weight is evenly balanced. My hands come up to protect my face as I watch Dalian and make sure he's ready for me. I pivot on my back foot and turn my knee inward as I strike out with my right hand. It's a clean punch, but Dalian is ready for me. He manages to bob out of the way before I can make contact.

"Good job, Ken." A huge smile appears on Connor's face as he nods his head at me.

"Told you I still got it." I feel pretty good, but then a loud voice booms across the gym, and everything inside me freezes.

"What the fuck is going on here?"

10

ZANE

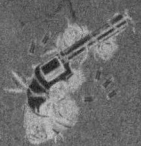

My hands clench into fists as I fight the urge to shove my hand down the fucker's throat. Whoever he is, he's much too close to Kennedy for my liking. Since we left Florida, shit's been running through my mind, and this only adds to it. I'm a bomb about to go off. My steps never falter until I'm standing right next to her. I've thought of nothing else but getting to her from the moment I saw the knife through that fucking photo. Against my better judgment, I called Connor to relay my concern because I didn't want to worry Kennedy, and it looks like it was a mistake on my part. The bastard decided to take matters into his own hands. Something we'll be hashing out later.

Asher and Axel are behind me dealing with Connor and their women, but it all blends into background noise. All that matters to me is getting Kennedy away from that fucker in front of her. I won't be able to settle the gnawing ache in my gut until I know that she's okay. My brothers can deal with the rest of this shit.

I grab Kennedy by the arm and pull her gently along with me and through the first door I see. It turns out to be the locker room. The door clicks shut, leaving the outside world behind us for now, and that's where it will stay until I'm satisfied.

A mixture of sweat and bleach fills my nose the second we enter, but I keep moving us farther into the room to the last set of lockers at the very end until we're far enough away from the door that I don't have to worry about her running off. After sitting in a car for the last thirteen hours, the last thing I want to do is have to give chase. It doesn't mean I won't if it's necessary.

I rip the gloves off her hands and toss them away somewhere behind me. They land with a soft thump on the cement floor as I lean in with my weight and cage Kennedy in. It takes a couple of seconds for her mind to catch up to the rest of her body. That's the only reason I managed to get her in this position as easily as I have. The moment reality sinks in, her body comes alive and jerks against me. But I have her caged in place, right where I want her. She isn't going anywhere.

The top of her head barely comes to the center of my chest, and it only reminds me of how tiny she is compared to me. She resembles a caged bird whose wings are about to be clipped, but instead of cowering, she spits out fire.

Her head tilts back as those blue eyes smolder with promises of incinerating my ass alive from behind her glasses. A deep crimson fills her cheeks and has her looking ready to carve my eyes out with her nails. "What the hell was that for?" The veins on her neck pulse as she continues to glare at me. Kennedy's like a lioness ready to pounce and refusing to bow down in fear. This is a new side of her. One that I haven't seen yet. It has my blood coming alive, pumping through my veins like a wildfire.

This is the first time we've been this close since we got back from Vegas, and I almost forgot how fucking beautiful she is. Mere inches separate us, but it's enough for me to see the tiny flecks of gold inside her blue eyes through the lenses of her glasses. My eyes slide down the rest of her face, taking in every detail. A light dusting of freckles covers the edges of her tiny nose. Plump pink lips that are begging for my teeth to sink into them. Images of her on her knees in front of me with those same lips wrapped around my dick flash through my mind. I have to fight back a groan.

Every inch of her is perfect, but I need to get my shit locked down and remember why we're standing in this position in the first place. I shake myself out of it before I do something fucking stupid and lift her shirt until it's above her ribs, revealing the smooth expanse of her stomach.

"Don't move," I warn as my fingers skim along the soft flesh. My healing knuckles are a stark contrast to her perfect porcelain skin.

"What are you doing?" Once again, she jumps at the contact and pushes against my chest to get away, but it's pointless. I'm stronger.

I grip both her wrists and lock them over her head with my free hand. The movement causes her tits to press up against my chest, and the friction against my nipple piercings has me biting back a growl. Pregnancy has made them bigger. I haven't said anything, but I've sure as fuck noticed. I notice everything about her.

"If I find one mark on you, I'm gonna rip that motherfucker's hands off and choke him with them." My teeth grind together at the thought of him standing so close to her like he had a fucking right to. Kennedy belongs to me. That makes me sound like a hypocritical asshole, considering how I've acted toward her, but I don't fucking care. She's mine. End of story.

My head is spinning, and I'm struggling with the urge to either stay in here with her or go back out there and beat his ass just for the hell of it. Then she speaks, and I'm ready to turn my ass around.

"Give me some credit. Dalian wouldn't hurt me."

I don't like how she says that name with such familiarity. It pushes me closer to the edge of my control. I'm wound up so tight that I can only handle so much before I snap and unleash a monster neither one of us is ready for.

I suck in a deep breath and force myself to calm down before I lose my shit entirely and end up spanking her ass. I grind out through my teeth, "Who the fuck is Dalian?"

When she remains quiet, I lean in closer until our noses are touching, pressing her deeper into the lockers with my chest, ensuring she gets the message not to test me, but Kennedy isn't one to bend easily.

She's trapped in here with nowhere to run, and still, she doesn't bend to me. "He's the *friend* I was sparring with before you came in barking orders like a damn crazy person." Her breathing becomes more frantic the louder she yells at me. The pupils of her eyes narrow, deepening the blue of her irises, the more her temper flares to life. They're like an ocean sucking me in, and I contemplate drowning in them for a brief second, but then her words penetrate through my fog and knock me back down into reality. The vein in the side of my neck throbs the more I let them sink in. It's complete bullshit.

"Are you out of your mind? You're pregnant. The last thing you should be doing is sparring with some dick-head. What if something happened?" Everything inside of me coils up tight at the thought of something happening to them.

"I said I was fine." Her voice comes out low and lethal. If it weren't for the slight tremble in her voice giving away her emotions, I'd think she was gonna lunge forward and attack me.

"Not good enough." I shake my head and bend down to continue checking her over. My fingers run along the top of her ribs, and she flinches again, trying to pull away. "Hold still."

"Your beard's tickling me." She squirms against the locker once more, but I'm not stopping until I'm satisfied. The knot in my gut won't settle until I have concrete proof that she isn't hurt. I've learned never to take anything at face value.

After I'm sure she doesn't have a scratch on her, I stand upright and stare her down. Everything over the last thirteen hours comes crashing into me all at once. From the time I hauled ass out of Isaac's until we pulled up here, my mind has done nothing but come up with what-ifs and had my self-control on edge. Thank fuck, none of them came to fruition.

"See? I told you I was fine," she smarts off and jerks her arms out of my grasp. I let her break free, giving her the illusion that she could get away from me. Truth is, my head's so fucked up right now that I'm not sure I can let her out of my sight even for a second.

"Yeah, you are." I lean down and press my forehead

against hers as I release a deep exhale, letting the shit from the last thirteen hours fall away. The heat of my breath causes her glasses to fog over, and if it bothers her, she doesn't say a word about it. My heart pounds in my chest, but she's safe right here in front of me. And I'm gonna make sure it fucking stays that way.

Silence stretches between us, and neither one of us makes a move to break our connection. We've found ourselves in a truce that neither one of us wants to be the first to break. The room is stifled with our mixture of heavy emotions, but I can't let her go. Not yet.

"You left."

Her shoulders droop as her words leave her on a small sigh. "You left first."

I open my mouth to argue, but she isn't done reminding me of what a giant dickhead I've been.

"You couldn't expect me to stay where I wasn't wanted."

Hearing her say that is like a punch to the gut. The last thing I ever wanted her to feel was like she was a nuisance that was in the way. I lift my head but keep my gaze firmly planted on hers and cup the side of her face. The hurt brewing behind those icy blue eyes is enough to knock me on my ass.

"I know I fucked up, but I thought I was doing what was best. Forgive me." My thumb traces small circles against the smooth skin of her cheek as I plead with her to see the truth in my eyes.

The softness of her soft skin is a welcome contradiction against the roughness of my own. She's soft where I'm hard. She leans into my touch, and I feel some of the tension leave her body. Her tongue darts out and licks her bottom lip, stretching the edge of my control even thinner. There's no mistaking the hunger behind that look, and it's the hottest fucking thing I've ever seen. Everything inside me coils up tighter, barely holding on to the sliver of sanity that I have left. It's been months since I've touched a woman—the same woman in front of me right now—and my dick presses against my zipper, demanding to break free and be buried deep inside her.

"Zane," she moans out my name like a prayer, and that's my undoing.

Something inside me snaps. I grab her by the nape of her neck and jerk her into me until our lips are crashing together. She freezes for a split second, but I'm not giving her a chance to stop me. Not now. After the hell that went through my head the entire drive over here, I'm not depriving myself of this.

"Open up for me." I bite down on her bottom lip hard enough that the metallic taste of her blood fills my mouth.

Kennedy gasps at my roughness, and when she does, I take full advantage. An explosion of sweetness mixed with that citrus lemon scent unique only to her overpowers me the second our tongues collide. She's the high I've been craving. The drug pumping through my veins. Everything about her is clean and good. Not tainted like me. Like the demons of my past. My tongue continues to work her over with promises of what I can do to her pussy later. Tasting. Devouring. Savoring what belongs to me.

She whimpers into my mouth as her hands claw down my chest, much like she did our first night together. Her fingers toy with the edge of my shirt, never going any further than that, but that's enough. That slight touch only fuels the fire burning inside of me. I tilt my head to the side to gain better access, deepening the kiss and pressing the frame of her glasses tighter against her face. My hands slide down and grip her ass, lifting her up and slamming her back against the lockers as her legs wrap around my waist.

Kennedy's moans hit my ears but quickly morph into something else. Something I can never escape, no matter how hard I try. I squeeze my eyes shut, trying to block them out. The louder their cries echo in my head, the harder I attack Kennedy's mouth, silently begging for her moans to block out the ones that haunt me every second of every fucking day.

"No. Please, stop."

My fingers dig harder into the flesh of her ass as I grind harder up against her. The metal protests from under the pressure of our weight, but I give no fucks. I'm not stopping. I slide my dick against the seam of her leggings, making her moan even louder this time.

"Help me."

I suck in a deep breath, letting Kennedy's lemon scent wash over me, reminding me of where I am. In the present. Not back there. It doesn't ease the ache in my chest, but then Kennedy shifts against me and moans my name like a prayer, making everything else fade away.

"Zane."

Her hips thrust forward, meeting me, stroke for stroke, bringing me back to reality. That's one thing I'll never forget. Kennedy gives as good as she gets. She grinds against me, riding me like I'm her lifeline, and I swear I could come in my fucking pants from the heat of her pussy alone. It isn't long before her body tenses up and convulses against me. Watching her let go like this has my dick pressing into the seam of my zipper so hard that I'm pretty sure the marks will be permanently embedded on my skin. Every bite of pain has my body coiled up tight and begging for more. Fuck me, if I don't get myself under control, I'm gonna end up fucking her into the lockers loud enough for her entire family to hear.

"Hey!" And just like that, a bucket of ice is thrown on my balls. Connor bangs on the door, reminding me of where we are. "Both of you get out here."

When I break the kiss to look at her, my heart damn near explodes out of my chest. I'm pretty fucking sure my balls are gonna be blue, but I can't take my eyes off of her. She's a fucking sight. Face flushed, lips swollen, glasses crooked. That *just fucked* look. It's perfection, and it's all mine.

I help her slide back down until her feet touch the floor, but my hands aren't ready to let her go just yet. My fingers splay across her waist as I stare down at her.

"Do me a favor?" She presses the palm of her hand against my pounding heart and gives it a small pat.

"What's that?" I straighten up her glasses and reposition them on the bridge of her nose.

"Stop acting like an ass to me." Her lips twist to the side as she watches me and waits for my reaction, digging the knife of guilt deeper into my back.

I nod at her request, trying to get myself under control, but it's damn near impossible. Her attitude is hot as fuck. "I want you back home." Where you belong.

"Not gonna happen." She lets out a small laugh and shakes her head.

"Fine. Then I'm staying with you at your place." I

kiss her again before she can argue. I've learned she's more pliant when I distract her with my mouth. "What time do you get off work?"

"Around six. Why?" She toys with the ends of my beard but watches me through hooded eyes.

"Because I'm taking you home." There's no way I'm letting her slip away from me again. Not with Isaac's threat hanging out there. And not with all the fucked-up shit wreaking havoc in my head.

"That's three hours away." Her forehead scrunches as she tilts her head to the side and looks at me like I'm insane.

"I'll wait." My meaning is clear—I'm not going anywhere.

"I rode with Connor." She tries to push me away again, but she needs to realize that I'll only push back twice as hard.

"Don't give a fuck who brought you, Ken. You're leaving with me."

"Boy, you're bossy." She shakes her head, but I don't miss the way her face lights up hearing me call her by her nickname.

"And don't you forget it." I lean down and press another kiss to her lips. Now that I've started, I can't seem to stop.

Kennedy and I lock eyes but don't move. Neither one of us is ready to break our connection just yet.

"Now!" Connor slams his fist against the door again, reminding me that the cockblocker is why we stopped in the first place, and I make a mental note to pay him back for this later.

"We should go. Otherwise, he'll come in here." Kennedy squirms against me, causing her stomach to brush against my groin. The second she feels how hard I still am, she freezes. A flush creeps back along her cheeks, and I'm second-guessing on telling Connor to fuck off.

I could give two shits if he walks in and finds us like this, but I know she does, and that is the only reason I comply with the bastard's demand. Kennedy keeps her gaze planted on the floor, and I can already feel the distance creeping back in between us. The woman who let me fuck her mouth with my tongue disappears before me. She's pulling away and retreating inside her head. It's a move I'm all too familiar with. One I can understand. It doesn't mean I like it. She fidgets one last time and moves to walk away, but I grab her wrist and slip her wedding ring back on her finger before she can.

"Don't take it off again." My voice brooks no argument. I'm still pissed that I found it on the chair when I walked in.

The muscles in her neck contract as she swallows at my demand, but the beast inside me is still not appeased.

"I'm not letting you out of my sight."

The tip of my finger traces along her bottom lip, the same one that is swollen and ripe like a mouthwatering treat from the way I devoured her, and I can't resist. I kiss her one last time, sucking that same lip into my mouth, and it takes everything I have not to strip her bare right here and spread her out over one of the benches so I can feast on her pussy. But I don't. Once I start, I don't plan on stopping there.

I let Kennedy take the lead as I readjust my aching dick before we head toward the door. Connor is smirking at me over her shoulder when she opens it, but I keep my face blank. My thoughts are none of his fucking business. Then he looks at his sister, and that grin is all wiped away. Good. Payback's a bitch.

Kennedy walks back out to where the girls and that fucker Dalian are. I make to follow her, but Connor puts his arm out, blocking my way.

I glance at his arm before meeting his gaze. "Problem?" My arms cross over my chest, and I wait him out.

A muscle tics in the side of his jaw, but he gives nothing away. We're too much alike in that sense. He's like a stick of dynamite, and I'm the match. This has been coming since he clocked me in the face. While we have spoken since that night, it's been short, clipped conversations only about Kennedy. This is the first time it's just the two of us up close like this, and he's not missing the chance to get in my face. Considering I just made progress with his sister, the last thing I want to do is beat his ass, but I will if he pushes me far enough.

"You have no idea what you've done." There's no missing his ominous tone.

"Then explain it to me." I cock my head to the side and study him. Eyes hard, face blank, but there's no mistaking the hint of something more hidden behind his blank expression. After all, like recognizes like.

He opens his mouth but hesitates for a brief

moment, and just when I think he's gonna explain, he clamps his mouth shut and shakes his head.

I don't have time for this shit. I knock his hand out of my way and head off in search of Kennedy. My eyes zero in on her without even trying. She's standing with the girls and that asswipe Dalian, but at least she's not geared up to do any fighting this time. I want to take her out of here and continue what happened a few moments ago in the locker room, but something tells me that wouldn't go over well. Instead, I do my best to ignore the ache building in my balls and go in search of my brothers.

Asher and Axel are sitting in the chairs off to the side of the mats. Asher has Lily in his lap, but he doesn't look any happier than I am to be here watching this shit. Axel, on the other hand, looks right at home. He has his legs stretched out in front of him and a bag of popcorn in his lap. I take the empty seat between the two of them and tamp down my urge to steal Kennedy away from here.

Connor walks back over to where they are but glares at me the entire way. If he's trying to sink under my skin by getting between us, then he's fucking with the wrong man.

"What's his problem?" Axel asks, shoving a handful of popcorn into his mouth.

"Nothing." I'm not getting into it right now because Axel can't keep his mouth shut for shit.

Asher shoots me a look but doesn't say anything. He doesn't have to. His body language says it all. He picked up on Connor's indifference too.

Connor places Kelsey and Charlee across from each other on the mat. At the same time, Kennedy motions with her hand for them to do something. Both of them nod and assume the proper stance. They put their hands up, protecting their faces, and square off. I lean back deeper against the back of my chair, watching Kennedy do her thing.

When Connor yells, "Fight," they begin sparring.

It's not full contact, which I'm sure is the only reason Asher hasn't shoved his fist down Connor's throat. Axel's the complete opposite. He's thriving on seeing his woman up there.

Thanks to Asher, Charlee's had more practice, so she's quicker at making contact, but Kelsey is still managing to hold her own. They stumble around the mat for the first few rounds but become more comfortable with each passing second, and both begin to hold their own.

"That's so hot," Axel grunts, keeping his eyes on Kelsey, and then shifts his attention onto me. "Too bad you sidelined Short Stack. I'd love to see what she can do."

I keep my gaze on the girls, ignoring him. He's digging in, trying to get a rise out of me, but I know my little brother well enough not to act on it. It doesn't mean he's not working on my last fucking nerve.

"Want some?" Axel shakes the bag of popcorn at me like he's a fucking kid.

I glance at the bag and then back up at him before turning my attention to Kennedy without offering him a verbal answer. Sometimes silence is better when dealing with him.

"Suit yourself." He shrugs and goes back to watching the girls.

Between watching Kelsey and Charlee, and Axel's

chewing in my ear, every last part of me is on edge and counting down until Kennedy's off of work. They go a few more rounds before Connor finally tells them to take a water break.

"My turn." Axel jumps up and hands me the bag of popcorn before stepping onto the mats and closing the distance between him and Kelsey before Asher or I can utter a word. "Come on, Short Stack. You're up."

"What the fuck?" I crush the bag of popcorn in my fist, ready to punch my fist through his face. I'm about to jump out of my chair when Axel holds his hands up like a little kid who got caught shitting in the corner.

"I promise. No contact on my end. I just want to see what she can do. That's it." Axel shrugs and gives me a smirk, but it doesn't stop the urge I feel to beat his ass.

"It'll be fine," Kennedy assures me, but I'm not fucking happy about this. Still, something tells me if I want to figure our shit out, I need to let her have this.

"One scratch, Ax"—I point my finger at him—"and I make a purse out of your nuts."

"Yeah, yeah." He waves me off, but I know I've made my point.

My teeth clamp down and grind together every second that Kennedy stands there. I'm still fighting with the urge not to murder my little brother as they bob and weave around the mat. Lucky for me, this shit doesn't last long. In all of his cockiness, Axel isn't at the top of his game. He's distracted, and that makes him sloppy. He leaves himself wide open, and Kennedy takes full advantage. She fakes a hook, and when he dodges out of the way, he leaves himself ripe for the taking. Kennedy hits him with a sidekick, but she's so short that it nails him right in the balls.

"Fuck." Axel folds onto the mat, holding himself like a little bitch. "What is it with you women and hitting me in my fucking nuts?"

"Popcorn?" I offer the bag to Asher while Lily lets out one of her high-pitched giggles. Even she likes watching her dumbass uncle getting his ass handed to him.

"Sure." Asher grabs a handful and tosses it back as we sit and watch Axel roll around in pain. Serves the fucker right.

11

KENNEDY

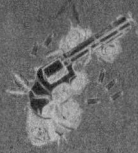

From behind my glasses, I stare back at my reflection, not recognizing the person I see. Dark loose waves flow down to the middle of my back. The top half of my hair is pinned up to secure the tiara that rests on my head. My eyes are done up in a smoky hue of gray and black, and the look is completed with a few coats of mascara on my lashes. For my lips, I opted for a neutral color to offset the heaviness of my eyes.

The beaded bodice of my dress molds to my breasts perfectly, stopping right above my navel and dipping in at the waist for a perfect A-line. My trembling hands smooth out the white chiffon skirt that has a split right up the middle that stops at the tops of my thighs. I lucked out finding this dress in one of the shops at our hotel on such short notice.

It takes me a couple of minutes to realize that this is, in fact, me. That this is happening. And it's not a dream. I am getting married.

A knock taps against the dressing room door, snapping me out of my thoughts. "Are you ready, Kennedy?" Ruth's salt-and-pepper bun appears in the mirror from behind me.

She and her husband own this little chapel that Zane managed to find off the Strip.

"As I'll ever be."

I paste a wide smile onto my face and press my hand against my stomach to tame the wild butterflies somersaulting around. Everything inside of me is spinning a million miles a minute. It takes a few slow, deep breaths to get myself under control and avoid hyperventilating. The last thing I want to do on my wedding day is have a panic attack.

"You look beautiful." *She hands me a bouquet of red roses tied together with a simple white ribbon.*

"Thank you."

My shaking hands grip the small bundle like it's a lifeline, and then I spin on the heel of my new white shoes. I usually don't wear anything taller than three inches, but I opted for the six-inch ones today because I didn't want Zane to tower over me as much as he usually does.

On unsteady feet, I follow Ruth out from the dressing room and into the tiny hallway, stopping at a set of white double doors. Sucking in a deep breath, I prepare to walk down the aisle. I can do this. I just hope my father will forgive me for this someday.

All of that is forgotten once the music starts. My heart beats wildly against my chest as "With or Without You" *by* 2CELLOS *fills the silence. When the doors open, my jaw drops. The small room is all done up with red roses that match my bouquet, and bows made out of white mesh are draped along the sides of each pew—pews that should have our friends and family sitting in them. I brush off the heaviness that attempts to settle inside of me.* It's not the time. *With my head held high, I place one foot in front of the other and make my way down the aisle to the tall, broody man that awaits me.*

He's wearing all black from head to toe. His long hair is pulled back into a smooth bun on the top of his head, and his beard is smooth and trimmed. He looks good enough to eat. His gaze is focused solely on me, and if I weren't close to hyperventilating at the moment, I'd find it sexy as hell. The closer I get, I can see the blues of his eyes darken into a storm of chaos. Hands hang loosely at his sides, but his attention never wavers from of me until I'm standing directly in front of him. A vein throbs in his neck as he stares down at me. His Adam's apple bobs against his throat as he visibly swallows. I can't tell what he's thinking, but judging by the hunger in his eyes, his thoughts aren't that far off from my own.

The priest, whom he managed to find on short notice, stands next to him, and my nerves subside. Being married by a Catholic priest might lessen the consequences of what we're doing. The priest begins to speak, but his words are lost on me the moment Zane takes my hand. The rough skin of his fingers rubs mine in small soothing strokes, reminding me that we couldn't be more opposite. Then again, they say opposites attract.

Words about love and commitment occasionally filter through my haze, but I keep my attention firmly planted on Zane's face. He's my anchor, keeping me from floating adrift and becoming lost.

We continue to go through the motions by reciting our vows and saying, "I do." The cold metal slips onto my finger, cementing us together as man and wife. I'm hit with the sudden reality of the situation. Of what I've just done. And my head starts to spin.

"You may kiss your bride." The priest smiles at us from his place at the altar.

I grip on to Zane tighter to keep my knees from buckling and lean forward, prepared to give him a quick peck on the lips so we can head back to the casino for dinner, but he has other ideas. His fingers slip through my hair and tighten. He pulls me in closer to him until I'm on the tips of my toes and have no choice but to hang on to him for balance. My fingers grip the sides of his lapels to keep upright as his lips crash down on mine. He nibbles on my bottom lip, teasing and tasting me with his tongue. This is no small kiss. It's a full-blown assault on my mouth that I'm feeling down to the tips of my toes. I should feel embarrassed that he's devouring me like this in front of a priest, but I don't. Nothing matters except for Zane and what he's doing to me.

Liquid heat pools deep in my belly down to my core. My thighs clench from the friction of our mouths as he continues to work me over. He tugs on my bottom lip with his teeth and then licks the side of my face. At the same time, a horrible smell hits me.

My eyes shoot open to find Thor in my face and his little body sitting on top of my chest. His tail wags back and forth like a weapon when he realizes that I'm no longer asleep.

I laugh and gently ease him away from me as I sit up and slip on my glasses. He takes that as an invitation to curl up in my lap and put his head down. I scratch behind his ear and stare down at him.

"How did you get in here, troublemaker?"

"That's what I'd like to know."

I jump at the sound of that gravelly voice. My attention was so focused on Thor that I forgot that anyone else was inside my apartment for a brief second. When I glance over at him, my breathing hitches.

Zane's standing in my doorway shirtless with his gray sweatpants sitting low on his waist, showing off the deep cut of his V and every muscle of his six-pack. His hands are shoved inside the front pockets, giving me an unobstructed view of his glorious chest. Tattoos that I don't remember seeing before cover both of his pec muscles. The silver of his nipple rings glints against the sliver of sunlight that's seeping into my room from my parted curtains. That does little to detract from the stoic expression he's wearing. His hardened gaze is planted on the bundle of fur sitting in my lap as he clenches his jaw. The messy knot on the top of his head hits the top of my doorjamb as he cocks his head to the side and continues to watch me. His massive form takes up the entire doorway.

"I take it you've met Thor." I gesture down to the reason for his morning attitude. "He's my favorite little thug," I tease.

"He's a little shit," Zane grunts out.

I cover his ears and shoot Zane a look. He's cranky this morning. "That's not very nice. He can hear you, you know?"

Zane rolls his eyes and removes one of his hands from his pocket to stroke the tip of his beard. "He's a dog, Ken. He has no clue what the hell I'm even saying."

I shake my head at him. "Still, that's mean. We're going to be parents and should probably start watching what we say."

"You been talking to Axel?" His head tilts to the side as he watches me with an expression that I can't quite read.

"No. Why?" My eyes narrow at him, unsure where he's going with this.

"No reason." He shakes his head and brushes off my question.

"How did he even get in here?" I nudge my chin at Thor.

"Not sure. I went out to get us some breakfast, and when I came in here to check on you, I found the little sh—" I clear my throat, and he corrects himself. "I found *him* on your bed."

"Oh." My lips purse into an O.

"Yeah, oh." He's not happy that he's been outsmarted by a dog. "You can bet it won't happen again."

"Why?"

"Because it's a safety issue, and I told you. I'm not taking any chances." His eyes drift down to my stomach and then meet mine. "With either one of you."

"He's a damn Maltese. What's he going to do? Drown me in his drool? This is insane." I gesture to Thor, who's still sitting in my lap with his head cocked to the side, staring at us.

I rub the top of Thor's head, ignoring the brute in my doorway because I don't do well with being told what to do. The second I do, Thor's tongue falls out, and his ears perk up. I hold him up against the side of my T-shirt and rub behind his ears, which gets a little growl of appreciation in return.

"Kennedy." Zane's jaw clenches as he holds me with his stare. "Put. The. Dog. Down." He speaks much slower this time, emphasizing each word. If he's trying to intimidate me into listening, he's got another thing coming.

"Why? He doesn't bite." I glance down at Thor and smile. There's no way something so cute could do something like that. "Do you, boy?"

Zane eats up the distance between us until he's

right before me, invading my personal space. He bends down at the waist and plants his fists on either side of my hips before whispering, "Yeah, well, I do." His lips brush against the shell of my ear, and the smile on my face dies. There's no mistaking the threat in his tone, and all of my earlier bravery goes out the window.

Heat fills my face as those tiny hairs on his beard tickle the sensitive skin at the nape of my neck. My core clenches as thoughts of the locker room yesterday come flooding back to me. It's not the time for this, but tell that to my body. I squeeze my thighs together to dull the ache that's building inside me and do my best to keep my breathing steady and controlled.

When Zane pulls back, his blue eyes have deepened into dark pools. There's no missing the promise in that gaze. He lifts his right hand and strokes the side of my cheek with the pad of his thumb as his eyes flick from mine to my lips and back again. The roughness of his skin against mine ignites a fire deep within me.

My heart pounds in anticipation of his next move, and he doesn't leave me to wonder long. He dips his head to meet my lips, and I lean forward, meeting him halfway, but just as our lips are about to touch, a shrill bark has us jerking apart.

Zane's dark eyebrows pinch together as he shoots Thor a death glare. He opens his mouth to no doubt lay into him, but he's cut off by the sound of my doorbell going off.

His whole body stiffens and goes on high alert. "Are you expecting anyone?"

"No. My brothers tend to stop by, but they usually call first to make sure I'm home." I narrow my eyes and try to think of who else could be here at this hour but come up blank.

"Stay here." He tosses a black T-shirt on and heads out into the living room without waiting for me to respond.

Thor jumps off my lap and follows after him, leaving me in my bed alone. I sigh as I wait for Zane to answer the door. The second he does, and I hear her voice, I jump out of bed and race after them both in nothing but my oversized T-shirt. The hardwood flooring is a shock to my bare feet, and for a split second, I debate turning around to find some pants but think better of it. There's no telling what Mrs. Baker will say.

When I come up behind Zane, he's taking up my entire doorway. I have to duck underneath his shoulder to squeeze in next to him. He drops his right hand and plants it firmly around my waist the moment I do.

"Morning, Mrs. Baker." I brush the stray strands of hair out of my face and try not to look like the mess I feel. Judging by her reddened cheeks, I failed.

"Hi, dear. I am so sorry to interrupt." She spares Zane and me a glance as she holds Thor tight against her chest.

"You're not interrupting anything." My voice comes out much too high, giving me away.

"I was just apologizing to this young man." She gestures to Zane with her free hand, ignoring the inflection in my voice. "I don't know how this little stinker keeps getting out. I bought a baby gate for my front door, but my grandson hasn't had a chance to put it up for me."

"Zane can do it for you." I smack him in the chest,

ignoring how solid his muscles feel against the back of my hand or the fact that he didn't even flinch.

Zane's head snaps in my direction the second the words are out of my mouth, and I can see his dark eyebrows arching out of the corner of my eye, but I keep my focus on Mrs. Baker. He shouldn't have tried to tell me what to do.

"Oh, I don't want to be a bother to y'all." Mrs. Baker tilts her head in Zane's direction and smiles.

"It's no trouble, ma'am." Zane clears his throat and attempts to soften his features when he answers her. He ends up looking more like he's in pain than anything else. "I can come over tomorrow after Ken's doctor appointment and set it up for you."

My body freezes momentarily, hearing that he called me Ken, but also, more importantly, at the fact that he knew about my appointment. I never told him when it was, but it shouldn't surprise me that he found out on his own. The man is more like my father than he'd ever admit. As if he can sense what I'm thinking, his fingers dig into my waist in a silent warning to keep quiet.

"That would be great." Mrs. Baker's face lights up at the offer as I force my smile to stay in place. "Thank you." Thor wiggles in her arms, reminding her that he's there. "Well, I better get this rascal home." She turns and hobbles back into her apartment.

As soon as she's out of sight, Zane drops his hand from around my waist and reaches for the knob. I back up next to my kitchenette, giving him ample space to shut the door as I attempt to cool my temper and wait for an explanation. In hindsight, I should have run.

That resounding click changes everything. It echoes

throughout my entire tiny apartment like an impending sense of doom. He flicks the deadbolt and turns around to face me with that blank expression he always seems to wear on his face. His body leans back against the door as he folds his arms over his chest and stares at me.

The silence is thick with tension. We're locked away from the outside world, and the air is sucked out of the room. I feel the weight of his stare down to my toes. I'm trapped. At least when I had Thor in my lap, he acted as a buffer. Now I'm on my own, and I'm so screwed. My heart pounds against my chest as I attempt to figure a way out of my current situation, but then I remember what he said, and a whole new set of emotions comes bubbling to the surface.

"How did you find out about my doctor's appointment?" I put my hands on my hips and glare right back. I didn't intend on keeping it from him, but the fact that he found out behind my back has my temper rising to the surface.

"I have my ways." He shrugs but doesn't say anything more, which only pisses me off.

"That's it. That's all you're going to say." I wrinkle my nose and fight the urge to scream at him.

Another shrug.

"You've ignored me for days to the point where I left your ass. Now you've insulted a poor dog and invaded my privacy. All I'm going to get from you is a fucking shrug?" I might be overreacting, but my hormones are all over the place lately. Not to mention, I'm still not entirely over how much of an ass he was to me. It hurt. We were supposed to be a team. In this together, but then he went off and disappeared on me.

All common sense leaves me the more my temper

flares to life. That's the only explanation for what I do next. Without a second thought, I pick up one of the magazines lying on top of the counter to my left and chuck it across the room, nailing him square in the middle of his chest.

The magazine lands with a thump against the floor, and my jaw drops right along with it. I can't believe I just did that.

"You're gonna pay for that." Zane presses off the door and stalks toward me. His steps are slow and controlled, like a hunter about to corner their prey.

"Oh shit." I waste no time spinning around to my bedroom with him hot on my heels. I'm through my bedroom door a few seconds later and make it to the farthest side of my bed as he enters the room. I jump on top of my bed and hold my arms out in front of me in a poor attempt at warding him off. "Don't be mad."

"I'm not mad." His voice is calm—a little too calm. It's unsettling. His arms hang loosely at his sides as he cocks his head to the side and watches me.

"I have to get ready for work. If I'm late, my father might show up." I attempt to distract him, but he has an answer for everything.

"Connor called. They gave you the rest of the week off."

My stomach plummets. Foiled by my own flesh and blood.

"I'm sorry, okay? I don't know what came over me." It sounds childish, but it's the truth. I grew up with four brothers and had to hold my own. That means I usually go on the offensive first.

He doesn't say anything as he steps deeper into the room. The closer he gets to the foot of the bed, the faster my breathing becomes. My pulse pounds against my ears in time with his steps. Once again, he's managed to dominate my space completely. I'm trapped with nowhere to go.

"Not yet, but you will be." His low voice skates across my skin, leaving chills in its wake.

My nipples harden at the commanding tone of his words, drawing his eyes straight to my chest. In all of my haste to get to the door earlier, I forgot to put a damn bra on. He has a front-row show of exactly how I feel about his little threat. His tongue darts out to lick his bottom lip as I see the rigid outline of his dick through his gray sweatpants. I bite my bottom lip to keep from clenching my thighs together, but Zane can see every emotion on my face clear as day.

His nostrils flare as he creeps up closer to the foot of my bed, caging me in. "Now we're gonna play by my rules."

Shit. I'm in serious trouble.

12

KENNEDY

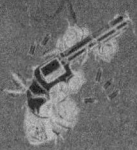

I fake like I'm going left in hopes of tricking him, but my feet get tangled up in the mess of blankets on top of my bed, and I end up tripping. My hair falls in my face while my knees hit the mattress with a soft bounce. Before I can even right myself, Zane's on me. His rough fingers circle my ankle and drag me down toward the foot of the bed. My T-shirt rides up the closer to the edge I get, exposing my lower body to the cool air in the room. I ignore the fact that my ass is on display for him and attempt to crab crawl away, but I don't even make it a single step.

Zane has me flipped over onto my back in a matter of seconds. He pins my arms above my head as the weight of his body comes down on top of me, cautious of putting too much pressure on my stomach and keeping me in place. His hips nestle between my legs as the few long strands of hair that fell out of his bun drape down, sweeping across the top of my chest. The hard ridge of his dick rubs up against my bare ass, and my insides tremble. A shudder of need rushes through me as I bite my lip to avoid letting out a moan, but it's pointless.

My heart pounds against my ribs from the heat of his skin seeping into mine. Each deep inhale I take pushes my breasts deeper against his rock-hard chest. My toes curl into the mattress as I fight the onslaught of emotions overcoming me. This position is far too intimate for the tongue lashing I want to give him.

Deep blue eyes bear down on me as he watches my every move, waiting to see what I will do next. I bare my teeth at him as I press my heels into the mattress and push with all the strength of my lower body in a poor attempt at flipping him over. I fail, and I can hear Connor telling me I fucked up the second Zane got me on my back. I know better, but Zane has my head in knots, throwing me off my game.

I try to push him off me once more, but he's like a ton of bricks weighing me down and doesn't budge. The only thing I succeed in is rubbing myself even deeper against him, and my core clenches from the contact. Nothing is separating us but the thin, soft cotton of his sweatpants.

Zane's fingers flex around my wrists as he stares down at me, but he's not even out of breath from our struggles. The bastard.

"You done?"

"No."

I squeeze my hands into fists, ignoring the weight of my wedding ring digging into my finger and how my glasses are pushing up against my nose. I attempt to twist to the side to throw him off balance, but it's no use. He isn't going anywhere. I end up winded and pissed the hell off.

My heavy breathing is the only sound in the room as we remain locked in our stare down. The rough material of my T-shirt brushes against my nipples, making them even harder, sending a shock wave of tingles through me that I feel down to my toes. The fine hairs on my arms stand on end as I clench my thighs tighter around his waist, trying to soothe the building ache. Everything inside of me is like a live wire ready to snap at any moment. Blood pounds in my ears as the sweetness of his gum mixed with a hint of cedarwood invades my senses and sends them into overdrive. It's earthy and sweet and all him.

"Fuck me. You're stubborn." He shakes his head, but there's a softness to his features that contradicts his words.

"You're just now figuring that out?" I raise an eyebrow at him, determined not to give in. The sensations that are starting to overtake me are making that almost impossible.

I expect him to argue, but he surprises me. His head dips down, and he kisses me. I'm a goner the second those warm lips connect with mine. They're soft and firm all at the same time. My eyes close, becoming lost in him as his tongue slips inside my mouth and intertwines with mine. The fine hairs of his beard scrape against my face as he tilts his head to the side, deepening the angle. His tongue continues to stroke and play with me until I've forgotten where we are or why we're even in this position.

He pulls back and whispers against my mouth, "Do I have your attention now?"

I open my eyes to find his hooded ones burning into mine. "Yeah," is all I can manage to say. I'm still in a Zane daze and only partially coherent at the moment.

"Good. Tell me why I shouldn't spank your ass for that shit you just pulled?" he growls out. The vibrations of his voice send shivers through my body, but I ignore them as my anger storms to the forefront.

Heat floods my cheeks as I shoot him a death glare. "Because you're an asshole, and you deserved it."

"I am." His chin dips in agreement.

My body tenses underneath him. "You're unbelievable." I let out a hollow laugh and shake my head at him. All the feelings I had for him moments ago disappear, and I fight with the urge to punch him. If my arms weren't still pinned to the bed, I would. "I tell you you're being a dick, and you just agree with me? No explanation."

"Would you rather have some bullshit excuse? You want a fight? Will that make you feel better?" His face hardens as the lines on his forehead deepen.

"Yes. No. I don't know."

I'm not used to his bluntness, and it's confusing the shit out of me.

"Or maybe you want something else," he says more to himself as he grinds up against my core once more.

My mouth drops open as those same urges that fled moments ago come rushing back with a vengeance this time.

"Oh, god." I'm so sensitive that it doesn't take much for that familiar ache to rebuild inside me. My head falls back against the mattress as a moan escapes me.

"Is that what you want?" A vein throbs along the side of his neck as his fingers dig deeper into the flesh of my wrists.

"Yes." I'm not above begging at this point. I'll worry about our issues later. "Please."

He switches my wrists into his left hand and slides his right one down my chest, past my stomach, and straight into my underwear. His fingers go straight to my clit, stroking in small smooth circles that have my insides fluttering.

"You're fucking soaked." His nostrils flare as the corded muscles of his neck become rigid.

"It's these stupid pregnancy hormones." I gasp as he hits the spot, and my entire body quivers.

"Hmm," he hums against my lips. His fingers pick up the pace as he continues to work me over and over. Taking me closer to the edge, but never letting me fall. He enjoys toying with me like he's in no hurry. My head begins to float the more his fingers continue to play with me, stroking the fire but never quite giving me the explosion of release I need. It's cruel.

"Stop teasing me." I don't care if I sound like I'm throwing a tantrum. I've been going without for too damn long, and the urge to come is overriding all my common sense.

"Only good girls get to come." He nips at my bottom lip. "Have you been a good girl, Ken?"

"Yes." A wave of tremors courses through me.

"I don't know." His lips trail down my neck as his fingers continue to scissor inside me. "Good girls do what they're told."

"Zane." I grind my teeth together as he continues to torment me in the best way.

"Quiet." His teeth nip at the sensitive skin where my neck and shoulder meet. "We're playing by my rules."

"Your rules suck." A whimper leaves me as he bites down even harder. I'm going to have a mark there later.

He lifts his head, and that's when I see the beast that's about to be unleashed. His fingers hook into the side of my underwear, and he rips them off, flinging them over his shoulder. He tugs at the edges of my T-shirt and growls out, "Off. Now."

I lift it over my head as fast as possible and throw it on the floor behind him. My glasses get knocked to the side in the process, and I go to remove them, but he stops me.

"Leave them on. I want you to watch me." He releases his grip on my wrists, throws my legs onto his shoulders, and slides down the bed until he's eye level with my pussy. His nose grazes along my inner thigh as he takes a deep inhale. "Fuck me. You smell like sin." His tongue flicks out and licks up along my slit. "And taste like heaven." He shoves his tongue inside me, and my hips buck up off the bed. He's working me over with so much intensity that his hair falls out of the rubber band and tickles the inside of my thighs. His shoulders hold me in place as he devours me like I'm his last meal.

I rip the hair tie out of his hair and slide my fingers through the long strands, fisting the sides, and grind my hips against his face. The feel of his mouth working me into a frenzy mixed with the slight tickle of his beard against my ass and the tips of his hair skating along the tops of my thighs has me in sensation overload. But it isn't enough. I still want more.

I tug on his hair, stopping him. He lifts his head to look up at me with my wetness coating his lips and his long dark hair covering his face. It's hot as fuck. I take my glasses off and set them down on the nightstand next to the bed and hold his blurry gaze to make a demand of my own.

"I want my mouth on you too."

He grips me by the ass and flips us over so that I'm on top of him. I brace my hands on the mattress, but before I can gain my bearings, I'm spun around until I'm eye level with his dick. He wraps his arms around my waist, locking me in place and bringing my pussy deeper into his mouth.

A rush of heat courses through me, but a flash of silver glints against the sunlight, and my mouth waters. "Holy shit." He's got an Apadravya piercing. That's new. I grip his dick and flick my tongue against the barbell that goes from the underside of his dick and out through the tip.

He groans against my pussy, and the vibrations send ripples of need through me. I suck him deeper inside my mouth, but he's so big that I can't take all of him. My lips wrap around the head as my tongue continues to play with his piercing. The salty taste of his skin coats my tongue and spurs me on to take him in even deeper. I slide down until I feel the metal of the barbell hit the back of my throat and smile as I'm rewarded with a guttural response as he shoves a finger inside of me.

Drool slides down my cheeks the deeper I take him, but I don't stop. I hollow out my cheeks, increasing the pressure as I slide back and forth, flicking my tongue against the head of his dick each time. He adds a second finger and continues to fuck me in rhythm with his tongue. His tongue strokes my clit, and I hum through a mouthful of dick as I feel the first stirrings of my orgasm stirring deep within my belly. The more he eats me and fucks me with his fingers, the harder I suck until my entire body convulses, and I can't think of anything else but sucking him in deeper.

"Come on my face," Zane growls out, and that's all it takes for my orgasm to overtake me entirely. My thighs shake as my entire body convulses, but he never stops licking and sucking as I grind down on his face and ride out the wave of pleasure.

Zane doesn't wait for the tremors to subside before flipping me over onto my back and coming down on top of me until we're face-to-face. I wait for him to slip inside me, but he doesn't. He stares down at me with my juices coating his lips, asking permission without words.

"I need you." My words are soft and breathless, much like I feel.

"Need me to what?" The bastard is toying with me and knows exactly what I'm begging for.

"I need you to fuck me. To make the ache go away." My fingers dig into the muscles of his biceps in an attempt to pull him in closer to me. "Please." I'm not above begging, and that's the only encouragement he needs.

My words are like gasoline to the fire. He aligns himself with my core and slips inside of me in one quick thrust with such force all the air leaves me. He's so big and thick that my muscles tense up.

"Fuck, you're tight." He growls out as he stills inside of me and waits for me to become accustomed to his size. "Ken, baby, I need you to relax, or this will hurt you."

"I'm trying. You're just so big." My head drops back against my pillow as I take a few deep breaths and will my body to relax. It takes a couple of times, but my muscles eventually get the message and slacken as they become accustomed to the invasion.

"Good girl." He slides out and slams back inside, pinning me deeper into the mattress.

"Holy shit!" I hum out a moan as the tip of his piercing hits me deep inside, nailing my G-spot. My heels dig into the mattress from the intensity of sensations running through me. Sex has never been this intense for me before. That little piece of metal is taking me to new heights I didn't imagine possible.

My fingers skate down his back, and what I find surprises me. There are small marks all along his upper back. Some are smooth, and others feel bumpy. Zane freezes for a brief second underneath my touch, but instead of freaking out like I'm expecting, he leans back and grabs my wrists. He presses them against his chest, and a flashback to our first night together comes to me. I know what he wants without asking. I dig my fingernails into the flesh of his chest until I feel his skin push in and try to alleviate some of the tension coiling up inside of me.

"Fuck." Zane sucks in a deep breath. "Hurt me. Make me bleed." I do as he says and press even deeper. I'm rewarded with a deep growl. The tips of my nails scrape down his chest, leaving a trail of red behind. Blood trickles down his chest, but he isn't satisfied with that. "More, Hummingbird. I need more."

Pain and pleasure are a fine line, and I don't want to go too far, but it's almost as if he needs this. Craves it.

I dig my fingernails into the bloody scratch marks on his chest until blood seeps under my fingernails, and Zane never loses his momentum. The more pain I inflict, the rougher he fucks me.

"Just like that." He groans and pounds into me harder, pushing my headboard against the wall.

My head falls back, and I drop my hands to the sides of his arms for balance as he thrusts into me. Over and over. Never stopping. It becomes a violent storm of skin slapping against skin. Then the pace changes. It becomes rougher. Harsher. And it hurts.

When I look back up, there's a glazed-over look on his face, and my heart stills. His eyes are a black void, and his face has lost all color. His body is here, but his mind is somewhere else. I cup the side of his face and stroke his cheek with my finger.

"Hey, come back to me." When he doesn't respond, I try again. "Zane," I say, a bit firmer, tightening my grip on his face. Still nothing.

His fingers sink into the pillow on either side of my head as his features harden and he slams back inside me. A gasp leaves me as a mixture of pleasure and pain fills me. Wherever he's trapped, it isn't good. Beads of sweat drip down his face, and the tendons stand out on the sides of his neck. An ache builds deep inside my throat as I watch helplessly underneath him as he falls apart before me.

I need to think of something, and fast. Or else things are going to get a lot worse.

I jerk his head down to mine and kiss him. At first, he doesn't kiss me back. I keep at him, coaxing him to open up for me. It takes a few moments for him to come out of his head, but once he is back with me, he takes control, shoving his tongue inside my mouth. Tasting myself on his tongue has my toes curling into the mattress. When he pulls back, I'm left breathless.

"I'm sorry." He presses his forehead against mine and sighs.

"Where did you go?" My heart pounds against my chest as I watch his color come back.

"Nowhere." He brushes off my concern as his hips pick back up at a much slower pace than before. It's as if he's apologizing to me for earlier.

I quickly succumb to the new rhythm and feel the peak of orgasm number two coming on when Zane stops. I open my mouth, ready to rip him a new one, but he flips us over until I'm straddling him. How he manages to do that without breaking our connection is a mystery. My knees press up against his sides as I gasp for breath. This position puts him even deeper inside me. I can feel him in my stomach. It's so intense that I can barely stay upright.

"Ride me." He slaps the cheek of my ass before gripping a handful of flesh.

I lean forward and brace my hands on the headboard and slam my hips back down on top of him. Zane takes advantage of this new position and sucks a nipple into his mouth. His tongue flicks and swirls around the sensitive flesh until it stiffens. And fuck me, does it feel good.

"You keep doing that, and I'm going to come again." I slap my hand against the headboard and try to get my breathing under control.

He groans in response but doesn't stop. A stirring builds inside me, and I'm overcome with the need to move. I pull back until he lets go of my nipple with a loud pop and takes charge.

My fingers hook inside the hoops of his nipple rings, and I tug on the little pieces of metal with each rotation of my hips. Zane's fingers dig deeper into my waist as he lets out a growl in response. I never stop grinding and tugging until that familiar ache builds. It isn't long until I feel my inner walls clench around him. I throw my head back and ride him as if my life depends on it.

"Fuck," Zane growls out as he throbs inside of me, spilling his release.

I rotate my hips a few more times and come again, not stopping until we're both wrung out and sated. Spent and limp, my body collapses on top of his firm chest. I listen to his heart pounding as I try to steady my rapid breathing.

The seconds morph into minutes as we lie like this. Connected and at peace. Nothing exists outside of this bubble we've concocted but the two of us. And I wish it could stay that way for a while longer, but Zane has other ideas.

He rolls us over until we're back right where we started, with me on my back. I wince from the loss when he pulls out of me, but he doesn't leave me for long. He lies down next to me and brings me up against his chest. His warm fingers strum over my back in smooth strokes, and it only adds to the cloud of pleasure my head is floating on.

"We need to talk."

"About what?" My head is still in the clouds, and I'm not sure I can even focus on words.

"Shit's gone down, and things will be a little crazy."

"What kind of shit are we talking about exactly?" I play with his nipple piercing as he talks, his deep voice rumbling underneath me.

"The serious kind."

"I'm afraid I will need more than that to go on." I roll

my eyes at him. He should know better if he thinks I'll be satisfied with vague orders.

"Do you trust me?"

"I'm learning to." There are still things I don't know about him, like what happened the night I left or where he went minutes ago for me to do that.

"That's fair. But, given who your dad is, I know that you're smart enough to know that when I tell you that shit is going down and you are not to leave my side, you know it's for your own good." I open my mouth to ask what, but he presses a finger to my lips, shutting me up. "Not done, Ken. I will do whatever I have to do to protect both of you. Everything I do, I do for a reason. You need to remember that."

"What if I think your reasons are shit?" I sigh against his chest.

He rolls me over onto my back and slips his fingers inside of me, then smears his cum over my clit.

"You'll learn."

13
ZANE

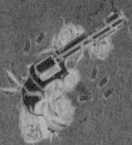

The stench of dirt and blood surrounds me, but it's
her soft cries that fill the room and set my rage on
fire. Tears stream down her face as she begs and
pleads with them to stop hurting her. Her dirty blond hair is
matted, and pieces are stuck to the side of her bruised face as
a mixture of sweat and blood drips down her temple. She
attempts to beg once more, but it falls on deaf ears. The
bastard violating her groans as he continues to use her for his
own pleasure.

My teeth grind together as the flame churns deeper in
my gut. "Get the fuck away from her!" I shout, but it's
no use.

They aren't stopping. Each of them takes a turn violating
her repeatedly. I jerk and pull on my chains with everything
I have, feeling them give a little more each time. The skin on
my wrists is raw and bloody, but I don't stop trying. The
moment I do, we're dead. Her cries burn in my ears, fueling
my need to break free.

When I glance over at her, a smear of blood coats the
inside of her thigh. That's the final snap on my thread of

sanity. The chains come down with one last pull, and every-thing fades into a red haze.

Toothless is the first fucker I reach, and I snap his neck before he can take his next breath. The machete, still coated in Nelson's blood, drops from his grasp toward the floor, but I swipe it up midair before it can hit the ground and move closer to the back of the room, where the other two still have her pinned down.

The short fucker rushes toward me, but I arc my hand, slicing him across the jugular with the blade. Blood coats my face and neck, but it doesn't deter me. I have a mission. One I will see through. I toss his lifeless body aside and head for the bald bastard huddling in the corner like a fucking pussy and using her for a shield.

He pulls out his whip and cracks it, taunting me, but I'm not chained up and defenseless. I'm free and ready for him. I grab the end of the whip and jerk him closer to me. I take the chain that's still dangling from my wrists and coil it around his neck. My hands squeeze with every last bit of strength I have until his face turns a deep shade of purple. His eyes widen, but I never let up, not until he stops breathing.

I throw him off to the side and make my way over to the girl. Her tear-stained face stares up at me as her naked body shakes. My eyes dart around the room and find a stained blanket that I toss to her. She's shivering and going into shock, which makes me feel like an ass for rushing her, but time isn't on our side. I'm not sure how many more there are or who might come.

"We're getting out of here." It's a promise. One I will keep.

She grabs the thin blanket and wraps it around herself. Once she's steady enough, I help her to her feet and take her hand. I keep her hidden behind me. Her hands hang onto the waistband of my cargo pants with a vise-like grip as I pull her along to the door. The machete stays stretched out in front of me while I lead the way out of this hellhole.

My heart pounds in my throat as we creep out into the darkened hall and head off to the left. I have no idea where the fuck I'm going, but I act purely on gut instinct and follow the moonlight. Judging by the damp coldness of the cement touching my bare feet, we're on the first floor.

Silence echoes around us as I strain to hear any little sound I can, but all I'm met with is silence. So far, so good. At the end of the hall, we come up to a door, but her hand is jerked away from my waistband before I can open it.

When I turn around, machete out and ready to strike, my jaw drops. The young boy from earlier—the one that knocked me out—stands with her pulled against his side and a gun pressed against her temple.

I try to talk him down, but he screams something back at me in Pashto, digging the barrel deeper into her skin the louder his words get. I can't understand what he's saying, but I can read body language, and his is threatening. She whimpers, but I tune her out and focus on the one thing I'm trained for—neutralizing the threat. I just never thought it would be a fucking kid.

"All right. I'm putting it down." I hinge at the waist and set the machete down on the ground next to my feet. I stand upright and raise my hands up in surrender. I'm doing my best to appear nonthreatening. "See." I take a hesitant step forward, trying to distract him with my words. All I need is an opening, and I can get her free. "I can help you." I keep my voice calm like I'm talking to a wounded animal. The last thing I want to do is spook him by making any sudden moves.

He shouts back more words that I can't understand, pointing the gun at me and then crushing it against her temple. He's jumpy and armed, which is never a good combination.

"I promise I won't hurt you." I'm trying to negotiate with him however I can to get us all out of this in one piece. But it's too late.

"No. Don't!" I lunge forward, but I'm not fast enough.

He squeezes the trigger, and I'm forced to watch the life leave her eyes. He tosses her aside and aims it at me, but I'm quicker. I tackle him to the ground and grab the butt of the gun, trying to get it from him, but the kid is stronger than he looks. It becomes a tug of war for the weapon, and then a loud crack breaks through the air. His eyes go wide as his body goes slack and blood trickles out of the side of his mouth.

"No!" I drop the gun as a coldness seeps into my body.

I've killed many faceless enemies in battle, but nothing prepares you for something like this. I suck in a few deep breaths and stand to my feet as I stare down at them. Just kids caught up in a war that's not their fault.

"God. Damn. It!" I run a hand through my hair and try to calm down enough to figure out my next move.

My muscles strain from exertion, but I know I have to keep moving if I'm going to make it out of here alive. I shake off my emotions and turn to find my way out, but I'm tackled from behind. Arms come around my throat as the prick behind me puts me in a headlock. I try to push off the ground and flip us over, but the fucker is too heavy.

My elbow cocks back, nailing him in the stomach and knocking the wind out of him. I use his distraction and flip him over onto his back. My knees cradle against his sides as I straddle him and use my body weight to pin him down. He manages to get a few punches in, but I'm bigger. My hands wrap around his throat and clamp down. I squeeze until I see *his eyes bulge out of his head. Fingernails slice down my neck, and this heat feels different.*

My eyes shoot open, and that's when I'm met with an explosion of color. "Fuck." Everything inside of me turns cold. My hands drop away from around her neck, and I jump the fuck off the bed like it's on fire. What the fuck did I just do? "Did I hurt you?"

Kennedy scoots up toward the headboard and grabs at her throat. Her tits are out on full display because we fell asleep naked after I fucked us into a coma, but I'm too focused on how they're heaving up and down as she struggles to catch her breath to care about anything else. Her face is a bit paler than normal, and that only sinks home how badly I've just fucked up.

"I'm fine." Her voice comes out strained and raspy, adding to the disgust I feel at myself.

I rush over to her side of the bed and move her hands to inspect what I'm pretty damn sure is lying beneath them. When I see the red fingerprints on her smooth white skin, I want to kick my ass.

"No, you're not." I fist the sides of my hair and squeeze until I can feel it pulling at the roots. I deserve the pain for what I've just done to her. "Goddammit!" I pace around the room in a piss-poor attempt at controlling my temper.

"Zane." She tries to get my attention, but I'm so disgusted that I don't look up. I can't. Seeing the fear behind her eyes will be my ultimate undoing.

"This is why I kept my distance. I knew shit like this was bound to happen."

"It's okay." Her hoarse voice shoves the dagger into my heart even deeper.

This is why I'm always alone. I'm dangerous to her. To our baby.

"Nothing about this is okay. I could have killed you." Every muscle in my body is corded tight and ready to snap.

"You're right. You could have, and now that I know this happens, I'll be sure not to try and wake you in your sleep." Her lips spread into a smile, but it doesn't erase the uncertainty that's warring behind her eyes.

"There isn't going to be a next time." I'll make sure of it. I grab my shit and exit out the door before she can stop me. I need to get out of here and out of my head, and there's only one person who knows better than me what I need.

I send a text to Connor before pulling my truck out onto the highway and head to the one place where I can think with a clear head and with no distractions.

When I pull up to the tree line, my temper still hasn't cooled. I check my phone and see that I have a few missed calls from Axel and Asher. No doubt Connor called them after I sent him a text. Kennedy left a voice mail, but I can't bring myself to listen to it. I'll deal with it later. I toss a piece of Juicy Fruit into my mouth, wishing like fuck it was a cigarette instead, and climb out of my truck. Before I disappear through the trees, I grab the ax that's lying next to the front porch of the small one-bedroom cabin and continue on my way to the clearing. The place used to belong to my mother's parents, and when she and my dad died, it became mine. It sits on the back edge of our family property and is far enough away that no one will even bother me out here.

My fingers itch to destroy something, to dull the shit storm I feel brewing inside of me. I grab a small log and set it on the large stump. I raise the ax above my head and slam down onto the log with one deep breath. It cracks down the middle, just like me, broken and jagged. My anger eases with each one I split, but nothing can fade the memory of those marks on her neck. I could have fucking killed her and our kid.

I'm several logs deep when I feel his presence behind me. I should have known if anyone found me, it would be him. Once a cop, always a cop. I continue chopping the wood and wait him out. I'm not sure who will break the silence between the two of us first. It's usually Axel that does that shit.

I'm so focused on my brother that I'm not paying attention and eventually run out of logs, which leaves me no choice but to acknowledge him. On a deep exhale, I turn to face Asher. He's leaning against a nearby tree with his arms folded across his chest, face blank.

He continues to watch me and pick me apart. Ever since Florida, he's been giving me looks, and I knew sooner or later we were going to end up here. He's working something out in his head. I have no idea what, but I still brace for what's to come. My big brother isn't dumb, and like me, he doesn't feel the need to waste words on bullshit.

"Do you know what happens to an ex-cop in prison?"

His question throws me for a loop. It's not what I expected him to say, but Asher never does what you expect.

"Ash." Muscles in my jaw clench as he brings up his past. Neither one of us likes to talk about this shit. We prefer our demons to stay dead and buried, which is why I am not sure why we're even talking about it now.

"It takes a toll on your soul. Every single day I woke up wondering if it would be my last." He takes a cigarette out of the pack in the back pocket of his jeans and lights it up. "If maybe it would be the day I'd see Lauren and our son again and be able to beg their forgiveness for letting them down that night."

"Ash, that wasn't your fault. And the bastards paid. We all made sure they were sent to hell where they belong."

"It doesn't make the shit any easier to live with." He takes another drag off his cigarette and shakes his head at me as he slips the pack back into his pocket.

"What's your point?" My fingers itch to steal the entire pack from him, but I fight the temptation and grind down on my fucking gum. It's flavorless and like chewing on grass, but that's one temptation I won't give in to.

Like he knows what I'm thinking, Asher blows a cloud of smoke in my direction. "My point is that we've both gone through some serious shit, which is why we aren't like Axel. Our demons are harder to slay but not impossible to manage. This shit will consume you until there's nothing left if you let it, little brother."

"So, what am I supposed to do?" I toss the ax onto the ground and cross my arms over my chest, facing him head-on.

"You find the light in the dark. The one thing that'll keep them quiet long enough for you to survive through the day, and then you get up and do it all over again until they're so quiet you can almost forget that they're even there in the first place."

His words hit home, and I know what he's implying without him saying a word.

"Kennedy." I let her name slip past my lips in a deep sigh.

"And your kid." He holds my stare. "You do whatever you have to do to keep them safe. Axel and I are here to help with that."

"What if they're safer without me?" It feels like I'm chewing on broken glass as I say those words out loud, but a part of me knows it's true.

"That's bullshit, and you know it." Asher tosses the butt of his cigarette on the ground and stomps it out as he narrows his eyes at me. "You telling me you'd be okay with someone else raising your kid and taking care of your woman? That anyone will protect them like you will? Because, brother, we both know you're fucking lying to yourself."

I hang my head and let his words sink in. Truth is, he's right. I may be a fuck-up, but they're mine. Mine to keep. Mine to protect. It doesn't make what happened earlier any easier to swallow. "What if it's me they need to be protected from?"

He pushes off the tree and closes the short distance between us. "Then Axel and I will be the first to kick your ass."

"Please tell me you didn't tell Axel where you went? I can't deal with his bullshit right now."

"Who do you think has Lily?" He cocks an eyebrow

at me, and the two of us lift the corner of our mouths in a smirk. If anyone can distract our little brother, it's Asher's kid.

"It'll be his turn to have one soon." I have no doubt Axel will want a kid of his own.

"Let's just hope it takes after Kelsey." Asher rolls his eyes at the thought and then makes eye contact with me. "You good?"

"Yeah, man. I'm good." And I am. I'll just have to be more careful.

"Good. Come to the house. I did some more digging, and there's shit you need to see."

Judging by the tightness in his face, I'm not going to like what I find.

"Why the fuck didn't you start with that?" I narrow my eyes.

Asher shrugs. "I needed your head straight first before adding more shit to it."

"It's straight now. Let's go." I turn and head toward my truck.

"One more thing," Asher calls over my back. "Connor told me to remind you of Kennedy's appointment tomorrow."

"I didn't forget. Show me the shit you found so I can get back where I need to be."

Little did I know that he was right. My head needed to be straight for all of the shit he showed me.

14

KENNEDY

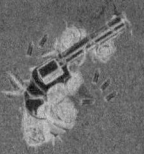

I sit on the bed to slip on my Vans and let out a small groan. Every time I move, reminders of what happened yesterday hit me. I can still feel Zane thrusting inside of me. Then I remember how things went downhill from there and that he left. I tried to call him once more after I left the voice mail, but after it went unanswered yet again, I gave up. I have more important things to worry about right now.

Movement out of the corner of my eye catches my attention, jerking me back to the present. When I glance over to the doorway, Rory is leaning against the jamb with his arms crossed over his chest. He's in the same jeans and navy T-shirt he was wearing the night before. After Zane left, my brother was at my front door with a bottle of Vitaminwater and two containers of chicken fried rice. I knew him showing up with my favorite food was his brotherly way of softening the disaster that has become my life. At least he didn't make me talk about it. We watched movies in silence until I passed out.

I woke up with a raw throat and aching chest. Sleep

came, but it was filled with nightmares of the haunting look on Zane's face when he saw what he had done to me. My thoughts must be projecting onto my face because Rory's expression hardens. It takes me a minute to realize his gaze is fixated on my reddened cheeks. If he notices my puffy eyes, he doesn't let on about it, which I appreciate. I feel a stray tear slip down the side of my face, and I wipe it away as quickly as possible, but he notices the movement.

The movement causes Rory to break his staring contest with my sad face, and he pushes himself away from the doorjamb into my room. He kneels in front of me and tilts my head to face him.

"He doesn't deserve those." His tatted thumb swipes underneath my glasses to catch another tear falling down my cheek.

"I know."

I'd like to blame my emotional meltdown on my pregnancy hormones, but that would be a lie. Some of it is because of one stubborn bearded baby daddy.

"You want me to kick his ass, just say the word." Rory's blue eyes deepen as he fights the urge to remain calm.

"Thanks, Ror. You're all heart." I sniffle and roll my eyes at him.

"The chicks don't complain." He shrugs and stands to his feet.

"Please don't tell me about your sex life ever." I wrinkle my nose at the thought of my brother's revolving door. "Unless you want me to cover you in regurgitated chicken fried rice."

"Noted." His lips twitch as he fights the urge to smile. "Are you ready to go?"

"Yup." I stand to my feet and follow my brother out to the elevator and into his truck.

I sit back against my seat and toy with the edges of my blue tunic, doing my best not to get lost in my head again. The familiar scent of tobacco and spice fills the cab, and a small smile plays on my lips. My brother has always loved to indulge in cloves.

The drive to the doctor's office is about what I expected. It's silent and awkward, except for the endless supply of U2 songs Rory plays on repeat. I asked him once what it was about that band, and his reply was simple—"Bono." Enough said in one word.

From the time Rory parks the truck in the parking garage to the time we make it into the waiting room is a bit of a blur. I'm moving on autopilot and hoping my morning sickness will remain under control. It's been hit or miss lately. Rory's phone goes off, and when he looks at the caller ID, his eyebrows scrunch together.

"I have to take this. Go check in, and I'll be right behind you." He's holding his phone up to his ear and walking off before I can nod my head. Whatever it is must be important. My dad's number one rule is family before business, but this must be important enough for Rory to take a call now.

I shrug it off and walk inside the office. It's eerily quiet except for the occasional ringing of a phone. A few women are sitting in some of the chairs, and they are much further along in their pregnancies than me. A wave of panic filters through me, but I don't let it pull me under. I square my shoulders back and walk up to the front desk to check in with all the confidence I don't feel.

The lady behind the counter greets me with a smile

as she types a few keys on her computer. "Name?" she asks.

I clear my throat a couple of times before I can get my name out of my mouth. "Kennedy Donnelly."

"Savage. It's Kennedy Savage," Zane corrects, making me jump. He's so quiet that I never even heard him come up behind me.

"Right." Her eyes grow wide as she stares at the tattooed giant behind me.

With his long dark hair down around his black T-shirt. A T-shirt that looks like it's two sizes too small, as it leaves little to the imagination. Her eyes widen as they come into contact with the outline of his nipple piercings, and an irrational burning sensation flitters across my chest. I stomp out the spark of jealousy before it makes me do something insane and end up needing to find a new doctor.

She darts her eyes back and forth between us before giving us a slight nod. "Go ahead and have a seat, and they'll call you back shortly."

"Thanks." I do my best to make up for the brute behind me, but the damage is done.

She nods and goes back to staring at her monitor.

I spin around on the heels of my Vans, walk right past the bearded pain in my ass, and plant myself into the nearest seat, which so happens to be a small two-seater bench. Zane slips into the space next to me, and luckily for him, there isn't an armrest separating us. He's so large that his body practically swallows up the entire space. I scoot over to give him more room, but it's pointless. His long muscular legs are still butted up right next to mine. The tips of my Vans bounce against the thin gray carpet as I do my best to ignore how good the heat of his body feels next to mine and glance around the small waiting room.

I cross my arms over my chest, trying and failing to keep my gaze from drifting to the behemoth of a man sitting next to me. The longer time passes without us saying anything, the more I stew on what happened the previous night, and I get angrier by the minute.

A heavy sigh escapes me. "What are you doing here?"

"We'll talk later. I promise."

Zane leans forward, planting his elbows on the tops of his thighs as the tips of his dark hair sweep down, acting as a curtain in front of him. He lifts his head and tilts it my way, giving me an unobstructed view of his face. The pain behind his eyes is almost enough for me to drop my ice queen facade, but then I remember how he took off last night with no discussion, and my temper flares all over again.

"Until you leave again." I shake my head as it takes everything in me not to smack him upside his beautiful head.

"I promise. I'll tell you everything, Ken. Full disclosure." The lines around his face deepen as he absently strokes the ends of his beard. "For now, I need you to let me be here for you both."

"Fine." I drop it because the last thing I want to do is cause a scene in the middle of my doctor's office. It doesn't mean he's off the hook, though.

My gaze roams around the waiting room to keep from meeting him in the eyes. The less I look at him, the better for me. Besides the two of us, there are only a handful of women here. The one that's a few rows over catches my gaze and offers me a small smile before her eyes shift onto Zane. There's no missing the lust that suddenly fills them, and my back stiffens against my seat. The nerve of her to check him out right in front of me. My hands ball into fists, but I remain quiet.

When I look at Zane, he isn't even paying her any attention. His entire focus is on her swollen belly, with a pinched expression marring his face. Since I've met him, this is the first time he seems lost, out of place.

I take pity on him and slide my hand off my lap until I find his and interlace our fingers together. The roughness of his touch is like a balm to my nerves. It keeps me grounded to know that he's here with me. I give him a gentle squeeze, and he only hesitates for a split second before his warm hand squeezes mine back. The rest of the tension leaves his body, and just for a moment, things between us aren't so strained. We've found a sort of truce for the moment, but it turns out that doesn't last long.

"What the feck are you doing here?" Rory's voice is calm and quiet behind me, which means he's feeling anything but.

I drop Zane's hand and go to stand, but Zane gets there first. He plants his body right in front of me, leaving me no choice but to stay seated.

"You spoke with Connor." It's a statement, not a question.

"I don't like it." Rory shakes his head.

"Not up to you." Zane squares his shoulders and glares at my brother.

A muscle jerks in Rory's cheek as the hands at his sides clench into fists.

My heart pounds in my throat. If I don't do something soon, there will be a brawl in the middle of this tiny room.

"It'll be okay, Ror. We need to talk," I assure him.

"Remember. Say the word, *deirfiúr*." He glances my way before shooting Zane one last look and spinning on his heels to head out the door.

I sink deeper in my chair, as that's one obstacle down—however many more to go.

We get a few minutes of reprieve before they call me back. Zane isn't as tense as he was when he first got here, but that didn't last long. He tried to come back into the bathroom with me to watch me pee in a cup. I put my foot down on that. That was not happening— ever. After I did my business and left the cup with my name on it, I thought the worst of it was over. I was wrong.

Now, we're back in the room waiting for the doctor, and things are just as silent and awkward as they were in the truck with Rory. I'm sitting on the edge of the table, swinging my legs back and forth to keep warm since I'm in nothing but those lovely paper gowns they give you. At least I got to keep my socks on.

The paper underneath me crinkles with every move I make as I swing my legs back and forth. I pretend to read the posters on the wall that are a road map of my internal lady parts and fight the urge to laugh from the awkwardness of my current situation.

Zane is standing next to me with his arms crossed over his chest, taking in the room. His dark eyebrows pinch together as he studies those same images on the walls. I'd give anything to know what's going through his head.

"What are those?" He points with his chin at the

gadgets of death outside my ankles. At least that's what I like to refer to them as.

"Those are stirrups." I let out a sigh as memories of how much I loathe them flash through my mind.

"And what goes in there?" His dark eyebrows scrunch together as he stares at them like they might jump out and bite him. If he only knew.

"My feet." My lips twitch with the urge to smile as I meet his blank stare.

The expression on his face is priceless right now. I open my mouth to explain further because he looks so lost. Things I will address later. Much later, when I'm alone, but before I can dwell on why, there's a knock on the door.

The knob turns a moment later, and in walks the doctor, clutching my chart in his hand. He's wearing dark blue scrubs with a white lab coat over the top of them.

"Hello, I'm Dr. Rourke." A smile spreads across his face that lights up his dark brown eyes, and I'm immediately put at ease. There's no hint at his actual age other than the flecks of silver mixed in with his short dark hair.

"Hi, I'm Kennedy." I smile and nod back, letting the last bit of nerves leave me.

His head swings in Zane's direction, and he's pretty much at eye level with him. "And you must be Dad."

Zane clears his throat and pushes his shoulders back, giving him his undivided attention. He's polite, but I can see him figuring Dr. Rourke out. It's a habit I've picked up on. He does it whenever he meets someone new.

"I am."

His warm smile stays in place as he holds his gaze. If he's picking up on any tension between us, he isn't letting on. Instead, he's professional and confident—everything I want in a doctor.

He goes through a series of questions and jots notes down in my chart as I answer. Zane remains where he is, pressed up by the wall and no doubt committing everything I say to memory.

It's all simple routine stuff. It's when he tells me to lie back on the table with my feet in the stirrups and pulls out a wand-looking thing that we hit a slight problem. He's rolling a condom over it and standing between my legs when Zane loses it.

He's pushed off the wall and has his hand wrapped around Dr. Rourke's wrist in the blink of an eye. "What the fuck are you doing with that?" There's no mistaking the wrath in his tone.

The doctor freezes with the wand midair and level with his mouth hanging open. "Um, well..." His voice trembles. "I'm doing an internal ultrasound. It's completely routine to do them this early in the pregnancy." Dr. Rourke visibly swallows, and I'm sure this office visit is anything other than routine for him.

I intervene before he can attempt to kick him out of the room. "Zane, look at me. It's fine."

At least Charlee explained to me ahead of time what to expect, so I'm not caught off guard. My mother's not around to ask, and she's the only other one I know that has had a kid. Judging by the vibes coming off of Zane, she better be right. My heart pounds in my chest as I hold Zane's stare, willing him to see the truth in my eyes.

I mentally count to five and brace for the storm I

know is coming when his posture relaxes and he releases the doctor from his grip.

"Will it hurt her or the baby?" He's still glaring at my doctor like he wants to rip his arm off.

Dr. Rourke gives him a tight smile and clears his throat a couple of times before answering him. "It will only be minor discomfort for Kennedy, but it won't hurt either one of them. I promise. This is standard procedure."

He nods, and Dr. Rourke goes back to what he was doing.

I force myself to relax as he inserts the condom-covered wand inside me, and he's right. It's only a minor discomfort. One that is soon worth it.

An underwater thumping sound fills the room, and all previous tension is forgotten when a little bean-shaped-looking thing appears on the screen. It's grainy, and we can't make out anything other than the basic shape, but it's our baby.

Zane shifts closer to me, slipping his hand into mine and giving it a slight squeeze. The move is so swift and natural that I don't think twice about returning his grip. We both continue to stare in awe at the screen of what we created.

"That's our baby." Tears fill my eyes as I tilt my head to meet Zane's gaze, but his eyes are on the screen. He's not blinking as he continues to stare at the image. His fingers squeeze tighter around my hand the longer it holds him captive. The more I watch him watch the screen, the more I feel something inside me shift, and I let go of my earlier annoyance with him.

"That's a nice strong heartbeat," Dr. Rourke says. He types on the keyboard with the hand that isn't holding the wand, taking some measurements before speaking again. "And looks like you are eight weeks exactly. Congratulations." He finishes up a short time later, removing the wand, and allows me to sit up. "Here you go." He hands me a small black-and-white photo. "You're all set. I'll see you in another month for your next appointment. You can schedule that on your way out at the front desk."

"Thanks." I stare down at the little bean-shaped blob and sigh as he exits the room. This is really happening. I'm having a baby with the bearded hothead next to me.

Zane's heat appears at my back as he leans down over my shoulder to look at the image. The fruity smell of his gum immediately invades my senses.

I sniffle as more tears fall. It seems to come at the most random times lately and is driving me nuts. I glance up and meet his warm gaze. "It's so small."

He lifts his thumb and wipes away my tears but never looks away from me. His features soften as he takes in my face. "It is."

Little did I know the effect that small image would have on our lives.

15

ZANE

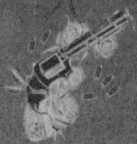

My head is still spinning from the time we leave the doctor's office to when we pull up to the pharmacy to pick up some vitamins for Kennedy. I guess pregnant women have to take more than just the regular shit. It's all new to me. Everything the doctor went over with us is still fresh in my mind, and I made mental notes of it all.

Seeing the image on the screen has changed everything. I knew she was pregnant, but looking at that grainy image on the screen had a tightness spreading across my chest. I glance down to Kennedy's stomach as she studies the best option of vitamins, and my gut tightens. My kid is really in there. Shit is about to get real, real fucking fast.

"What?" she asks without taking her eyes off the shelves.

"Nothing." I clear my throat and shake out the shit running through my head. Being out in the open like this has me on edge. Ever since Asher showed me the shit he found in the files, I haven't been able to think of anything else but getting to Kennedy.

Being out in the open like this has my body crawling with tension. I don't like crowds. It leaves too many possibilities for shit to go sideways. Anything can happen at any time. It's taking everything in me not to toss Kennedy over my shoulder and lock her away in my room, where I know my brothers will be able to help keep them safe. "Are you almost done?"

She grabs the first bottle she initially looked at and shoves it into my gut with a little more force than necessary. "I am now." She walks off toward the registers, grabbing a bag of black licorice, some chocolates, and a jar of pickles on the way.

I shake my head, knowing this is just the tip of the iceberg of the shit storm ahead of me. She's been easy-going about all of this, but everyone has their breaking point. I know that when she does lose it and explodes, it's going to be fucking nuclear.

We stand in the checkout lane with a mound of random shit that has me feeling like I'm back in high school with Axel doing a midnight munchies run. The guy rings our stuff but doesn't comment on it. It could be the death glare I give him when I catch him staring at Kennedy's tits. I pay and grab our shit before I grab him by the throat. I've already done that once today. It's a good thing Kennedy's doctor is on her dad's payroll, and I won't have to worry about the cops showing up at my door.

The second we're back inside the cab of my truck, Kennedy is digging through her bag of snacks. I set my wallet down on my center console and tilt my head to watch her. This woman never does what I expect.

She must feel me staring because her head snaps to the side and pushes the frame of her glasses farther up her nose as she narrows her eyes at me. "What?"

"I half expected you to fight me about paying for your shit."

"I thought about it, but I figure this is just a taste of the apology you owe me." She shrugs and rips open the package of licorice.

"Fair enough." I nod and pull out onto the highway. "Do I get to eat any of that?" It's my half-assed way of diffusing the underlying tension that's constantly there between us. I have no other idea what the fuck to do, and channeling my inner Axel might help.

She glances my way and twists her mouth to the side, taking her sweet time coming up with an answer. "Here." A piece of black licorice is shoved in my face. I fucking hate that shit, but I take it like the olive branch it is.

"Thanks." I snap a piece off and force myself to chew and swallow it down. A fucking MRE tastes better than this stuff any day, but I'm not going to say anything that'll land me in deeper shit than I already am with her.

"Don't mention it." She goes back to staring out her window, and I let her. It's too confined of a space to risk pissing her off just yet.

I focus on making my way through traffic and finding the quickest route to get us back to her apartment complex. It's a sunny day out, but I can see the small patch of clouds lingering in the distance. One thing about Georgia, you can get all four fucking seasons in one day.

I glance in my rearview mirror to change lanes

when something catches my eye. The same gold sedan that was behind us when we left the doctor's office is a couple of cars behind us. It could be nothing, but my gut says otherwise. There's no such thing as coincidences. I casually switch lanes, waiting to see if they follow, and sure enough, about twenty seconds later, they get into the same lane as me, about three cars back.

I'm doing my best to keep calm, but Kennedy must be able to pick up on it. "Everything okay?"

My eyes glance back to the mirror and find the car still cruising three cars away. "I don't know yet. Just in case, open my glove box."

Times like these, I'm thankful her family is who they are. She doesn't even bat an eye when she pulls out my Glock 9 and hands it to me. I rest it on the cup holder in front of me and wait. It's too populated for them to try something out in the open like this, but I'm not taking any fucking chances when it comes to Kennedy and our kid.

She leans back against her seat and watches through her side mirror. "The gold car, right?"

My eyes narrow as I spare her a quick look, waiting for her to explain.

"I noticed them when we pulled up to my doctor's office. It reminds me of a grandma's car." She sighs and scoots down in her seat.

I'm going to rip Rory a new asshole for not watching his surroundings better when he's with her. I'm about to verbalize that when the sedan changes back into the right lane and turns off down a side street. I let out the breath I didn't know I was holding and relaxed against my seat. My head is so fucked up that it has me all thrown off.

We change lanes, turn right at the next light, and take a side street to avoid traffic. The faster we make it to her apartment complex, the better. I'm hoping to convince her to pack up her stuff and come back to my property where I can keep a closer eye on her. Something I know she will fight me on, but I'm putting my foot down. There are too many unknown variables at her place. Like how that fucking dog got in.

A jolt from behind has us jerking forward, knocking my Glock off the center console and underneath Kennedy's seat. I glance in my mirror to see a blacked-out SUV reversing and getting ready to plow into us again. "Shit."

"Oh my god!" Kennedy grabs on to her seat belt to protect her stomach and keep from flying forward. "What the hell are they doing?"

My eyes skate across the road, weighing my options as fast as I can. "Hang on, Hummingbird."

I slam my foot down on the gas and turn through the red light. Horns blare and tires squeal as I cut across oncoming traffic, but I barrel on through. The SUV follows right behind us.

Kennedy spins around in her seat to get a better look. "They're gaining on us."

My foot presses down harder on the gas. The engine revs higher, and I just hope my engine doesn't get too hot and blow. We need more of a distance between us. I jerk my wheel and flip a U-turn, hopping a curb and destroying a couple of plants.

"We're going to die." Her breathing becomes more erratic as she's jostled around the cab. Her face looks a little green.

"No, we're not. Look at street names, Ken. I need to

know where we're at." I keep my voice neutral as I give her orders. The last thing I want to do is cause her to panic even more. It's not good for her or the baby. Instead, I try to distract her with something to do. "Call Rory and put him on speaker for me." I'd much rather call my brother's, but I know hers are closer.

She sniffles next to me but does as I ask. I hear the phone ring a couple of times before Rory's voice comes through. "Ready to call in that favor already, Ken?"

"How far away are you from your sister's place?" He must sense the urgency in my tone because he doesn't give me any shit.

"I just pulled up to Morrigan's." All humor has left his voice. He's all business now.

"I've got a blacked-out SUV with no tags on my ass. Fuckers hit us from behind." A few seconds later, I hear a commotion and tires screeching, then Connor's voice is on the line.

"We're heading to you now. ETA is about ten minutes." I don't need to ask how he knows where we are. If Kennedy were my sister, I'd have her shit tracked too.

Another big jolt has more metal grinding behind me. The ass end of my truck fishtails as we skid across four lanes, leaving more tread of my tires behind. I grit my teeth as I jerk the steering wheel to straighten out. My truck better hold up on us a bit longer.

Then shit goes from bad to worse. Loud pops go off—a few ping off the tailgate. One hits the rear window of my cab, and it shatters, sending shards of glass everywhere. The next one nails Kennedy's side mirror.

"Fuckers are armed." I reach out and cup the back of

Kennedy's head. "Give me the phone and get down, Ken."

She's in shock but manages to do as I tell her and scoots down lower in her seat.

"Hang tight. We're almost there. Five minutes out." Connor's voice is calm, but I can hear the tightness in it. He's as pissed off as I am about his sister being shot at.

"We don't have five minutes." It's taking everything I have not to lose my shit on him right now, but every second counts.

"Head toward our dad's place. It's closer to you and safer than Ken's apartment. Take the next street on your right and then the first left. His house will be at the end of that." Connor's issuing orders at me, and under any other circumstance, I'd bite his head off, but in this case, it's warranted.

"On my way." With my left hand gripping the wheel, I turn right down the street he mentioned.

Kennedy has grown quiet next to me, and I'm not sure if that's a good thing. "Talk to me, Hummingbird. How are you doing?"

"I don't want to die." She sniffles into her hands.

"We won't. I promise." At least I fucking hope not. "We're almost to your dad's, and you'll be safe." I keep my voice calm, but my heart is pounding against my chest inside. It's another two minutes before we can reach Finn's place, and a lot can happen in that time.

Out of the corner of my eye, I can see the SUV making its way to Kennedy's side of the truck. The rear driver-side window is cracked, and the reflection of metal peeks out. Another pop goes off, and Kennedy's window shatters. She screams as shards of glass rain down on her back.

"What was that?" Connor asks.

"They're firing at us again. They just hit Ken's window."

"Motherfeckers," Rory shouts through the phone.

"How's your aim, Ken?" I glance down at her before sweeping my eyes back on the road.

"What?" Her voice goes up an octave at my question.

"Can you shoot, Hummingbird?" I hope Finn prepared her for the trouble his lifestyle brings.

"Yes."

Thank fuck for that.

"Good. Reach down on the floorboard between your legs and grab my gun." I don't want her involved in whatever this is, but they leave me no choice. I'd rather her take one of them out instead of her lying in wait for one of their shots to get her.

Out of the corner of my eye, I can see her crouch down into position and aim at the SUV.

"Aim at the driver, Ken." I struggle to keep my voice calm, but inside I'm ready to tear that fucker's head off.

"Are you sure?" She hesitates with her hands crouched out in front of her.

"I'm sure." That should buy us some time. Worst-case scenario, they lose control of the vehicle if she nails him and runs into us. Of course, I'm not telling her that. She needs all her focus and not to be distracted by what-if scenarios.

Kennedy aims, and I hear the gunfire. She hits the window, but it bounces off.

"Shit." My palm slams down against the steering wheel.

"What's wrong?" Connor asks.

"They have bulletproof windows." I should have seen that coming.

"It'll be fine. Teegan can see you." Connor's voice is a slight relief in this clusterfuck of an afternoon. He pauses for a brief second as Rory tells him something. "Fuck."

"Fuck what?" That's never a good fucking sign.

"He says there's a problem at the gate. It won't open. We're pulling up right behind you now."

I glance in the rearview mirror and see Rory's lifted Chevy closing the distance. They're close, but not close enough. All it takes is one bullet to hit their target, and it's all over. "I can't stop. I do, and they'll be on us." And I'm not letting that happen.

"Don't stop. Crash into the left side and go right through to the front door. We'll take care of the rest." It's all the permission I need.

The familiar three-story house comes into view. Four white pillars extend outward to the concrete stairs that split off on either side and meet the driveway. Green shutters cover each of the many windows that line the front, and I'm sure there are several more along its backside. Large shrubs surround the entire thing, blocking out the view of the house from the street. To say the house is fucking huge is an understatement. It's almost a shame we're about to plow through and rip it all up.

"Brace yourself, Ken." Fucking shit, this is going to be bad.

She curls into the fetal position in her seat as I barrel straight through the left side of the iron gate, narrowly missing one of the poles. The force cracks my windshield, splintering my view, but I can make out enough to keep going. What becomes of the SUV is suddenly a memory after that.

We're off-roading through Finnegan Donnelly's front yard, ripping it to shreds. Pieces of green and Georgia clay fly all over the place, landing on the hood of my truck. I don't stop until the nose of my hood is right up against the steps that lead up to the front door and slam it into park. Kennedy is my first priority.

I bend down and pull her up into my lap against my chest. My hand strokes the top of her head as her body shakes against me. "You okay?"

Her head tilts back, and what I see punches me in the gut. Her glasses are cracked, and there are minor scrapes on her face where the glass cut her. She's got minor wounds that are bleeding, but nothing too serious. "No. That was bloody nuts." The more upset she gets, the thicker the Irish lilt to her words becomes. "What the feck happened?"

"I don't know." But I'm gonna find out. And they're fucking dead. Every last one of them.

I help Kennedy out of the truck and inside the house. Rory and Connor pull in and follow after us, but I'm not waiting. The faster I can get Kennedy inside the house, the better I'll feel.

Inside the house, it's just as I remember the few times I was here with my brothers. Hardwood flooring throughout with off-white walls and splashes of green is all I see. I manage to take in a bit more and find several family pictures along the walls this time. One, in particular, catches my eye. I recognize all of the Donnelly kids, but it's the woman that Finn has his arm draped around that has me stopping where I stand. Everything about her is identical to Kennedy, from the dark hair to the glasses on her face. The only thing Kennedy inherited from her father is those infamous Donnelly blue eyes.

"My mother, Siobhan," Kennedy says, answering my unspoken question.

I clear my throat and glance over at her, doing my best to ignore the tension that courses through me when I catch sight of the scratches on her face. "You look just like her."

The corner of her mouth lifts into a smile that doesn't reach her eyes. "My dad says I act a lot like her too. She was murdered when I was four." The way she says it with such a neutral voice leads me to believe that Finn never hid the truth of what happened or how he handled it from them.

I keep my expression blank. This isn't news to me. That's one of the first things Asher looked up when we found out Kelsey was his niece, but I have a feeling if I tell her that, she'll punch me in the nuts.

She taps the glass of the framed photo and starts back up the stairs. When we walk up to the open office door, I come face-to-face with the last person I ever expected to see at Finnegan Donnelly's house.

16

KENNEDY

"What the fuck are you doing here?" Zane's entire body goes rock solid next to me. Gone is his calm demeanor from earlier when he checked me over. He glares in the direction of my father's desk at a blond in a tan suit. The temperature in the room instantly drops by several degrees, and all conversation stops when the blond lifts his head and his hazel eyes glance our way.

While Zane is busy lost in whatever pissing contest this is, my nausea decides now is the perfect time to make an appearance. I suck in a few slow, deep breaths, hoping like hell I can keep the licorice down. Something tells me that it will not be so hot coming back up.

I look to my dad for a distraction and possibly an answer for what is going on, but his gaze is also fixed on Zane. My dad is sitting behind his big mahogany desk in one of his favorite black pin-striped suits with a cigar in his hand and an open folder on his desk. The familiar blond, whose name escapes me, is leaning a hand against the side of the desk, tilting his head to the side with his head bent over the pile of papers. I've seen him around here a couple of times, but other than a few small pleasantries, we've never exchanged many words. If we're interrupting something important, neither one of them lets on.

"I'll take care of our little problem as long as ye do yer part, Rosenberg." My dad leans back in his chair, dismissing him.

"Consider it done," the blond, who I now remember, answers with a chin tilt as he grabs his briefcase from off the floor by his feet and heads toward the door, putting himself directly in our path. A smile spreads across his face the closer he comes to us and holds his hand out for me to take. "It's always a pleasure to see you again, Kennedy."

"Mr. Rosenberg." I suck in another deep breath to control my rebelling stomach and place my hand in his, prepared to shake it when his fingers tighten around mine.

"I've told you. Call me Barrett." Barrett smiles, showing off the whites of his teeth. He attempts to lift my hand to his mouth, but my husband gets there first.

"I don't fucking think so." Zane grabs my hand out of Barrett's grasp before his lips make contact. He pulls me in tighter next to him and drapes an arm around my shoulders, locking me in place. He might as well have peed on me to mark his territory. Heat fills my face at the move, but Barrett isn't fazed.

He ignores that comment and Zane's caveman behavior as his gaze darts from me to my husband. Those hazel eyes light up as his lips twitch, suppressing another smile that wants to break free. "I hear congratulations are in order." Barrett leans in closer to press a kiss to my cheek, and that's when Zane loses it.

He shoves Barrett in the shoulder, knocking him back a couple of steps. "Touch my wife, and you won't live to regret it."

Barrett laughs and shakes his head. "There's that Savage temper. Tell your brother I haven't forgotten about him." With that, he winks and walks out the door.

Zane drops his arm and stomps forward until he's right in front of my dad's desk. He bends forward and presses his fists down on top of the stack of papers. "What in the fuck is the district attorney doing inside your office?"

My dad leans back in his chair and gives Zane a once-over, letting the silence linger for a couple of beats. I've seen this tactic lots of times before. It's something he does when he's trying to assert his dominance and let others know that it's his house and he's in charge. He'll do things in his own time and in his own way, whether you like it or not.

"You think it was wise to threaten him?" My dad's dark eyebrows arch as he tilts his head to the side.

Zane stands upright and puffs out his chest, mimicking my dad's domineering posture from earlier. "If he's in here with you, I'll take my chances." He shrugs.

My dad stares at him for a beat and then shakes his head. That's as good of a sign of respect as Zane will get. Then his gaze shifts to me, and his features soften. It's then I have to admit that Connor was right. Being the only girl in this family does tend to work out in my favor most of the time. He adjusts the ends of his suit jacket before standing to his feet and setting his cigar down in the ashtray to the right. He crosses the room and wraps me up in a tight hug. I sigh into the familiar warmth of my dad's chest, just like I used to do as a little girl.

When my dad pulls back and glances down at me, his dark eyebrows pinch together. "Everythin' okay, *a stóirín*?"

"Yeah. I'm fine." I press my lips together in a firm line and ignore my turning stomach. If I don't think about it, then it's not nearly as bad.

"Ye sure? Ye look a wee bit pale." My dad's dark eyebrows pinch together as he studies me.

"I'm just a little shaken up from being chased and shot at, but I'll be okay." I attempt to shrug it off, but my dad can see right through me.

"Aye, that ye will." He kisses me on the forehead. "I'll make sure of it." Those words hold a double meaning in the world of Finnegan Donnelly, and I've learned not to question them. He'll find out who did it and make sure that Zane and I don't make the news. "How did yer appointment go?" he asks, changing the subject.

"Good. The baby's healthy and right on track where it's supposed to be." I reach into my pocket and pull out the grainy photo to show him.

His blue eyes light up the second they land on that image, but his expression takes a nosedive when his gaze lands on the diamond ring on my left finger. "That's grand news." He kisses the top of my head once more, and then he hands me off to Connor. He and Rory are standing quietly on the sidelines, watching everything unfold, and I forgot they were even there.

Connor wraps his hand around the top of my head and pulls me into a hug, careful to touch the broken lens of my glasses. "Scared the feck out of us, Ken."

"I'm sorry. It's not like I planned on getting shot at," I mumble against his chest.

"I know." He pulls back and taps me on the chin. "Good to know you can still aim at least."

I roll my eyes and get ready to say something smart back at him, but without warning, there's a sound of flesh hitting flesh. When I turn around, my dad has his fist up, and Zane's got a cut on his bottom lip.

"What are you doing?" Nausea be damned, I'm not going to stand here and watch without doing something about it. I move to stop my dad from hitting him again, but Connor's arms tighten around my middle like a vise, keeping me in place. It's obvious to me now why I was passed on to my big brother in the first place, and I should have known better. My dad is always ten steps ahead of everyone.

"Don't even think about it, *deirfiúr*," Connor says to the back of my head as I continue to struggle to break free. "He had it coming, and he knows it."

"That's for treatin' me daughter like a feckin' slag." The muscle jerks on the side of my dad's jaw as he glares at Zane, but he's not done with him yet. Another blow comes. This time from the left. "That's for shittin' all over our Catholic traditions."

My hands come up to my mouth to stop the scream that wants to break free because I know it will do no good. There's no stopping this until they're done. And it seems my dad isn't. He slams his fist into Zane's stomach, knocking the wind out of him. "And that's for fecking with me business."

Connor tenses up at that last comment, but I'm too fired up to wonder why at the moment.

Zane grunts, and he folds in half from the impact.

My heart pounds in my chest as I watch him suck in a few shallow breaths before gaining his sense of balance and standing back upright. He spits out a mouthful of blood at my dad's feet and wipes at the corner of his mouth. I'm not sure if he has a death wish or enjoys taunting my dad to see how far he can push things. He's lucky that I swore my big brothers to secrecy on the rocky terms our so-called relationship has been thus far. "You done?"

"I don't like ye or yer brothers, but ye've got balls, Savage. I'll give ye that."

"You are all insane." I jerk out of Connor's grip and wave my finger at every Neanderthal in the room. I hope this baby is a girl. I'm so tired of being outnumbered and surrounded by stubborn-ass men. "You know that, right?"

"Some more than others," Rory feels the need to add, and I can hear the humor inflected in his voice. Such a shit stirrer that one. He could give Axel Savage a run for his money in that department.

"Shut it, Ror." I hold my hand up to keep whatever bullshit remark he wants to make trapped in his mouth where it belongs. The last thing he is is a damn saint.

My dad flexes the hand that he just buried into my husband's face, drawing attention to the ripped skin of his knuckles, and another swarm of heat flushes through me. I've had enough excitement to last me a lifetime today. I want to shower and wash the crap from the last forty-five minutes off. They can stay in here and act like the little boys they are.

I spin on my heels and stomp my way down the hall into the bedroom I stay in whenever I have to stay here. The cream walls are bare except for a few of my favorite paintings on the far wall. This isn't a room I spend much time in, so I haven't put forth the effort to decorate it to my liking. The patterns meld perfectly with the maroon bedding that's resting on top of the four-poster California King bed that's in the middle of the spacious area.

Each of us may be grown, but we all have a designated bedroom, complete with its own bathroom at my dad's insistence. And given my family's line of work, I guess he isn't too far off the mark with that.

I keep walking into the en suite bathroom with the same color scheme as my bedroom and straight to the shower. It's one of my favorite places to think and regroup. The raindrop showerhead is much nicer than the basic one I have back at my apartment and just what my sore, achy muscles need at the moment. My hands make quick work of my clothes and glasses before I slip inside the steamed-up space.

My hands press against the marble wall, and I hang my head, letting the heat of the water seep into my weary bones and trickle down my back. The only plus to come from this crap is that my nausea seems to have gotten itself under control.

I let the crap that has been weighing me down wash away. With each spray of the hot water, I feel the tension leave my body. The longer I'm under, the more it fades away until it becomes a distant memory. That is until I feel a warm, firm body at my back.

17
ZANE

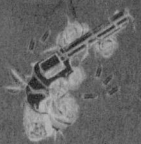

I hold Finn's gaze as Kennedy leaves. The second we walked in and saw Rosenberg, I knew that there was more shit to this than I knew. My gut tells me that part of the reason he sucker-punched me was to get Kennedy to storm out of the room like she did so that he can tell me what he really wants to say.

Finn straightens his suit and calmly walks back over to his mahogany desk, where he leans over and grabs a thick manila folder. My heart jumps at the sight. Things didn't end well for us the last time we were all together, and he had one of those, but in the end, it helped us to save Kelsey. He plants his ass on the corner and calmly flips through it, looking at who the fuck knows what.

"Ye've got an interestin' background." His head tilts up as he flashes me a smug grin, letting me know in that one expression he read everything in it.

"Where the fuck did you get that?" Everything inside me tenses up as I grind my teeth to keep from putting his ass through the nearest fucking wall. "That's a classified file."

He lets my words hang in the air until they become a strained silence weighing down the room. Without taking his eyes off me, he tosses the folder to the side. His finger runs along his top lip as he continues to stretch out whatever it is he wants to say. Finn enjoys playing the long game of making you sweat it out. Too bad he's barking up the wrong fucking tree with that bullshit.

When he finally realizes that I'm not going to break, he pulls out a cigar from the wooden box on top of his desk and grabs the silver metal cutter. Holding my gaze, he snips off the end in one final attempt. He tried the same tactic with Axel last time we were in his office, and it didn't work then, just like it's not working now. The moment he realizes it, I'm rewarded with a slight nod of the head, and he moves on.

"I told ye I've got friends in high places."

"I haven't forgotten." I stand taller, not taking kindly to his unvoiced threat, but Finn isn't done.

"As I said, ye fecked up an important business deal that took me a lot of time to set up." His words cause my temper to spike. I know what he's talking about. The business arrangement he made to marry Kennedy and my kid off to some prick in Boston. Hearing the callous way he's talking about her like she's a fucking commodity has my fingers clenching into tight fists.

"She's not a fucking bartering chip, and neither is my kid." I close the few steps that separate us, ready to get in his face if I have to.

"Aye, she's not, and neither is me *grandchild*." His voice hardens on that last word, making sure that I know no matter what, my kid will always be a part of his family as well.

I decide now is the perfect time to bring up what happened this afternoon. After all, I can give as good as I get. "Family or not, if I find out that your bullshit is why Kennedy and I were shot at today, you'll be dealing with me."

"Fair enough." Finn bites down on the tip of his cigar, watching me like I'm a wild animal waiting to strike. "But ye can expect the same from me, Lad."

"What are you planning on doing with that?" I jerk my chin in the direction of that fucking folder, ignoring his threat. I'm hoping he'll burn it, but something tells me that would be too easy, and nothing ever is when it comes to Finnegan Donnelly.

"Ye stop actin' like a feckin' gobshite, nothin'." That's as good of an answer as I'm going to get from him. "Yer truck is fecked. The two of ye will stay here tonight." It's not a question, and if I disagreed that it would be best for Kennedy, I'd tell him to get fucked and have my brothers come and get us. They're going to find out and be worried as fuck as it is. But I'm putting my wife first. Even if that means we have to stay under her father's roof for the night.

"We're leaving in the morning." I dare him to argue, but he doesn't. And thank fuck for that. I don't want to spend any more time under this crazy fuck's roof than I have to.

He nods his head. "Fine, but know I'll be watchin' ye. Ye may be family now, but I don't trust ye."

I let that roll off my back and move to get out of there before he says something else to piss me off. "I'm going to find my *wife*."

"One more thing," he says to my back. "Tell yer brother to be careful. Word is he's diggin' up ghosts that want to stay forgotten." There's no missing the underlying threat to Asher, but that's something I'll deal with later. For now, I have a wife to find. The sooner we have it out, the better. I know she's still pissed at the way I left her apartment, and that's one thing I need to rectify before we pile more shit onto my plate.

I'm two steps into the hall when I hear water running. My feet carry me toward the sound and through a cream and maroon bedroom that has Kennedy written all over it. It may be simple, but I'm learning that's what she likes. I shut and lock the door before Finn can change his mind and come barging in.

The bathroom door is closed but cracked just enough that I can make out her figure through the steamed-up glass. If my head wasn't on straight before then, it is now. All that kept running through my mind in my truck was that if we get out of this, I need to listen to Asher and stop being such a fuck-up. It took being shot at to finally get my head the rest of the way out of my ass.

I disrobe and leave my shit in a pile on the floor without making a sound. I'll deal with not having any clothes later. I should call my brothers, but that can wait too. Right now, the only thing that matters is getting my hands on Kennedy. I know she told me she's fine, but I need to see for myself that she is. My head's been even more fucked since we left the doctor's office, and the only thing that will settle the beast within is feeling her flesh for myself.

I open the door, letting a curtain of steam swallow my vision as I step inside, my steps a silent whisper against the white marble shower.

Kennedy's hair clings to her back, the wetness

making it almost black against her pale skin. A trail of water trickles down her spine and onto her heart-shaped ass. All of the blood rushes straight to my dick at the sight. My fingers itch to squeeze that ass in my hands.

Everything about her is soft and perfect. That's one of the first things that drew me to her that night in the club. Things may have started as a way for us to gather information, but I knew after a few minutes of talking to her that she was special. That she could be more. It's part of why I left and never looked back after that night. It took everything I had to forget her and continue my shitty existence. It was hard as hell, but I did what I thought was best for her. That all changed the moment I found out she was pregnant.

Now, she's mine. She belongs to me. And I plan on keeping her. For the first time in as long as I can remember, I'm taking what I want and not feeling guilty about it. But first, I need to lay my demons at her feet and see if she still wants me around. Stripped down and bare is the only way this is going to work. She doesn't trust me, and with good reason. I've abandoned her, not once but twice. This time I need to prove that I'm staying if she'll have me while also doing what I need to do to make sure Isaac isn't a threat.

I press up against her back, burying my hard dick between her ass cheeks, and dig my fingers into the indent of her hips, letting the water soak us both.

"Zane! What the hell are you doing?" She jumps, but I don't release my hold on her.

"We need to talk, Ken."

"Then get out and let me get dressed like a normal

person." She tries to shut me out, but I don't miss the slight hitch of her voice.

"No." I rest my chin against the space where her shoulder and neck meet, enjoying the way she squirms from the tickling of my beard. "We do it in here, where we can leave this shit behind us and move on."

"Can I at least turn around?" She tries to spin around to face me, but I press the weight of my body forward, keeping her in place.

"I can't, Ken. What I have to tell you, I can't—" I choke over my words. "I need to do it this way. Please?" My throat goes dry as it seems like I wait for an eternity for her to answer.

"Okay." She nods as she lets out a small sigh.

"Thank you." I press my lips to her wet flesh and let out a breath I didn't realize I was holding. I close my eyes and bare my soul's darkest secret. "Since I can remember, my brothers and I wanted to make a difference in the world. Asher became a cop, and Axel went into Special Forces. I became a Navy SEAL with my best friend, Nelson. We even graduated at the top of our class. Thought we were hot shit." A hollow laugh escapes me as I think back to how arrogant and naive we were.

"We were teamed up with Isaac and Grady not long after graduation, and the four of us completed every mission they assigned us. We were so caught up in the high that we couldn't wait for the next one. I think that's why they approached us for this one." A tightness builds in my chest as the memories flash through my mind like a movie.

"Eight years ago, our superiors called us into their office and said they had a special mission for us. They made sure we knew it was off the books. If we got caught, there'd be no record of us there, and we were on our own."

"What was it?"

"Admiral Wallace's daughter was on a mission trip in Kandahar with her church. She was taken and sold to a well-known group that deals in human trafficking. The higher-ups wouldn't sign off on it because they said there were too many political factors involved." My fingers flex around her waist, and she places her hands on top of mine. I take this as a sign of good faith and keep on going.

"Things were fine at first. We made it in without a problem. Then—" I let out another deep breath as I picture those brown eyes. "Then it all turned to shit. A boy was wandering around, and I grabbed him to keep him safe. He struck me from behind, and the next thing I knew, I woke up in a damp room underground, chained up to a wall by my wrists. Nelson was strung up next to me. I found out later they killed Grady, but Isaac managed to escape. They tortured us for days, trying to find out who sent us. I'm not sure how long exactly because there were no windows, and everything bled together."

"The scars on your back?"

"Yeah, the scars on my back." I'm not surprised she put that together. She felt them the other night.

She sucks in a small gasp, and I wonder if I should stop now, but she needs to know the worst of me.

"They kept asking who sent us, and when torturing us didn't work, they tried a different tactic. They cut off Nelson's head right in front of me."

"Oh my god!" Her body attempts to break free, but I keep her still.

"There's more. Her name was Kara. She was eighteen and so full of fucking life."

"Was?"

"She's dead, Ken." She whimpers, and I rub small circles with my finger against her hips as I continue purging my sins to the one woman who can break me. "When they brought her in, I barely recognized her. She was dirty and so fucking skinny. They—" My mouth tastes like ash as the memories surface. "They took turns raping her in front of me."

She lets out a muffled whimper but doesn't interrupt me.

"I broke free and killed every last one of them."

"The boy?"

"I had no choice. He had a gun, and it was him or me." I hope like hell she understands. "So, you need to think long and hard about what you want from here because that's the monster you married. That's whose kid you're having." I drop my hands and step back away from her, letting everything I just told her sink in. If she tells me to get the fuck out, I'll respect it and leave. But, if she turns around, she's mine for keeps.

My heart pounds against my chest. I wait for what seems like an eternity for her to make up her mind. Every muscle tenses as a sense of unease crawls through me. And suddenly, I've never wanted anything more than I do for her to turn around and accept me.

Her blue eyes are glassy as she holds my gaze, but mine drop to the cuts marring her face, and my hands clench into fists. Those assholes will pay whether she tells me to fuck off or not. She cups the side of my face and stares up at me with wide doe eyes. "It wasn't your fault."

"What?" Not what I expected her to say.

"What happened wasn't your fault, and you need to let it go." She grabs my hand with both of hers and places it against her stomach. "For the both of us. Can you do that?"

"I'm working on it." I clench my jaw and stare down at the slight bump. The doctor said it might be too soon to show, but I can see it.

"Then I'll work on it with you." She tips up on her toes and presses her lips to mine.

I take that as my answer and lift her by her ass, bracing her against the marble wall. She lets out a gasp of shock from the cold, and I take full advantage. My tongue slips inside her mouth, deepening the kiss until I'm not sure where she ends and I begin, only pulling back when the lack of oxygen finally gets to us. I rest my forehead against hers and let out another long breath. My thumb strokes the seam where her hip and thigh meet, going no further. There's nothing sexual about it. I want her to know that this means everything. For the first time in forever, I exist in the moment. I don't get caught up in all of the bullshit that filters through my head.

Her soft hands rub across my back, showing special attention to every scar, every imperfection on my skin. She's letting me know without words that she's accepting all of me—all the jagged and rough pieces. Fuck me. She's perfect.

"Fuck, Ken." The hand that's still around her ass clamps down, and like she can read my mind, her hips tilt up, grinding her core against me. "I want to go slow and make this good for you, but I don't think I can."

"Then don't." The blacks of her pupils almost swallow the blue of her eyes whole as she rests her head against the marble and bites down on her bottom lip. "I want you to fuck me."

That's all the permission I need, and I slam into her in one hard thrust. She's wet and tight and like coming fucking home. Her heels dig into my ass as I pump in and out of her. My Apadravya piercing hits that place deep inside her that has her toes curling. I slip the hand that was on her hip down and pinch her clit between my thumb and forefinger. Her head falls back, and her pussy instantly clamps down on my dick.

"The doctor wasn't kidding. You really are extra sensitive down here." I grit my teeth and focus on anything other than how good her pussy feels. Otherwise, this will be over before it's even started. And I'm not ready for this to be over. I want to draw this feeling out as long as I can.

"You remember that?" She gazes up at me through hooded eyes.

"I remember everything when it comes to you." A muscle in my jaw jerks as I see the tears pool in her eyes.

"I do too," she whispers as she places her fingers through the hoop of my nipple piercings and gives them a light tug. "Do you still need it?"

I stare down at her, a knot forming in my throat when I realize what she's asking. "Please." My voice is as thick as the demons trapped inside my head. I've laid my soul bare, but this isn't something that'll ever change.

She tugs until I feel the first bite of pain ignites my blood. My balls tighten as I pull all of the way out and slam back inside her welcoming heat, relishing in that realization. I get lost in the motion, reveling in the feel of her pussy wrapped around my dick.

The water has chilled around us, but neither one of us gives a fuck about that. Nothing exists in this moment but her and I.

"Where's my Hummingbird?"

She hums, and I let out a groan of approval. With each thrust of my hips, her cries of pleasure get louder and louder. I cover her mouth with the palm of my hand to muffle her screams. Her moans of pleasure belong to me and me alone.

"Quiet, or your dad will hear how bad of a girl you really are." I suck the lobe of her ear between my teeth and bite down. Her body shudders under my touch.

She nods, but I need to hear her say the word. "That's not good enough, Ken. I need to hear you say it."

"Yessss," she hisses out. "I promise."

"Good girl." And since she's such a good girl, I reward her. My hips thrust inside her even deeper, yet it's still not deep enough. My toes curl as my feet dig into the marble for traction, and my balls tighten. I explode inside her with a loud groan. My heart is racing as I watch her plump tits heave up and down. Her perfect pale skin is now a pink flush all over. Both of us are painting as we just watch the other.

"Can we do that again?" She smiles up at me, and fuck, that's everything.

"We have all night." Once we're out of the shower, I keep to my word. I fuck her until we're both too exhausted to remember or care about the bullshit that awaits us tomorrow. It can wait.

18

KENNEDY

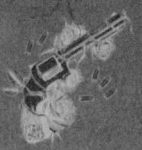

I wake up tangled in the same black sheets as I have for the last four days—alone and in a room that isn't mine. After the heart-to-heart we had in the shower, things haven't been as strained between us. Zane still refuses to sleep next to me. He'll come in and screw me into exhaustion. I pass out and wake up to an empty bed.

He hasn't been going out of his way to avoid me, but there's still something messing with his head. I can see it in the way he looks at me when he thinks I'm not paying attention, like I might disappear at any moment. The dark circles under his eyes aren't helping matters. I'd be more worried if it were just him, but his brothers have also been acting stranger than normal.

My full bladder reminds me of how other things are changing. I drop my gaze down to my chest, which seems to have doubled in size even more, and I groan. I'm falling out of the only bra I have with me.

I throw the sheets aside, grab my glasses, and stumble into the bathroom to do my business. When I look in the mirror, I look like a hopeless mess. The cuts from the car chase have scabbed over and are starting to heal. I'm in nothing but one of Zane's oversized T-shirts that comes down to my knees. If it weren't for Charlee or Kelsey showing me where the laundry room was, the only pair of clothes I brought with me would still be dirty. I can't keep scrounging for clothes from the small bag we packed from my dad's place. I'm sure it will not go over well, but I need to swing by my apartment today to check on things and grab some more clothing. With how overprotective Zane is being, I'm sure convincing him to stay at my place is off the table.

A heavy sigh leaves me as I slip my only pair of black leggings on underneath Zane's T-shirt. I'm too lazy to change my top half, and it still smells like its owner. I pinch the top of the collar and bring it to my nose, inhaling deep. The familiar smell of Juicy Fruit and sandalwood hits me and causes a rush of heat to gather between my legs. My thighs squeeze together as I remember how his beard tickles my inner thighs and his tongue strokes my clit. These damn hormones are making it hard to think of anything else.

I fight the urge to take care of myself and walk out to see what everyone else is doing, and I find the entire family having breakfast at a long oak table in the kitchen. It seats at least ten and is overflowing with food. The mixture of so many smells is overwhelming to my senses and has nausea churning in my stomach. I breathe through my nose, doing my best to let it settle. The last thing I want to do is spend another morning puking. It usually hits me mid-afternoon, but it's becoming more of an all-day thing the last few days. To take my mind off of the overwhelming feeling building inside my stomach, I focus on the people around the table.

Charlee's at the far end feeding Lilly, who's in a high chair next to her. Lily is shoving tiny handfuls of scrambled eggs into her mouth, and what doesn't make it ends up on the floor. Her dark hair is sticking out all over the place as her green eyes follow her mother's every move. Asher is on the other side, watching them with that same stone-cold expression on his face. I'm not even sure the man knows how to smile. Kelsey is sitting next to Axel, and they are lost in their own conversation. But it's the brooding, bearded man at the end that makes my pulse quicken.

Zane's long dark hair is thrown up in a messy bun as usual, and his biceps strain underneath the fabric of his navy shirt. His head hangs over his plate, and his beard almost ends up in his pancakes while he eats. His blue eyes are zoned out in front of him, and he's lost in his head, wearing that same strained expression that I've seen on his face once before.

I lean against the wall and take in more of the family scene unfolding in front of me. It's all very normal, something I haven't had since my mother died. A small sigh escapes me as I continue to watch, feeling like an outsider looking in. All eyes come to me the second they hear me, and I realize I was louder than I thought. I'm also standing there in Zane's T-shirt. It's a little unnerving for me to be the center of attention. I shuffle on my feet as I push my glasses farther up my nose, wishing for the room to swallow me whole.

"Morning." My cheeks heat up as I give them a small wave with one hand and press the other one to my stomach, hoping it will stop churning.

Axel's blue eyes light up, not bothering to hide that his gaze has followed my hand, and then the corners of his mouth twitch. "Is that Z's shirt?" He flicks his chin to the oversized T-shirt I'm currently swimming in.

I shrug. "They're more comfortable." Heat fills my cheeks as I brace for him to comment on why my clothing might not fit as well, but he surprises me by remaining quiet.

Zane finally glances up at me from his seat, and what I see has my stomach plummeting to the floor. The bags underneath his bright blue eyes are even heavier, as is the strain that mars his features. They're a dead giveaway that something is seriously wrong. His beard may cover half of his face, but there's no hiding the evidence. I can sense the tension radiating off of him from here. His blue eyes drift from my face, doing a complete inventory of me, stopping on the hand resting over my stomach. He clenches his jaw, and that's the only outward sign of emotion I'm given from him. A dark shadow crosses over his features, but it's gone so fast that I almost wonder if I've imagined it. Millions of reasons fill my head for that reaction, but Zane speaks before I can dwell on it.

"Hungry?" He grabs a plate and starts piling a mound of food on top of it without waiting for me to answer. My stomach chooses then to stop turning and growl instead.

Axel's eyes crease at the sound as he laughs. "Guess that's a yes."

"I might be a little hungry." I hesitate for a brief second, playing with the hem of Zane's T-shirt, not wanting to intrude. Then Zane stands up and pulls the chair next to him out for me. No words are exchanged, but it means everything. I slip into the empty seat and smile at the rest of the family while he slides my chair in and takes his place next to me. The smell of grease and sugar floods my senses and makes my mouth water. I just hope that I can manage to keep it all down.

Axel laughs as Zane sets the overflowing plate down in front of me. "Eat up, Lil' Sis."

My fork stops halfway to my mouth as I shoot him a look. "Why did you call me that?"

"Because you're pocket-size, and you are technically my sister now." Axel waves a forkful of egg at me before shoving it into his mouth.

"So is Charlee." I tilt my head to the side and purse my lips together, wondering if I'm missing something. He never calls her that.

"She is, but she isn't." Axel shrugs and presses his lips together like he might be second-guessing his words.

"What do you mean?" My eyebrows pinch together, causing my glasses to slide back down my nose. It's too early for riddles, and since caffeine is out for the next several months, I'm not functioning on all cylinders.

"You're a Savage now"—he points his fork at me, then swings it in Charlee's direction—"Hellcat's still a Vega."

The room is swallowed in silence as Axel's words drop like a bomb into the center of the room. All eyes go to him, and I instantly feel bad for bringing the whole thing up. The tension is so thick you could cut it with a knife. I keep my gaze on my plate like it's the most fascinating thing I've ever seen to avoid the heavy weight that fills the room.

"Excuse me." Charlee's chair screeches against the

floor as she slides it out and power walks out of the room, but not before I catch her wiping at a few stray tears from her cheeks.

"What? What did I say?" Axel glances at her retreating back as Asher slaps him upside the head and gives him a stone-cold glare.

"Axel." Kelsey shakes her head at him and looks as if she wants to say more but doesn't. Something tells me that he will be getting a talking-to later, though.

"Fucking idiot." Asher hands him a squirming Lily right before stomping off after Charlee.

Axel glances around the table at all of us before the corners of his eye crease once again. "He had that coming, and y'all know it."

"You did that shit on purpose." Zane clenches his fist and glares at Axel. It's a statement, not a question.

"Yup. She'll thank me later when he finally gets his head out of his ass and meets her at the altar." Axel smiles as he bounces a smiling Lily in his lap. "Ain't that right, Wildflower?"

Lily answers him with a high-pitched giggle as she waves her fistful of eggs at him.

"See, the kid gets it." Axel cocks his head at his brother like he's always right.

Zane holds his glare, unimpressed, and the two of them are locked in a heated stare. Silence ticks by, and if it weren't for Kelsey's neutral expression, I'd be a bit more worried. My brothers do the same thing; the only difference is it tends to end with one or more of them bleeding. I'm not sure what to make of this situation at all.

I push my glasses back up my nose, take a big bite of my eggs, and decide now is the perfect time to throw something else into the mix in hopes of diffusing this bomb. "I need to go by my apartment and get some more stuff today." We haven't had time to discuss our living situation with everything going on, and I'm smart enough to know that now is not the right time.

Zane's darkened gaze switches from Axel to me and softens just a fraction. "You sure that's a good idea?" He runs a hand through his hair as he tries to keep his voice soft. I'm sure it's his way of attempting to sweet-talk me out of it. Instead of doing what he wishes, I meet his gaze head-on and stand my ground.

"I am. It's been four days, and I can't keep wearing your clothes." I push around the grits on my plate so it looks like I've eaten them. The last thing I want to do is be rude, but I've never been a fan of them.

Zane's gaze dips down to the T-shirt that's swallowing me whole, and a muscle jerks in his cheek. "They look better on you."

I ignore that comment because the last thing I want to do is jump his bones at the family table. "I'm not going to hide out forever while you find the dipshits that shot at us."

Axel snorts. "You've got balls. I like you, Short Stack." He cranes his head in Zane's direction, emphasizing the nickname he's given me this time, and is met with a shake of the head from his brother.

"Uh, thanks." I turn to Zane as another thought comes to me. "So?"

Zane takes his time swallowing his latest bite of scrambled eggs, no doubt running it all over in his head, and just when I'm about to lose my patience, he nods. "After you eat and get ready, we'll go get your stuff—and your car." Zane adds that last bit as an afterthought.

Since his truck is totaled, it makes perfect sense to have my car here. He jerks his chin toward my plate, and it takes me a bit to realize what he's said.

"I can't eat all of this." I shake my head and glance down at the mountain of food that he piled onto my plate.

"Ah, ah, ah." Axel shakes a finger at me like I'm a little kid. "We can't leave until you finish all of your food like a good little girl."

"Fuck off, dickhead. You ain't invited." Zane glares at him and then turns his attention on me. "Eat what you want and leave the rest for Axel."

"Really? How were you planning on getting there then? Walking? Your truck is fucked, and there's no way I'm letting you drive Willie Mae," Axel taunts in a singsong tone as he bounces Lily on his lap, causing her to show off a gummy smile. I fight not to do the same myself at their banter, and the way it reminds me of my own family as I take a few more small bites of food.

"Gertrude," Kelsey corrects him.

"No way, Wildcat. We've talked about this." Axel points his fork at her. "That is the name of someone's grandmother. Not a lifted beauty like her."

"Well, I won the bet, and I say it's Gertrude." She shrugs and stuffs more scrambled eggs into her mouth.

"You still owe me a rematch." He wriggles his dark eyebrows, and something tells me that whatever the stakes are, they'll both be declared a winner.

"Fine." Zane's teeth grind together as he realizes that Axel has a point. "You can come, but if you talk too much, I'm shoving a gag in your mouth."

Axel rolls his eyes at him but grins so big his dimples show. When he sees me staring, he just shoots me a wink and goes back to playing with Lily. "Uncle Z is a softie at heart."

She giggles and claps her hands together like he's said the funniest thing ever and then steals a tiny fistful of egg off his plate. It's halfway to her mouth when Axel reaches down and snags it from her. Lily laughs again, lightening up the somber mood, and that's how we spend the rest of our breakfast.

When we arrive at my apartment complex, I can't jump out of the truck fast enough. It was an awkward and tense drive. My stomach has been in knots ever since we left. I'm not sure if it's just nerves or if my breakfast wants to come back up. I can't wait until I have the privacy of my own vehicle again.

Axel wasn't the only Savage brother to invite himself along to collect my things. Asher didn't give Zane a choice to turn him down, so the four of us drove over here. Axel drove with Asher riding passenger and Zane in the back next to me, but it didn't stop Axel from talking my ear off the entire way. The easygoing banter between us helped make things less awkward, but the underlying tension couldn't be ignored. Other than a few grunts thrown in as an answer, Zane remained quiet and lost in his mind while he chewed on more gum. I don't miss the way his fists tighten, and his head is constantly scanning the roads, looking for any signs of the car that shot at us.

Things don't get any better from there. When we

exit the elevator and walk up to my front door, we find the jamb busted and the door barely hanging by its hinges. Splinters of wood cover the surrounding ground.

The body language of all three Savage brothers instantly changes. They stiffen and pull out their guns from the waistband of their jeans. What happens next is a bit of a blur. One minute I'm standing in front of my door with my keys in my hand, and the next, I'm looking at the back of Zane's head as Axel grabs the crook of my elbow and gently pulls me back next to him. The move is slight, but it's enough to jostle around the food in my stomach and spark my nausea back to life.

Asher takes up the space beside Zane, ready to go in after him. They've made a shield out of their bodies and barricaded me in the middle.

"Stay behind us, Ken," Zane orders without a backward glance.

"I've got her." Axel pulls me in even closer until his side is pressed against mine and wraps an arm around my shoulders. He's so close that all I can smell is the fruitiness of his gum. "You two go inside, and we'll wait out here until you give the all-clear."

Asher nods but doesn't say anything else. I've learned that about him. He's like my brother Connor. They don't like to waste their time on unnecessary words. He and Zane make their way into my tiny apartment with their guns raised. The further they go, the harder my heart pounds in my throat until they're out of sight. I clutch the ring of keys in my hand tighter against my chest as the floors creak from underneath their weight.

Doors slam open so hard I hear the drywall crack,

causing me to jump. My nerves are shot. Every little noise is putting me on edge.

Axel puts a hand on my shoulder. "Easy there, Short Stack. We aren't going to let anything happen to you." His words ease my pounding pulse enough for me not to feel like I'm having a mini heart attack.

I switch my keys over to my left hand and wipe the palms of my sweaty hand on my leggings. Even the humid August air isn't enough to calm my nerves. It takes everything I have to control my rapid breathing, but there's no stopping the butterflies somersaulting inside me. My hands press against my stomach, where our baby is growing. We better make it out of this in one piece.

Seconds tick by as we wait. The entire time, Axel's head never stops roaming the hall, scanning our surroundings. He's on constant alert, which is putting me on edge.

"What the fuck!" Zane shouts from inside.

Axel shoots me a look and rushes in to see what all of the commotion is about, leaving me standing there by my lonesome.

I'm torn between being out here alone or taking my chances inside with them. The latter option wins out.

When I step over the threshold, my insides shrivel up. Everything I own is trashed. Stuffing from the few throw pillows I own litters the floor in a sea of white, like a giant snowstorm came through. My couch is tossed on its side and torn apart as well. Things are just as bad inside my kitchenette. All of my cabinets are open, with the contents littering the floor. Broken glass and food are everywhere I look. Nothing has been left untouched. They purposely wanted to destroy any shred of me they could find. I can't even imagine what my bedroom must look like.

When I get to my bedroom doorway, Zane has a man I've never seen before pressed up against the wall and a gun pressed to his temple. His dark skin is covered in tattoos like Zane's, and his clothes look like they have seen better days.

Asher is standing next to him, watching it all unfold. Axel is leaning against the wall next to the door, mimicking Asher's stance. None of them are aware that I've even entered the room, so I stay quiet and watch.

"Talk, Issac." Zane slams him back up against the wall as every muscle in his body goes rigid. "Why the fuck did you trash the place?"

"It wasn't me." Isaac holds his hand up in surrender. "I came to ask you for help and found it like this."

"Then why the fuck were you hiding in here like a little bitch?" Asher asks.

"I thought it was them coming back to finish the job." Isaac's dark eyes drift over to Asher.

"Bullshit."

"It's the fucking truth. I swear." Isaac sags into the wall and hangs his head.

Zane stays stock-still for a beat, but then he eases the gun away from Isaac's temple and backs up a step. "Let's say I believe you. It still doesn't explain what you're doing here."

"They fucking killed her, man." He runs a hand over his face, exposing more tattoos on top of his hand. "Left her there like she was trash." His voice cracks as he speaks.

"Who's they? And don't bullshit me. I know when

you're lying," Asher asks, with his arms crossed over his chest.

Isaac lifts his head and stares at Asher. His black eyes are glassy as he lets out a deep sigh and shakes his head. "I don't know. That's what I need your help with."

I move to step closer in the room, and that's when they finally register that I'm inside the apartment.

"Careful, Ken," Axel says, coming up next to me and grabbing me by the elbow to usher me over to the only space on my mattress that isn't sliced up and sitting me down in the only usable chair.

Tears fill my eyes as I glance around at what's left of all of my belongings. Nausea fights its way to the back of my throat. "Who would do this?"

All three brothers share a look with Isaac before Zane brings his gaze back to me. "Not sure, but we're going to find out."

That's all it takes to lose the battle I've been fighting all morning, and I throw up all over the floor next to Axel's feet.

19
ZANE

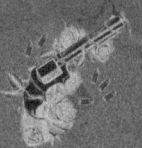

Axel jumps out of the way, but not in time before Kennedy's breakfast comes back up all over his shoes.

"Oh my god. I'm so sorry." Kennedy covers her mouth with her hand and slumps her shoulders as her body sags deeper into the chair. Her eyes are glassy as she fights the urge to cry, and I glare at Axel, daring him to say anything that'll upset her further. She already feels like shit with this nausea, and I'll be damned if I let anyone else make her feel worse about it. Lucky for him, he makes the smart choice.

"It's fine, Short Stack." He holds on to the wall as he slips out of his shoes and socks. "I'm just going to rinse my feet off in the shower." He jerks his thumb over his shoulder toward Kennedy's tiny bathroom.

I offer him a chin tilt in appreciation and then turn my attention back to Isaac as I cross my arms over my chest. Water starts running, but I let it become background noise. The only thing of importance right now is finding out why the fuck Isaac is here. He says he didn't do it, and everything in my gut believes him, but my past has taught me the hits usually come from where you least expect it. I'm reserving my judgment until I know more.

"Give me one reason why I shouldn't string you up by your nuts for threatening my wife." I cross the room and put my hand on Kennedy's shoulder, letting her know without words it's okay. Her muscles spasm but soon relax under the comfort of my touch.

Isaac's black eyes swing from Kennedy to me as his forehead wrinkles. "I've already told you, Z, that wasn't me." The message is clear. He's not saying who he suspects in front of Kennedy.

"Then who the fuck was it?" Asher asks.

"The same motherfuckers that hired you to seek me out and killed my woman." Isaac tugs at the collar of his stained T-shirt as a muscle tics on the side of his jaw. The red haze has cleared, and now I'm taking in the rest of his appearance. He's covered in dirt and grime and has heavy bags under his eyes. Even his usually clean-shaven face is covered in at least a few days' worth of hair growth. He also looks like he hasn't had a good night's sleep in days. I should know. I'm looking pretty much the same way at the moment.

"And the money in your account?" I ask as Kennedy attempts to get up from the chair to clean up the mess she made on the floor. "Leave it, Ken. I'll take care of it." Translation: Axel is going to do it. The fucker owes me one. Besides, none of us are bothered by the smell. We've trained under worse conditions. A little sour milk smell isn't going to bother us.

"All legit." Isaac leans his head back against the wall and holds my gaze out of the corner of his eyes.

"Bullshit." Asher isn't buying it. Then again, his cop instincts make it hard for him to believe that things like that just happen to people the legit way.

"I've made some investments, and they paid off." He shrugs as his lips twitch. "You never did believe in investing in jack shit." He shakes his head. "I told you to play the long game, and it'll pay off." He taps the end of his nose.

"Then why put it in Cindy's name?" That's one thing I haven't been able to figure out. With the dirt Asher's managed to dig up, we have a pretty good idea who did this, but I wait Isaac out to see if he's going to lie to me some more or not. The investment story is a matter of semantics. I know what he means by it and what he's been doing down in Florida to get that kind of money. Not that I give a fuck about how a man makes his living. Fuck if my brothers and I don't toe the line of what's legal or not, so I'm no one to judge. But if his lies hurt me or mine, we have a problem.

Isaac's body tenses up at the mention of his girl-friend, and a part of me feels like a bastard for twisting that knife deeper, but I need him to be straight with me. "Why do you think?"

"If I knew, I wouldn't be asking." My patience is running thin with him. Not only do I still have to have a conversation with Asher about who I saw in Finn's office —a conversation I have put off as long as I can—but the faster we get out of here, the better for us all. I won't feel safe until we're back at the house, and then we can get to the bottom of this. And exactly what we signed up for with this job.

"Big brother is always watching. I wasn't going to risk them pulling me back in and using that as leverage to do it." He digs his clay-stained sneakers into the wooden floor as he stands up away from the wall, finally coming clean and letting me know without words what I've suspected all along. He was laundering money. "It still managed to fuck me in the end." He shakes his head as his eyes drift off into the distance before landing on Kennedy. "They still managed to take what I treasure most."

It's a bit of a relief to know that I was right about Isaac all along. He's not dirty. He's just trying to make a life away from the shit that is our past. Still, his words hit too close to home. Kennedy and I have had too many close calls for my liking lately.

I'm about to ask him another question when a white blob zooms past me and stands at Isaac's feet.

"Thor!" Kennedy's face lights up seeing that damn dog.

Isaac bends down and picks him up. "Cute dog. Yours?" He scratches behind Thor's ears, and the little shit's tail wags back and forth like a whip.

"No," I grind out through gritted teeth. I've been so caught up in getting answers from Isaac that I forgot Kennedy has no fucking door, and anyone off the street can come in. Hence why that little shit managed to get in.

"It's my neighbor's," Kennedy offers by way of an explanation.

"Hello?" Mrs. Baker's voice calls from the living room, and everyone stills. All eyes shoot in the direction of the front door. Fucking hell, this shit just keeps becoming more and more complicated.

"Goddammit." I pinch the bridge of my nose to keep from losing control.

Thor squirms against Isaac's hold, and he sets him down. I follow after the furball, hoping to keep Mrs. Baker from entering and noticing the clusterfuck that is Kennedy's apartment.

When I get there, she's standing at the doorway. Thank fuck she's got coke bottles for glasses and can't see that well. Or at least I hope not. Still, her gray eyebrows pinch together, letting me know she can make out some of the disaster that was Kennedy's apartment.

"Mrs. Baker." I fight to keep my voice neutral and not let on to the chaos surrounding us.

"Oh, hi." The wrinkles around her mouth disappear as she smiles. "I was hoping you could help me put up that gate so this little prankster will stop sneaking out and causing trouble. My grandson still hasn't gotten around to it."

My fingers clench. Her grandson sounds like a lazy piece of shit. One thing our parents taught us was to respect our elders. We dropped everything anytime one of our parents or grandparents needed us.

Her head peeks around me, and her brown eyes widen. "What happened in here?"

"Redecorating." Isaac comes up behind me and offers her a smile that's all teeth.

"Who are you?" Her head tilts to the side as she studies him like he's the most exciting thing she's seen all day.

Thinking fast, I say the first thing that comes to mind. "He's the decorator Kennedy hired."

"I sure am." Isaac shrugs, immediately catching on and slapping me on the shoulder much harder than needed. The fucker. I don't get off on lying, but the last thing I want to do is scare the shit out of an old lady who lives by herself. Something tells me that letting her know about a burglary that happened right under her nose wouldn't go over so well.

"So that's what all the commotion was about yesterday." Her attention swings back to me as Thor wiggles against her hold.

"Commotion?" My eyebrows cock as her words have me standing up taller.

"Oh yes. It was pretty loud too." She narrows her eyes in Isaac's direction.

"My apologies, ma'am." Isaac places a hand over his heart and does his best to look humbled by this news, even though I'm sure his mind is spinning a mile a minute like my own. He always was quick at thinking on his feet. That's part of what made him so good at what we did.

"You're new." Her brown eyes widen over my shoulder, and I know that she's just gotten her first glimpse of Asher without glancing back.

"Ma'am" is all my older brother says, but that's enough.

She nods her head, causing the gray bun on top to move back and forth, and then glances back at me, waiting for an answer to her earlier question.

"Now isn't really a good time." I move to shut the door, but then she gives that same soft look my mother used to give me.

"It'll just take a second. Please?" She adjusts Thor against her side as she waits for me to answer.

Everything inside me is screaming to tell her no, but even I'm not that much of a bastard. And maybe I'll be able to get more information from her about those visitors. "Yeah. Just give me one sec to grab some tools."

"All right." She spins and shuffles back to her apartment.

"Who was that?" Axel asks as he comes out of the bedroom with a washrag.

"Neighbor. Where's Ken?" I swing my head around him and come up empty.

"Bathroom." He wrinkles his nose, letting me know what she's doing in there with that one look—more puking.

An uncomfortable feeling settles in my chest. I hate that she's so sick, but there's nothing I can do for her. "Can you stay here with her while I handle this?"

"Yup." He nods and tosses the washrag onto the counter and spins around to head back into her bedroom when I stop him.

"Make sure she packs all of her shit."

Axel grins, showing off his dimples from over his shoulder. And I know damn well what he's thinking. I don't offer him an explanation because he's right. Kennedy isn't coming back here after this shit is all said and done. She just doesn't know it yet.

"Can I get y'all anything? Pecan pie? Cookies? Sweet tea?" Mrs. Baker asks for the umpteenth time since we've been here. She's been hovering around us ever since we came over with a plate full of cookies in hand, offering us any kind of drink or food she can think of to stuff us with.

Thor is nowhere to be seen, so I assume she locked

the little fucker up. Which is a small favor. The last thing I want is him pissing on my feet while I set up the gate.

"No." Asher gives his typical one-word answers, but it doesn't deter her from trying.

"No, thank you, ma'am," Isaac cuts in, making up for the proper manners my big brother and I lack.

She soaks up all the attention Isaac shows her, but it's nowhere near the attentiveness she's been giving to my older brother. Come to think of it, she has yet to leave Asher's side. Since he stepped inside her apartment, she's been no more than a few inches away from him. Something I've found interesting, but judging by the stern expression on my big brother's face, he doesn't.

Her place is similar in size and layout to Kennedy's, but that's where the similarities between the two apartments end. While Kennedy had family photos all along her walls, Mrs. Baker's are all bare. There is only one single photo in her living room that I glanced at earlier. Everything about it feels impersonal as hell. It lacks all the warmth that made Kennedy's place a home before those fuckers destroyed it. It must be another thing she was waiting on her grandson to do for her.

Asher does his best to avoid Mrs. Baker and comes to help me with the gate. I'm damn near done, but I let him pretend for an escape from her attention.

Isaac has gotten even more into character and taken to roaming the apartment pretending to offer her decorating advice. Some of it sounds believable, while some of it sounds just plain nuts. Where he manages to come up with this shit, I have no fucking clue, but he sells it.

I test the gate out a few times to ensure it works properly. Once I'm satisfied that it'll stay in place and keep Thor locked inside until she lets him out, I stand ready to get down to why I came here. "This should keep him from escaping now, Mrs. Baker?"

"Oh please, Mrs. Baker was my mother's name. Y'all can call me Ella Mae." She grins.

Asher and I share a look at that little piece of information as he comes to stand next to me, coming to the same conclusion as me—we will, without a doubt, be giving Axel shit about this later.

"Baby gate is up." Asher clears his throat and shoves his hands in his pockets.

"That was fast." Her face falls, and I can see her mentally calculating something else for him to fix.

"I have one just like it at home." Asher shrugs but doesn't offer her any more of an explanation than that.

"Really? Lucky lady." She laughs, and a light shade of pink coats the apples of her cheeks. "Oh my. You are a big fella, ain't you."

Asher tugs at the collar of his shirt, looking like he would rather be anywhere than here. He takes a few steps back to avoid any more awkward conversation and gets out from under her scrutinizing gaze.

"Ella Mae?" Isaac steps in front of her, drawing her attention away from Asher as he steals a cookie off her plate.

"Hmm?" Her mouth presses into a small line.

"You mentioned that the noise was bothering you?" He bites into the cookie and smiles at her. Isaac always was a smooth bastard with the ladies.

"Oh yes, it shook the wall in my kitchen where our apartments connect. The darn vibrations almost knocked all of my precious china from my wedding off the counter." She narrows her eyes at Isaac as she remembers that little detail. "They were my husband's favorite."

"Do you happen to know around what time that was?" When she stares at him in confusion, he tacks on, "I had my assistants over, and I want to make sure they know what time is too late to be working. The last thing I want is to be unneighborly."

She taps a finger against her chin as she thinks about his words. "It must have been around eight. That's when my *Murder, She Wrote* marathon starts." She casts a sheepish look at Asher. "I like a good bit of mystery."

"Angela Lansbury is a true treasure." Isaac is laying it on thick, and I have no fucking idea how he even knows what she's talking about, but I'm willing to let him roll with it if we can get our answers.

"That she is." She nods. "Anyway, Thor was going crazy and barking so loud I couldn't even hear it."

"Did you happen to catch a glimpse of them leaving?" It's a long shot, but it's still worth asking, just in case.

Her lips purse together as her head tilts to the side. "Why?"

"So I know who I need to tell," Isaac offers by way of explanation.

She thinks on it for a solid minute while the entire room goes silent, waiting on her answer. "Well, no. But I did hear one of them talking into a walkie-talkie thing like my grandsons used to play with."

"Could you make out what he said?" I'm hoping she can give me something that'll tell me who he is.

"Not really. The television was up pretty loud to drown out the noise, but I know it was in Spanish. My husband was fluent in it, and I picked up enough to recognize it when I heard it."

That's something we didn't know before, at least.

Kennedy did mention that she is the eyes and the ears of their floor. Her having missed whoever was in here tells me all I need to know. They're professionals, which means we need to up our game and get ahead of this before it's too late.

20

KENNEDY

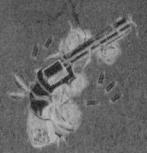

Zane is sitting as far back as the seat will allow, but there isn't much room in my Honda Civic for a guy of his size. He might as well be driving one of those clown cars for as out of place as he looks. He's hunched over the steering wheel because his head hits the roof. The fit is so tight that he had to take his hair down because otherwise, he wouldn't make it inside. Even his oversized hands swallow up most of the steering wheel.

"What?" His dark eyebrows pinch together as he catches me staring.

"Nothing." I bite my lip and do my best to fight the urge to laugh. It could be from the trauma of having my apartment trashed, but there's just something about seeing the broody bastard driving my car that has me busting out in a fit of giggles.

He spares me a glance before shifting his gaze back onto the road. "I've never heard you laugh like that." His hand tugs on the seam of his jeans as he clears his throat. "Now you have to tell me, Ken."

"You just look huge, is all." I gesture to his hunched seating position. "It can't be very comfortable driving like that all bunched up against the steering wheel."

"I'll admit I miss the room the cab of my truck had." His eyes narrow as he undoubtedly remembers what a mess his truck is now. I asked if he would take it to a shop, but he said he would cut his losses and get a new one.

"And that's why you should have let me drive." My humor fades a bit. I'm still annoyed that he pulled that macho crap about driving, but he did have a valid point. After he, his brothers, and now the newest addition to the group, Isaac, checked over every inch of my car, Zane and I argued over who was going to drive. Just because he's the man doesn't automatically mean he gets the keys.

Then he reminded me of our last car trip together, and I caved. I do not want to be behind the wheel if we're shot at again. Axel and the other two guys may be following behind us, but it's still a risk I do not want to take. My dad always said to pick your battles, and this is one that I'll happily let slide.

"Hopefully, the trade-in value for this is decent," Zane's voice cuts into my thoughts.

"Excuse me? Trade-in value?" That has me sitting up straighter in my seat and cocking my head at him.

Zane nods but doesn't take his eyes off the road. "I prefer you and my kid in something that won't crush like a fucking tin can if something happens." I want to be angry at him, but he is making sense, and damn if that doesn't irritate the crap out of me even more.

"And asking me what I want was just out of the question for you?" It's a struggle to keep my voice neutral when I really want to shout at the top of my lungs at him.

Zane must sense the hostility brewing in the air between us because he switches course and takes a different approach. "No. But you're a smart woman, Ken, and something tells me that you too want what's best for our family. And that's what we are now—a family. You, me, and that little one inside you." His hand gestures to my stomach without taking his gaze off the road.

When he's rational like this, it drives me insane. I can't lash out because he's making sense, yet again. A heavy sigh escapes me as his words resonate, hitting his designated target and my weakness. Still, it doesn't mean I have to comply so easily. I am no doormat. "That may be true, but it's one thing to have someone make decisions for you without asking or including you. As a *family*, these are things that should be discussed together."

Zane stays silent, working over what I've just said in his head. "Fair enough."

"Thank you." That was easy. I expected him to put up a bigger argument about him being the man and all that crap again—the same song and dance my dad and brothers always give me.

Satisfied at that, I stare out the window, mentally calculating everything I will have to replace in my apartment.

"Do you have comprehensive coverage on this piece of shit?" Zane asks, and I know exactly what he's getting at.

"And you were doing so well too." I shake my head as the corners of my eyes crinkle, but there's no fight behind my words. He knows that he's won another round because it's the smart thing to do. I want my child to be as safe as possible, and if that means I have to concede and buy something the size of a tank, I will.

We sit in silence for a few more minutes when my curiosity gets the better of me. "So, that was *the* Isaac? The one that was in Afghanistan with you?" I add that last bit as an afterthought to ensure he knows what I'm asking.

"It is," he grunts out. "Why?"

"Just curious." I pick at an imaginary piece of lint on my leggings as I prod him for more information. After all, we're married, and as his wife, I can ask him these things. Whether he'll tell me or not is another story entirely. "How long has it been since you've seen him?"

"We lost touch after everything that happened and went our separate ways. I tried everything to get back to normal. Even therapy. None of that shit worked." He takes his right hand off the steering wheel and begins to twist the ends of his beard. A nervous tic I'm not even sure he realizes he does, but one I've picked up on.

"Therapy?" My ears perk up at this piece of information. He's never told more than what happened in Afghanistan. I haven't learned what happened after, but if he's opening up to me now, it tells me it's something he's not doing lightly. Maybe being trapped in this small space is acting as his confessional?

"What happened over there fucked with our heads, and they wanted to make sure that we weren't going to be sent back out into the field and blow a civilian's head off because they sneezed at us wrong."

"Did it work?" I push my glasses farther up the bridge of my nose and twist in my seat until I face him, hanging on his every word.

His forehead wrinkles as he thinks over my question. I can see the wheels turning in his head like it wasn't something he ever really thought about before. "Don't know."

"What do you mean, you don't know?" My eyebrows dip down at his answer.

"I'm still fucked up, aren't I?" His fingers clench tighter against the steering wheel until the stiff plastic protests under the immense pressure. He's disappearing inside his head, and the last thing I want to do is lose him to whatever darkness sucks him under. I reach over and pull his hand away from his beard and interlace our fingers, letting him know without words that he isn't alone anymore.

"Considering who my family is, I don't think I'm one to judge on that." My tone is lighthearted, but there's a certain truth hidden behind my words, and of course, he picks up on that and turns the conversation over to me.

"What about you?" Zane asks, and I sit up straighter in my seat.

"What about me?" I slip my hand out of his and lean away from him until I feel the armrest on the door digging into my back.

"I get the feeling that Finn didn't shelter you from what he does? From who he *really* is?" He takes his eyes off the road for a split second to look me in the eye as he quizzes me on my childhood before they drift back onto the road.

I don't answer him right away. The truth is how I was raised is difficult to explain to outsiders, but then again, with what Zane has experienced, he may be just the one who does get it.

"He didn't. You remember me telling you how my mom was killed?" My throat becomes scratchy as the memories come back to me full force. Zane answers with a slight nod of his head, so I continue. "She was on her way to pick me up from preschool when her car was boxed in."

My hands rub against the tops of my thighs as I practice my box breathing. In for four. Hold. Out for four. Hold. He catches on to what I'm doing without me having to utter a word. He grabs my left hand and plays with the diamond on my ring finger, twisting it around in time with my breathing. This goes on for at least a couple more seconds before the ache in my chest subsides enough for me to continue talking.

"They gang-raped her and then sent her back to my father in pieces." There's a slight tremble to my voice as I force out the worst of it in one long breath. Delivering news like this is similar to ripping off a Band-Aid, and it's best to do it as fast as possible. Even knowing it still makes my insides ache with the torment my mother must have endured at the hands of those monsters. The atmosphere in the car grows heavy with tension, but I need to get out the rest so that we can move on to a different topic. One that won't make me want to throw up yet again.

"Fuck, Ken. I'm sorry." He squeezes my hand a fraction tighter and lets out a heavy sigh. When he glances my way, his dark eyebrows are pinched together, but it's the darkness behind his eyes that has a tingle spreading from my stomach and down between my legs. I clench my thighs together to try and gain some sense of self-control, but my hormones have a mind of their own.

The fact that he resembles the same expression my

dad wore that dreadful day hits home. I might have been too small to remember everything accurately, but that is something that has stuck in my mind through the years. I wanted someone to feel that deeply about me. My father loved my mother. She was his world, and after they took her from us, he made sure everyone knew what happens when you fuck with a Donnelly.

"There's more, isn't there?" A pained look crosses his face.

I nod and swallow down the lump building in the back of my throat. "They sent him pictures of me, from everywhere. There were some from school and even some from me in our yard. Told him that I'd be next if he didn't back off."

"That's why your dad is so protective of you," he says more to himself, like it's an afterthought.

"Yeah. And my brothers. They figured the best way to keep me safe was for me to know what was going on. My dad thought if they did that, I wouldn't take any unnecessary risks where my safety was concerned. They also taught me how to use a gun and some self-defense moves."

"You were only four." His eyes narrow, but something tells me that he will be just as protective as mine if we have a daughter.

"In this life, it's better to be prepared from a young age. It's kill or be killed." It's harsh but true. "Teegan and Keegan were only two when she died, but they grew up the same way."

"That's fucked up." He shakes his head but doesn't loosen his grip on my hand. A few beats of silence pass before he asks, "What happened to them?"

"What do you think happened to them?" I know

better than to admit outright what happened. I may have only been four, but Connor and Rory told me and swore me to secrecy. "There's a reason my dad has the reputation he does." I shrug.

"Good," Zane grunts.

And that's the end of our conversation. We drive in comfortable silence the rest of the way back to the Savage property. A sense of relief fills me that I could share my upbringing with Zane, and he listened without judgment. And I am beyond relieved that we weren't shot at once the entire drive over.

When we pull up the long dirt drive, Zane parks my car right in front of the porch where Kelsey and Charlee are sitting and waiting. Lily is nowhere in sight, so she must be down for a nap. With all I've been through today thus far, I have half a mind to join her.

I move to get out, but Zane stops me. "Stay there." When I give him a blank expression, he explains, "I'll come around and get your door."

"I can do it." I attempt to reason with him, but he isn't having it.

"Please, let me do this. For my peace of mind." His blue eyes hold mine, his expression saying everything his mouth isn't.

"Okay." I sag against my seat and watch him climb out of my Civic. It almost feels like I'm watching child-birth as he contorts himself in half out from under the steering wheel to make it out of the small space. After some growling and grunting, he's out and around to my side of the vehicle. His long hair blows across his back as he opens my door. I hear Charlee and Kelsey laughing behind me, and I can't help but join in.

The second I set foot on the Georgia clay, he interlocks his fingers with mine. It's safe to say that since we left my apartment complex, he hasn't wanted me out of his sight. He takes one look at my face and shakes his head, but not before I see the corner of his mouth twitch.

Axel's truck pulls up next to the front of Asher's house. He's out and headed our way, leaving Isaac and Asher standing next to the truck and deep in conversation. Whatever is being said must be intense, judging by their stiff body language.

"Thank fuck I'm out of there." Axel pulls a cigarette out of the pack he draws from his back pocket and shakes his head. He pinches the end between his lips and goes to light it, but Zane yanks it from his mouth before he can and tosses it to the ground.

"What did I tell you about lighting up in front of Ken?" Zane smacks him upside his head.

"Shit. I forgot again. I'm sorry, Short Stack." Axel smacks the side of his head.

"It's fine." I wave him off, but Zane isn't having it.

"What the fuck do you me 'again'?" Zane pushes his shoulders back and stares down his baby brother.

Axel's eyes widen as he realizes his slip-up. "Umm." He scratches the side of his cheek, doing what he can to stall and come up with an explanation. "Did I say that?"

"Yeah, you did."

Axel's blue eyes drift to mine, and I can't help but feel bad for him, so I do what any good sister-in-law would do and take one for the team.

"Oh no." I hunch over and place my hand on my stomach like I'm going to be sick.

"What's wrong?" All of Zane's focus shifts to me. "Are you going to throw up again?"

Axel catches on to what I'm doing and calls out, "Wildcat!" As he passes me to go to Kelsey, he whispers in my ear, "I owe you one."

"No. I'm feeling a little lightheaded."

Zane's eyes narrow as he tilts his head to the side, studying me. "That right?"

"Mm-hmm." I suck in a deep breath and do my best to sell it.

"Then why are you holding your stomach if it's your head?" he asks.

Well, shit. He's got me there.

Zane shakes his head, but I can see the slight humor behind his eyes. "I'm in a fuckload of trouble if you're already covering for Axel."

I shrug and open my mouth to explain when Asher's raised voice catches our attention.

Zane glances over to Asher and Isaac, working out something inside his head. The cords of his neck are tense as he absently twists my wedding ring around my finger. He watches Isaac's every move like a predator, waiting to pounce on him at any moment.

"You sure it was safe to bring him here?" They had no problem driving him over here, but seeing the expression on Zane's face, I'm having second thoughts about this.

"Didn't really have a choice. At least this way, I know exactly where he is." His eyes drop down to mine. "And that's one possible threat against you accounted for." The hand not holding mine strokes the ends of his beard as he continues to watch the two of them. "You okay to go inside with the girls while we take Isaac to Asher's place to talk?"

"Yeah." I'm not naive enough to think that they'll

just be talking, but I have something else on my mind. "You still going to avoid sleeping next to me?" It's probably not the best time to bring it up, but timing has never been my strong suit.

He pulls me in tighter against him and kisses the top of my head. "We shouldn't be too long, and then you and I are going to have another talk."

"Fine." I nod as he lets go of my hand and starts to make his way over to where Asher is.

"Let's go, Ax." His steps never falter as he calls him over his shoulder.

"Yeah, yeah," Axel grumbles but follows behind Zane. "I'm coming."

Charlee steps up next to me with Kelsey not far behind her and crosses her arms over her chest. "Who's that?" Her green eyes narrow in Isaac's direction as her mama bear comes out.

"Isaac" is all I offer by way of explanation. I don't know much else to offer her.

"Hmm." She's all Vega as she studies the newest person that's come into the mix. It doesn't go unnoticed that she never crosses over to greet Asher, and I have to wonder if what Axel said at breakfast holds a bit of truth. "If Asher let him come on the property, he must have a good reason."

Her dark eyebrows pinch together, still not happy that there's a stranger on the same property as her daughter. And I have to agree with her. I just hope the guys know what they're doing by bringing an outsider home. My dad always says to keep your enemies close because it's easier to see the knife coming if they can't reach your back.

21

ZANE

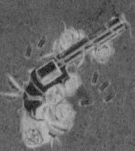

My brother catches my eye and leads Isaac into his house. We pass the row of kid toys that litter the path to his front door—a reminder of what's at stake if we fuck this up and head inside.

I'm not sure what else Isaac is going to drop on us that he didn't want to spill in front of Kennedy, but my gut tells me that Isaac is as innocent as I thought before we took this job, and that only leads to more questions than answers about what the fuck is going on.

Asher leads us into his office in the back of the house, just past the kitchen, and goes straight to his safe, where he keeps all the confidential files of the jobs we take. We may be morally gray, but there is no such thing as black and white in this world. And since we loosely operate within the fringes of the law and have a few important people on our payroll, it never hurts to have all of our shit covered.

Isaac only gets two steps in before I grab him by the

collar of his shirt and slam him up against the wall. "Talk."

His nostrils flare as his dark brown eyes stare me down. "You know I'm getting real fucking tired of you slamming my ass up against the wall like I'm your fucking enemy. You forget, brother. I was there with you. I watched them kill my partner too. Grady may have been an asshole, but he was the asshole that always had my back."

The words hit, but I don't let go. I wait him out to see what he does next. Sometimes when cornering an animal, it's best to wait and see how they fight their way out of it. That's the most telling of all. I know he can break through my hold, but he doesn't, and that says more than his words to me at this moment. He's giving me the upper hand to prove his point. That he's not out to fuck us over.

My hands ease away from his shirt, letting him push away from the wall to a standing position. "Fine. Now, talk."

He shakes out the wrinkles I made on his filthy shirt and narrows his eyes at me. "Look, I have a business to run, and I can't afford any more complications if you get what I'm saying." His dark eyebrows pinch together as he waits for me to catch on to what he's getting at.

"Your drug business doesn't interest me. As far as I know, it has nothing to do with why Ken was shot at or threatened. I don't give a fuck how you make your living." I push my chest out and stand up taller to drive home my point.

"I already told you once that wasn't me, and I'd like to think that since we used to be as tight as brothers, you know I'd never do that to you."

"As much as we're enjoying this little reunion, can y'all get to the fucking point already?" Axel props himself up against the doorjamb, waiting and watching. He may appear casual, but he's not. He's blocking Isaac's only way out in case shit doesn't go our way.

Asher has taken up residence next to his desk and sits on the corner with his arms crossed over his chest, taking it all in. The file he took out rests on the desk next to him. He'll share what we have after Isaac spills first. It's the only way to know if we're being played.

Isaac glares over at my little brother, and if he wasn't my blood, I'm sure he'd be kicking his ass. Instead, he does as Axel demands. "You know what shit was like when we got back."

I nod, not needing to voice it out loud. Everyone in this room knows what he's saying.

"Therapy didn't do shit."

A grunt escapes me because he's right. Sitting on a couch while some stranger takes notes on whatever you say doesn't do dick. My family has helped me more than anything, and I'd be lost without them, which is why I'll also kill to protect them.

Isaac jerks his chin at my noise of agreement and keeps going. "I couldn't hold down a job to save my ass. And that bullshit pension they gave us could barely pay my bills. I had to find something that I could make a decent living at."

"And drug dealer was your answer?" Axel asks.

"I prefer the term 'importer.' I don't deal directly. I just help them bring their product in." Isaac shakes his head at Axel, like the distinction between the two is huge.

"Oh, big difference," Axel smarts off. "My mistake." He waves him on with his hand. "Continue."

Isaac's nostrils flare. "You're a real smart-ass, kid."

Axel opens his mouth to snap back, but Asher gets there first.

"Ax," he barks at our little brother. Axel shuts his mouth, trapping whatever comment he wanted to say inside, and thank fuck for that. He pushes it too far sometimes and needs to be reined in before he gets his ass kicked.

Once Axel grows quiet, Isaac starts back up. "As I was saying, I know the ports and how they operate, so I use that to help them smuggle their product into the States. And the money was rolling in. Things were good."

"Until?" My eyebrows arch as that tidbit piques my interest.

"Until they sent some new business my way. I had a gut feeling that this fucker was bad news to begin with, and I never should have gotten into bed with him."

"Bad news, how?" Asher perks up from his spot because this is news to us.

"Bad." Isaac swallows as he runs a hand through his hair, and it's clear that whatever it is, it's a hard limit for him. He glances my way, and what I see has my gut tightening. "You have to know that I had no idea, and once I did, I put a stop to it."

The floor drops out from under me as I catch onto what he's telling us.

"I would never willingly do that shit. Not after everything we've been through."

"Would y'all like to explain it to the rest of the

class?" Axel glances between Isaac and me, trying to make heads or tails of this shit.

"Humans." My voice comes out rough and raspy as I force that word out. Everything inside of me coils up tight, ready to explode.

"Not just any humans. They all had a black paw print on the side of their necks." A muscle jerks in Isaac's cheek as my whole body tenses, but that coincides with what Asher found.

"There's more." It's a statement, not a question. Asher doesn't dwell on the bomb Isaac dropped because he's quick to see the bigger picture and connect the dots. It's what made him such a good cop.

Isaac nods. "After—" He swallows down the bile that I'm sure is stuck in his throat as memories of our past surface. "You know I don't stand for that shit. I couldn't stop doing business with them, or else I wouldn't be able to put an end to it. So, I did what we were trained to do."

"You watched them." I know because that's exactly what I would do if the situation were reversed.

"I did." He nods. "I started keeping tabs on them. Every *delivery* that was made, everyone that went out, and to who. I saved it all."

"I don't get it." Axel pushes up off the wall and walks deeper into the room. "Then why didn't you go to the feds with all of it?"

"I did, but they said it wasn't enough because I didn't have the big fish. They wanted the top dog, and these were just throwaways." The corner of Isaac's lip curls back at the thought.

"And you never found out who that was?" My fingers

itch to wrap my hands around the piece of shit's throat that is responsible.

"No." He shakes his head. "After I went to the feds, all deliveries stopped, and they went radio silent on me."

"Of course." Asher shakes his head as his nostrils flare. "Fucking dirty cops." He has his own reasons why that hits too close to home, and I don't blame him. He lost his wife and unborn son because of a dirty cop—his own partner, of all things.

"That's why they trashed your place," I say more to myself, but he manages to hear me.

"That and because I have this." Isaac pulls a flash drive out of his back pocket and holds it up for us to see.

"What exactly is on there?" I tilt my chin at the small device between his fingers.

He says one word that changes the entire game. "Everything."

"Fuck." My heart pounds against my chest as some more of the picture comes together.

"Now, your turn." Isaac closes his fist around the flash drive and puts it back in his pocket. He knows we want what he has and just dangled a giant fucking carrot in front of us to get his answers.

Asher opens the folder on his desk and pulls out everything that he's managed to dig up without drawing too much attention to us. He lays all the images and printouts across his desk for Isaac to see. Including the ones of the women's naked bodies that have been found mutilated all around the Georgia-Florida area. Each has that same fucking black paw on their neck.

"We were hired to bring you in. They said you were

a traitor. Selling secrets to the enemy." I run a hand through my hair as everything replays in my head.

"And you believed them?" The lines on his forehead deepen as he takes in everything on Asher's desk.

"No, but there were things that didn't add up. The beachfront property. The money. The account in Cindy's name. None of it looked good." A tightness builds in my chest as I think back to the picture they painted. Against my better judgment, I fell for their shit.

"Fuck you, man!" A vein pops out the side of his neck as he glares up at me before going back to the papers. "Y'all are a piece of work. You already knew everything I just shared."

"Had to make sure you'd tell us the truth." Asher shrugs, giving zero fucks on Isaac's opinion.

"Fucking Savage." Isaac shakes his head at my brother.

"What the fuck was I supposed to think, Isaac?" I know damn well if things were reversed, he'd be thinking along the same lines as me. He's just too pissed off to admit it to himself.

"That you know me, and you know I'd never betray our country like that. I mean, fuck, Z. A traitor? Really?" He runs a hand down the side of his face, scratching at the stubble as the full weight of it all sinks in.

"You're right." I hang my head, feeling like complete and utter shit. "I should have known better. I'm sorry, and I'm going to make it right for both of us."

"How?" Isaac paces a few steps and then stops and slams his hand against his chest. "They killed my woman!" His eyes gloss over at the mention of her, and I can't blame him, but he's not the only one with something to lose.

"And they shot at mine!" I punch my chest as my temper flares to life at the shit Kennedy's been through.

Axel whistles, drowning out the rest of our argument. "Yo! Can y'all save who has the bigger dick for later, so we can figure out just what the hell is going on?"

"It doesn't make sense. If they knew we were coming to bring him in, why would they take care of it themselves?" Asher asks the very same thing that I've been wondering myself.

"That's a good question. We need to find out just how deep this rabbit hole goes." Isaac's jaw sets as he stares each of us down.

"We do, but not right now." Asher pushes off the desk, and he's getting ready to head out, but our conversation can't wait any longer.

I offer him an olive branch in the only way I know how. "You look like shit."

"Feel like it." Isaac lets out a hollow laugh.

"Ax, can you take him inside our place to clean up? I'm gonna hang back for a bit."

Axel's eyebrows pinch together as he studies me. He knows something's up. "Sure." He glares at me one last time, and I know he will ask me about it later, but he does as I ask.

I wait for the sound of the front door shutting so that I can break the news to Asher. If he finds out that I knew and didn't tell him, he'll be pissed as fuck, and I don't blame him, but that'll only distract him from the other shit we have going on.

"Something on your mind?" Asher cocks his head to the side, waiting me out.

I toy with the end of my beard and struggle with the

best way to tell him what I've got to say. There isn't a good way to deliver this type of news, so I just lay it all out there for him.

"When Ken and I were at Finn's, he had a visitor." My tongue sticks to the roof of my mouth as I watch my words sink in. I almost wish Axel's dumb ass was here for a diversion.

"Who?" Asher narrows his eyes at me.

"Rosenberg."

Asher's whole body goes rock solid like I just dropped a bomb with that one word, and I may as well have. "What the fuck was he doing there?"

"Turns out he's one of Finn's and why he never came after us for what we did."

"And you're just telling me this now?" He grinds out through his teeth.

"I didn't want to just spring this shit on you." I glance down at his clenched fists and cock my eyebrow at him. "And judging by what I saw earlier, it was the right call."

"We're fine. Charlee's just being emotional and shit." A muscle jerks in his cheek, letting me know I hit the nail on the fucking head with my earlier observation. I knew Ax struck a chord at breakfast when he said that shit in front of Charlee, but I've been too busy dealing with my own problems to give it much thought.

"I hate to give Ax any credit, but he's right, man. You're not fine, and you need to figure your shit out before it's too late."

"Like you?" He turns the conversation back around on me. It's a tactic I'm all too familiar with because I do the same shit myself.

My temple throbs, but I fight back the urge to kick his ass. "I'm working on it."

"Looks like it." His jaw tightens as he cranes his neck to the side. "That's why you're still sleeping on the couch every fucking night."

"I said I'm handling it." I grind my teeth together to keep from lashing out. He's pissed about Rosenberg and not hearing me.

"You handle your demons your way, and let me deal with mine." His words are final, but I can see the war brewing behind his eyes.

We're locked in a stare down—both of us too fucking stubborn to be the first to break it. The only sound in the room is the pounding of my pulse in my ears as we continue to watch the other.

"I fucking knew it." Axel breaks the silence and comes storming into the room like the loose cannon he is.

"Where's Isaac?" I ask, not even touching his comment. He's quick, and I'm sure he'll put the pieces together.

"He's getting cleaned up." He crosses his arms over his chest and turns his head from me to Asher and frowns. "Something told me that I needed to come back here and check on both of y'all."

"We're fine, Ax." Asher won't look up as he collects all of the papers on his desk and tucks them back inside the folder.

"Y'all are too fucking stubborn and can't get your heads out of your asses to get your shit together without me." He shakes his head, not convinced and knowing us better than we know ourselves.

"Ax," Asher warns, but our little brother isn't listening to either of us.

"I can see you ain't ready for the shit you need to hear, but don't come bitching to me when they pack up and leave your stupid asses." Axel shakes his head, but Asher is done with this conversation.

"Won't happen." Asher gives him one last look before walking out and leaving the two of us standing there.

"You always have to push, little brother." I run a hand through my hair as I stare him down.

"Y'all can thank me later." Axel winks and takes out a pack of cigarettes from his back pocket. He puts it in his mouth, but before he can light up, I smack him upside the head, knocking the cigarette to the floor.

He grabs the side of his head and glares at me. "What the fuck was that for, Z?"

"I warned you not to light up in front of Ken." I shrug. He had it coming, and he fucking knows it.

He rolls his eyes and picks up the cigarette off the floor. "So fucking touchy, Z." He wipes it off against his T-shirt but puts it back in the pack instead of lighting up.

"Maybe you'll remember that next time then." He mumbles something under his breath, and I know he's bitching, so I offer him a bone. "Meet in the basement." I walk off and head into our house, down into the basement. All of the shit going down has me crawling out of my skin, and I need to work it out.

Axel's right about one thing, though. I need to get my shit together. And I'm trying, but it's not something I can conquer overnight. I hope she can understand that some demons aren't meant to be slain. They're meant to be walked with.

22

KENNEDY

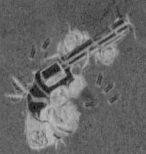

T he second I wake up, I become aware of two things. There's an excessive amount of heat hitting the front of my body. And I can feel someone watching me.

When my eyes blink open, I find a pair of legs covered in gray sweatpants and stretched out along the bed. My eyes trail up Zane's body, taking my fill as they do. His naked chest has heat flooding my face. Even though he's a bit blurry without my glasses on, it doesn't stop my mouth from watering with every one of his tattoos on full display. The piercings on his nipple glisten in the morning sunlight, and my fingers itch to tug on them until he's groaning. I continue my path to his face to find his eyes on me.

"Were you watching me sleep?" I cock an eyebrow at him as I fight back a grin. I'm not freaking out that he was because at least I woke up to him next to me, and that is progress. I'll take my wins where I can.

He lets out a deep sigh but doesn't answer me. His left hand lifts, toying with the end of his beard, and that's when I get the first glimpse of his knuckles. They're red and swollen.

"Nightmares or old memories?" I ask, knowing it has to be either of the two that would cause him to do that. Since he came clean about his past, it's helped me understand what's going through his head better, and I'm trying not to push him but at the same time get him to become comfortable opening up to me.

"Both." He glances down at me, his eyebrows drawing together as he loses himself in his thoughts. Something is troubling him, but he's having difficulty articulating it.

"What is it?" I grab his hand and start rubbing slow, soft circles on the inside of his palm with my fingers, letting his warmth seep deeper into me and paying close attention to his wedding ring. All tension instantly leaves his body from my touch, and I wait him out. I have learned with Zane that patience will always be rewarded. He may take a bit to voice things, but when he does, those words are worth the wait. In his silence, he's working out the ever-warring battle in his head.

"I'm sorry. I thought I could sleep next to you, but I can't." He shakes his head. "I don't want to hurt you."

"Is that the only thing bothering you?" I press a kiss to his swollen knuckles.

"Axel said something last night." He swallows as a muscle twitches in his jaw.

"What did he say?" I freeze, narrowing my eyes. That wasn't what I thought he was going to say.

"I don't want you to leave again." His fingers tighten against mine in a death-like grip. "Promise me it won't come to that."

The turmoil behind his eyes is like a knife straight to

my chest. I sit up and straddle his lap, interlocking my fingers behind his neck and facing him. His hands circle my waist as I do, but he keeps his head down.

"Look at me." I keep my voice soft like I'm talking to a wounded animal. The longer we're together, the more I'm figuring out what makes this man tick and how to navigate through these tricky waters with him.

He lifts his head, and the turmoil swimming behind his eyes has an ache spreading across my chest.

I press a kiss to the side of his mouth, enjoying the way his stubble tickles my cheek. "I promise you I'm not going anywhere." My lips move to the other side and give him another kiss. "I want to dance with your demons, but you have to lead the way." I lean my forehead against his and hold his gaze. "Can you do that?"

His hands tighten around my hips as I feel him harden underneath me. He lets out a deep sigh that fans across my cheeks. "I'm fucking trying, Hummingbird."

"I told you, we'll figure this out together." I cup the side of his face and rub my thumb along his jawline.

The silence stretches between us, and I could be the first to break it, but I wait him out. He's locked in his head, letting my words sink in, and it's something he has to come to terms with on his own. It doesn't mean that I can't give a visual to help smooth things along.

I lean forward onto my knees and slide the waistband of his sweats down until his dick springs free. My fingers circle around him as I stroke him from root to tip. I swirl my thumb over the precum dripping out of his tip, rubbing it over his swollen head.

His head drops back against the headboard as he lets out a low growl that vibrates through my whole body. Thanks to my pregnancy hormones, I'm already wet and aching for him to fill me. I lift up onto my knees, ready to slip off my underwear, but he's in no mood to wait. He rips them off one-handed and tosses them to the floor. I almost laugh at his eagerness, but it matches my own.

My teeth dig into my bottom lip as I slowly sink down onto his length until he's buried inside me. He's so deep I can feel him in my stomach. I feel full and hungry all at the same time.

I sit there for a moment staring into his gaze and enjoying our physical connection. He throbs inside me, and everything inside of me is begging for my hips to move, but I keep still. I want him to feel it. Feel us. Feel what we're creating here. I could tell him how I feel, but sometimes our bodies say what our words cannot.

He continues to watch me, not moving a muscle and letting me take the lead. A muscle in his jaw twitches as his fingers dig deeper into my hips.

"You feel it?" I grind myself down onto him until he's buried so far inside me that I don't know where I end and he begins. Each movement is slow and controlled, with a purpose.

"Hummingbird, please?" He lets out a growl so deep I feel it vibrate against my entire body. He's getting there. I just need to push him a little further.

"Tell me you feel it, and I'll give you what you need. What we both need." I continue my torturous pace, coaxing what I need him to understand.

"Yes. I feel it." His blue eyes burn brighter than they were a few moments ago.

"You do what you have to do to make sure we're all safe, and I'll be here ready to wash the sins from your soul one kiss at a time." I lean forward, take his bottom lip between my teeth, and give it a slight tug.

"I'll walk through hell for you. For you both." His fingers dig into my skin as he lifts me and slams me back down onto his dick. He repeats this move a few more times, each more forceful than the last. A heaviness settles low in my belly as he hits me in all the right places.

"I don't need you to. I just need you." My toes dig into the mattress as I press my knees deeper into the mattress for better balance.

"You have me." My hips move in a circular motion, causing him to stumble through his next words. "Holy fuck, do you have me."

"Good. You do whatever you need to do, and we'll be here. Battered and bruised, as long as you come back to me, we'll survive. Got it?"

"I got you." He does a slight nod of his head, and that's all that needs to be said. He moves me up and down his length until I feel my core clamp down on him. The orgasm hits me hard and fast. Zane follows right behind me, and the two of us groan at the pleasure our bodies are ringing out from the other.

Our heavy breathing fills the room as we both come down from the clouds of ecstasy. I stay where I am, letting his warmth settle over me. He's still buried inside of me as my fingers toy with the long strands of his hair that have come loose.

"When's the last time you cut your hair?" I ask.

"I don't like anyone to touch it. Not after what happened." He shrugs.

"You let me mess with it all the time." My eyes narrow.

"You're different." His tongue darts out to lick his bottom lip as he clears his throat. "Always have been."

Heat fills my cheeks at hearing that, and my insides light up as if they've just been given the best gift. "That's one apology down, but you still owe me."

He rubs his thumb along my bottom lip. "Name it, and I'll do it."

"Anything?" I tease.

"Anything." He presses a soft kiss to my mouth.

The corners of my mouth lift into a wide smile. "Remember you said that."

"How many more times do we have to kneel?" Axel whispers from next to Zane.

"Ax," Zane growls out in response but never turns his head.

"I'm getting rug burn on my knees," Axel whines.

"Axel, behave." Kelsey slaps him on the shoulder.

I chew on my lip to keep from laughing in the middle of Mass. When I asked Zane for my favor last week, I never thought it would turn into a full-blown family affair. I guess it makes sense since Kelsey is my cousin, but I don't think they had any idea what they were getting themselves into.

Axel and Kelsey are on Zane's left, and I'm stuffed in the pew between Zane and Connor. Asher and Charlee opted to stay home because Lily's teething and fussier than usual, which is entirely understandable. I think they also did that so that Asher could keep an eye on

Isaac. I'm just wondering if Axel is the one who needed babysitting.

At least Zane convinced his brother to wear a pair of black dress slacks and a navy button-up shirt that matches his. That was a battle, but Axel agreed, thanks to Kelsey mentioning how hot he'd look all dressed up.

This morning was a series of wins. I was also able to keep my breakfast down. My hand rests on my stomach as I sigh. The black baby doll dress I'm wearing is loose enough in the middle to not bother my tiny bump. In the last week, I've popped. It's not huge, but it's noticeable to me.

Father O'Dea keeps going with Sunday morning Mass, but I don't miss the way his gaze darts from the general crowd to Axel. I almost want to scooch down lower to avoid being seen. If we were in the back, it would be much easier to hide, but we're in the same front row that my family has occupied since I can remember.

"Let us go in peace to love and serve the Lord," Father O'Dea says, signaling the end of Mass.

There isn't a set system on how anyone exits the church, but my family is usually the last to leave. The main reason is that my dad likes to hang back and chat with Father O'Dea. He's the same priest that married my parents over twenty years ago, and it helps my dad feel a bit closer to my mom when he does.

Dressed in his Sunday best of an expensive pinstriped suit and matching fedora, my dad stands and makes his way over to where Father O'Dea is standing. My brothers follow in line behind him, dressed in a similar style. One thing my dad always made sure of was that we wore our Sunday best for church.

My eyes drift over to where they're standing, but I stay seated a bit longer—the more space between us, the better. Having a conversation with Father O'Dea about my less-than-traditional wedding is the last thing I want to do today.

They shake hands and stand around conversing. My brothers join them with smiles on their faces. They don't talk long because other people begin to gather around, eager for Father O'Dea's attention.

My dad gives him one more handshake and makes his way down the aisle to the front door with my brothers in tow. I stand too and follow out after him with Zane, Axel, and Kelsey behind me. It's a good thing I wore my flats today because I'm so focused on making it out of there undetected that I almost trip and fall. Zane catches me before I can face plant into the green carpet.

At the door, I dip my hand in the holy water and do the sign of the cross before continuing on my way outside to the car where my dad and brothers are waiting.

The sun hits my face, and I smile. It's a beautiful August summer day in Georgia, with a few clouds decorating the sky. Judging by the overwhelming humidity in the air, a rainstorm is coming.

"Kelsey." My dad kisses her on the cheek. She doesn't flinch, but I don't miss the way her posture stiffens underneath her blue maxi dress. She's still coming to terms with the fact that we're family. That word means something entirely different to men like my dad than most people. Blood is thicker than water in his eyes, and he'll make a deal with the devil himself if it's in our best interest. I don't know much about her dad, but I'm guessing he wasn't as affectionate with her as mine is with us.

She presses her lips into a tight smile and steps back next to Axel, who snakes his arm around her waist and jerks her back against him. He and Zane are still apprehensive when it comes to my father, but I hope that's something that will change with time.

"How are ye feelin' today, *a stóirín?*" My dad wraps me up in a hug and kisses the top of my head before pulling me back to look me in the eye.

"No nausea, so that's a plus." I press a hand to my lower stomach and smile up at him.

"That's grand. Glad to hear it." My dad smiles down at me, the corners of his eyes creasing and hinting at his actual age. My father may be in his early forties, but you'd never know it by how he carries himself.

Zane's warmth hits my back as he comes up right behind me and winds his arms around my middle, pulling me back against his chest.

A vein pops in the side of my dad's temple as he watches, but he doesn't say anything about it. "Savage."

"Donnelly." Zane's politer than I expect. "Everything all set to go?"

"Aye. Teegan and Rory will be over first thing in the mornin'." My dad nods his head while he pulls a cigar out of his jacket pocket.

"What about Connor and Keegan?" Zane's chest tenses against my back.

My dad tilts his head from side to side, studying Zane as he pinches the cigar between his lips. It's a look I've seen him do a million times before. He's gauging how much info to share. "They're needed in Boston to tend to some business matters for me."

That piques my interest, and my head snaps up to meet Connor's gaze. "You going to see Fiona while you're there?"

"Yeah." Connor's nostrils flare as his eyes harden, but I've learned to ignore him when he's in one of his moods.

"Will you tell her to call me? I've tried a few times, and she hasn't answered." I think back to the last phone call we had, and it's not like us to go so long without talking.

"Promise, *deirfiúr*." His gaze travels over to my dad, and I get the feeling that he wants to say something more but holds back. "I'm going to pack." He spins on his heels and heads off toward his truck without another word. Rory shoots me a wink and walks off to follow after him.

Teegan and Keegan remain standing off to my dad's right, but I can tell by their stiff body language that they aren't happy with Zane's question. They're nineteen and cocky. Having Zane question that is a massive hit to their egos.

"What happened with Kelsey wasn't our fault." Teegan tugs at the collar of his black dress shirt.

"Exactly." Keegan adjusts the red feather on his fedora as he shoots Zane and Axel a look.

"No one is blamin' ye for that."

"Speak for yourself," Axel mumbles loud enough for everyone to hear.

"That right?" Keegan moves to step forward, but my dad stretches his arm out across his chest to stop him.

"Easy, lads." My dad ignores Axel's comment and keeps his attention on Zane. "Everythin' is set. The boys will be there first thing in the mornin'."

"Good." Zane's deep voice rumbles against my back.

"A Donnelly always keeps his word," my dad says around the cigar in his mouth. "Ye might want to remember that." My dad gives me one last smile before turning and getting inside his car.

Zane's fingers tighten around me, but he's not getting out of this. I twist out of Zane's hold and push the bridge of my glasses up my nose to stare at him.

"What was that about?"

"Nothing." Zane does a slight shake of his head, but I know better. He can't weasel his way out of this.

"Don't you 'nothing' me. I know it most certainly means something if my dad said that." I put my hands on my hips and wait him out.

"Oh shit. Her hands are on her hips. You're so fucked, Z." Axel snickers.

"Shut up, Axel." Kelsey slaps him upside the head and rolls her eyes. "I'm sorry," she mouths. "I'm sorry."

"That's it, Wildcat!" He bends down, props her stomach against his shoulder, and then carries her off in a fireman's hold. "Looks like I need to you teach a lesson." He slaps her on the ass.

"Don't you dare! We're at church, for crying out loud." She laughs as they disappear into background noise.

Once they're out of sight and Zane sees I'm not giving up on this, he finally caves. "It's no big deal, Ken."

"It is, or you'd be telling me what it is." My hands go from my hips, crossing them over my chest.

His eyes follow the movement as he toys with the end of his beard. "He just promised that I'll never have another kid if something happens to you."

"Why do I get the feeling that you're giving me the G-rated version of what was said?"

"Because you're not wrong." He's not going to elaborate any more on that.

"Just promise me one thing." I know when to pick and choose my battles, so I'll let this one slide.

"Anything." He doesn't even hesitate, and that makes my heart smile.

"You come back to us in one piece."

"That's a promise, Hummingbird." He pulls me into his arms and kisses me until I forget my name.

If only I knew that I would be the one to break that promise.

23
ZANE

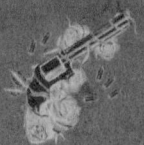

Rain pelts against the roof of the SUV as I tug on the end of my beard while the four of us sit and wait. We've been sitting here in the woods in the back parking lot for a couple of hours, and my gum is out of flavor, but it's the only thing keeping me from losing my shit.

Axel whistles as he rips open a bag of Doritos. "Do our women know we're going inside a sex club? Because I don't know about y'all, but I like my balls attached where they are."

"What do you think?" Asher keeps his gaze planted on the door as he lights up another cigarette. He's damn near smoked half a pack since we got here. Something is up with him. He's been moodier than usual, and if I'm starting to notice, then it's serious. We'll have to have a talk when this shit is all said and done.

"They don't need to know." I grind down harder on my gum and twist around to face the back seat, resisting the urge to steal a smoke from him.

Isaac laughs. "Trust me, kid. They already know.

They probably knew where we were going before we did."

"You tell them?" I lock eyes with him, not finding the humor in any of this. The last thing I want Kennedy to know is where I am right now.

"Nope." Isaac exhales a cloud of smoke in my face. "They're women. Enough said." He cocks his head at me like that's a foregone conclusion.

"Meaning?" My eyes narrow as he takes forever to get to the fucking point.

"Meaning they're better than the FBI when it comes to that shit." He pinches his cigarette between his fingers and holds my stare.

Axel laughs and shoves a handful of Doritos into his mouth. "We're so fucked when we get home."

"Ax," Asher grinds out, reaching the limits of this conversation much like I am.

Axel opens his mouth wider than normal and crunches down harder on the chips. He's purposely pushing his buttons and itching for a fight. If we weren't in the middle of something serious, I'd pull them both out of the car and watch it play out for myself.

"He'll show?" I change the subject to avoid beating the shit out of both of my brothers.

"He'll show." Isaac steals a chip out of Axel's bag and shoves it in his mouth.

"You're sure?" Because I'm sure as fuck not.

"I am. He's been coming every Thursday night at eleven for the last five years." He dusts his hands off and goes back to staring out the window.

"And this chick he's banging is good with us cutting into her pocket like this?" Axel licks the cheese powder off his fingers and tosses the empty bag behind him, without a fuck to give.

Isaac doesn't answer him right away, and an unsettling feeling stirs in my gut. "Destiny and I go way back. She's cool with it."

"Destiny? That her real name?" I cock my head to the side and study him. In all the years we've known each other, he's never once mentioned her.

"It's her real name." Isaac shifts in his seat. "We grew up next door to each other."

"Right." I file that info away for later in case it's needed and go back to staring across the back lot.

A few minutes later, the back door opens, and a woman dressed in all leather with a blue wig appears. She leans against the block wall and lights up a cigarette.

"There's the signal." Isaac puts out his cigarette and opens his door, ready to sprint across the lot in this downpour. He's as eager as I am to have a chat with our former leader. "Time to play."

The three of us follow behind him, scanning the parking lot and watching our backs as the rain soaks our clothes. Isaac has been trustworthy so far, but I'd be a dumbass if I didn't still keep my guard up.

When we come up to the back door, the woman in the blue wig watches us for a beat. She props a foot on the block wall and takes a drag off her cigarette. Her red-painted lips stain the butt. "Interestin' company you keep these days, Isaac."

"Zane's an old friend." Isaac slips his hand into his back pocket and pulls out a wad of cash. "Brought you a gift."

"Ain't you sweet." She smiles at him, but it doesn't

reach her eyes. Isaac slips her the cash, and as she's counting the money, she says, "Last door on the left with the red D on it. Make sure the red light stays on."

"Red light?" Axel pipes up from behind me.

She eyes him up and down a second before blowing a cloud of smoke. "Think of it as a 'Do Not Disturb' sign."

"Thanks, Des." Isaac's voice softens a fraction as he speaks to her. I have a feeling they have more to their history than being childhood friends.

"Whatever." She rolls her eyes at him. "I'm on a smoke break and never saw you."

"And the cameras?" he asks, standing in her space.

"Wouldn't ya know? The damn things are busted." She shrugs as she flicks ash onto the ground.

"I owe you one." Isaac jerks his chin her way.

"Don't worry. I'll be around to collect." She pinches the cigarette between her lips and goes back to watching the parking lot, signaling this conversation has run its course.

We go to move inside, but she calls out behind us, "Just remember, a girl's got to have her fun."

I shoot Isaac a look, wondering what the fuck that meant, but he rolls his eyes and waves us inside. The scent of sweat and smoke hits me when we step into the darkened hallway. Sex is seeping out of this building's pores. "KILL4ME" by Marilyn Manson pumps through the black walls. There's a series of doors with different letters on them. Each has a different color. It's as if they are color-coded for a reason. Each has a small square window that's covered with a blacked-out panel. On the top left of every door is a small red light. Most of them are off, so we keep walking.

Axel stops and hesitates when we reach the last door with the red D on it.

"Open it." I jerk my chin at the handle, but he doesn't move.

"Oh no." Axel holds his hands up and takes a step back, away from the door. "You open it this time."

"Axel," Asher grinds out. "Stop being a pussy and open the fucking door."

"Nope." Axel shakes his head and crosses his arms over his chest. Stubborn shithead is wasting time. "Not doing this again."

"Fine. I'll do it." Isaac shakes his head and turns the knob, giving way to something that wasn't what I was expecting.

"That's not something you see every day." Axel cranes his head from side to side, studying Wallace like he's a science project he can't make heads or tails of as the four of us step farther into the room.

The good admiral is strung up on a set of hooks like a Thanksgiving turkey with his wrists bound to a set of poles. He's naked from head to toe with a ball gag in his mouth and looking like the perfect sacrifice. His dark eyes widen the second he sees us. The only other thing in the room is a red velvet chaise lounge that's covered in plastic.

Asher shuts the door behind us and locks the deadbolt before crossing the room to stand next to Axel.

"Evening, Admiral. It's been a long time." My eyes drift down his body, not missing the circular scars that mar his chest. I'd bet money they're from a cigar or something similar in shape and size. A black cord runs along the floor behind him that's hooked up to what looks like a car battery. I'm not exactly sure what the fuck it is, and I also can't make out where it's connected to him in the back.

Drool drips down his jaw as he attempts to talk through the gag in his mouth. He struggles against the rope at his wrists, but Destiny is a pro. There's no give. He's stuck and at our mercy, and he knows it.

Axel cranes his head to the side, looking around Wallace to see where the cords go, and then his face pales. "Is that where I think it is?"

"It is." Isaac's standing behind Wallace, staring at his ass with disinterest.

"Really?" Axel crosses his arms over his chest, and I can't tell if he's fascinated or shocked by that. Probably a bit of both, knowing my little brother.

Asher stays planted by the door, no doubt taking it all in. He's lying in wait, letting me know that this is my show, and he'll jump in when needed.

I walk around the room. The wall at the back of the room holds my interest. It's like a gold mine of kink for anyone up for it. There are several items hung up and at my disposal, but the last thing I want to do is anything that'll bring the bastard pleasure. I take my time looking each device over until I find one that'll do the job.

"Ax." I pick up the set of nipple clamps on the table with a small remote and motion for him to take them.

Axel cocks an eyebrow at my request but takes them from me without a word. He's curious to see where I'm going with this and willing to go along with it.

I cross the room until I'm standing back in front of Wallace. Sweat coats his skin as his bloodshot eyes watch my every move like a wounded animal. A rush of heat fills me at watching the bastard squirm. This is someone I respected. Someone I would have given my life for—and almost did.

"We're going to play a game." I watch Wallace as his gaze follows Axel and the nipple clamps he's holding. "You give an answer I don't like, then it's going to be a rough night for you."

"Hold still, asshole." Axel moves to put the clamps on Wallace's nipples, but I stop him, having a much better idea in mind.

"Not there." I jerk my chin where I want them. "There."

Axel's hand freezes midair as he narrows his eyes at me. "Fucking really, Z?"

"They say pleasure and pain is a fine line. Let's see how true that is." I shrug and wave the remote at him.

"Crazy motherfucker." Axel chuckles but does as I ask and kneels to attach the clamps to Wallace's nuts.

Wallace jerks against his bindings, but there's still no give. He's stuck, and he knows it. The light dims in his eyes the second he realizes just how fucked he is, and not in a way he likes. He flinches when he feels the pinch but doesn't make a sound otherwise. His face reddens as he mumbles something unintelligible.

Axel stands to his feet and cups his hand over his ear. "What's that? I can't hear you." Then he turns his head my way. "Your call, Z."

I jerk my head in agreement. I'm willing to hear what bullshit is going to fly out of his mouth. It'll either be what I want to hear or fuel my fire to fuck him up.

Axel unbuckles the ball gag from his mouth, letting it fall to the floor. He wrinkles his nose and wipes the drool off his hands before stepping back and letting me take over.

"What the fuck do you want?" The prick speaks for the first time since we walked in, and it's not anything I want to hear.

"Don't play fucking dumb with me. You know damn well what we want to know." I glance over to the friend in question, and his hands are balled up into fists. Isaac's itching for a crack at him, and I plan on delivering. I just need the information we came for first.

"I don't know what you're talking about." Wallace struggles to speak. Every breath he takes causes his body to shake. It's only feeding the craving I have for his blood.

"That wasn't an answer." I put my finger on the button and press down.

He whimpers like the pussy he is. "I swear I had nothing to do with it. You have to believe me." His wrists are starting to bleed from rubbing against the rope, but we are far from done with him.

"I don't have to do shit." I wave the remote at him. "Now talk."

"It wasn't me." It seems the admiral can hold out longer than I thought. Time to change up my tactics and up the ante.

"Fine. If that's the way you want to play it." I motion for Isaac to step behind him and next to the machine behind him.

I keep my finger on the remote while Isaac flips the switch. He holds my gaze, and together we fill him full of enough electricity to push him past his threshold.

"Damn, man." Axel cringes next to me, but I ignore him. I'm too focused on what I'm doing to pay him attention.

Wallace's whole body convulses and swings on the

hooks, causing them to tear into his flesh, but he doesn't cry out. If he wasn't such a piece of shit, I might respect him for that. We keep at him for another few seconds before letting him come up for air.

"Ready to talk yet?" I crane my head to the side and wait him out.

His body is limp and hangs there as he struggles to catch his breath, but he's still conscious, and that's the only fucking thing that matters.

I give him another ten seconds until I decide it's time to push him again. "Wonder how high these things go?"

"We've got all night to find out," Asher says from behind me. My big brother is calm and collected on the outside, but I know he's reaching his limit for bullshit like I am.

"No!" he gasps. "Please. They already took one daughter from me. I can't lose another."

"I have a family too. And someone shot at them." A muscle jerks in my cheek as I think back to Kennedy's face when she hunched down in the seat covered in glass.

"You don't understand." He hangs his head and sighs. "This goes deeper than you can imagine. These people have connections that can bury us both."

"That's a chance I'm willing to take." My hands tighten around the remote until I feel the plastic crack from under the pressure. "Talk."

"All right. All right. I'll talk." A string of drool runs out the side of his mouth as he forces his head up to meet my stare. "I set you up." His eyes drift to Isaac. "Both of you. And it was a way to get a little bit of payback for your fuck-up in Afghanistan."

A muscle jerks in Isaac's cheek at that revelation. "You made me look like a fucking traitor. But it's been you all along."

Wallace nods. "I hired Savage, knowing that he'd go bring you in. The plan was to turn you against each other and let the problem sort itself out. Then we could continue business as usual."

"You piece of shit." Isaac slams his fist into Wallace's stomach. The admiral winces as his body sways on the hooks. Blood trickles down his shoulders, but not one of us gives a fuck. "Cindy was innocent."

"So was my daughter!" Wallace's face reddens as he bares his teeth.

Silence swallows the room like a shroud of death at his comment. Neither Isaac nor I argue his point because he's not wrong. She was an innocent, and the guilt has eaten me alive for the last eight years.

"You don't understand." Wallace's voice hitches as he speaks. "He threatened to take my other daughter and sell her. I can't lose her too."

That gets my attention, and my focus is back on track. "Who the fuck is he?"

"I can't tell you." He shakes his head. "He'll kill my family and make me watch."

"You think we won't kill you first?" Mercy isn't an option, nor is it anything this fucker deserves.

"A name." Isaac raises his fist, ready to slam it into his stomach.

Sensing he's out of options, Wallace opens his mouth to speak but never gets the chance. The sound of the glass on the window shattering cuts him off.

"Gun!" Asher shouts and plasters himself against the wall and out of the line of fire. The rest of us duck behind the chaise lounge for cover and pull out our guns. He waits a few beats, and when there are no more shots, he creeps out the door to find the fucker.

"Where the fuck did that come from?" Axel asks as he peeks his head around the side of the furniture.

"I don't know." A heaviness settles in my gut that someone found us, and we didn't see them. "Go back up, Ash."

"On it." Axel does as I say and follows out the door behind our brother.

"Fuck!" Isaac leans over the opposite side of the lounge in Wallace's direction and jumps to his feet with me on his heels.

Fuck is right. Wallace has a bullet hole dead center in the middle of his chest. Blood drips out the side of his mouth as he gasps for air.

"Who is he?" I have one last shot at finding out who the piece of shit we're looking for is, and I've come too far to lose now.

More blood pools out of his mouth, but he manages to choke out one word before the light leaves his eyes permanently and screws us completely.

"Lobo."

24
KENNEDY

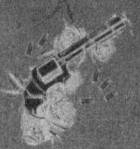

I've been sitting in the same spot for the last few hours on the couch next to Rory, watching reruns of *Castle* as I try to refrain from watching the clock. I don't even know what episode we're on because my mind is elsewhere. I haven't even changed out of my pajamas. Kelsey is in her art room drawing, while Charlee is at her house taking care of Lily with Teegan keeping watch, so it's just been the two of us.

Something explodes on the television, but I'm too caught up in my head to pay it any attention. I bite down on my thumbnail as my bare feet bounce up and down. Despite what I told Zane, sitting and waiting has never been my strength.

Rory places his hand on the top of my knee to stop me and gain my attention. "Everything will be fine, Ken."

I drop my hand and sag back into the couch, letting my head fall back. "I hope so," I say to the ceiling, so I don't have to face him and let him see the concern I'm trying so hard to hide.

Rory twists his body toward mine, and I tilt my head down to meet his gaze. "This conversation never happened, and as much as it pains me to admit it." He pauses, looking like he's about to swallow something sour. "They're good at what they do."

"As good as you, you mean." I bite the corner of my mouth to keep my jaw from dropping. My brother has never given anyone outside of the family a compliment like that.

"Now, I didn't say that." Rory shakes his head, but I don't miss the humor in his eyes.

"Yeah, you did." I cock an eyebrow at him.

"I admit nothing." He rolls his eyes at me and falls back against the cushion.

"Thanks, Ror." I smile, feeling a sense of lightness for the first time today.

"Anytime." He shrugs and goes back to watching Castle. "Just promise me something."

"What's that?" I push my glasses up the bridge of my nose, wondering where he's going with this.

"That I get first dibs on holding my future niece or nephew." He jerks his chin toward my growing stomach as his lips curve into a smile.

"Deal." I laugh at what he's just signed up for because my other brothers will be giving him shit for this when they find out. My phone vibrates against the table, making me jump. When I see the unknown number, my eyes narrow. It rings a few more times, and I debate sending it to voicemail.

"You gonna answer it?" Rory asks as he lounges farther back against the couch.

"I don't know the number." My eyebrows scrunch together as to who it could be.

"Want me to get it?" Rory offers.

"No. That's the last thing I want. I can only imagine what you would do." I answer it before he can, prepared for it to be a solicitor asking about my car's extended warranty. "Hello?"

"Kennedy! Thank God. You seriously scared the shit out of me." A deep sigh exhales into the phone as Fiona's voice comes through the other end, her voice cracking as alarm bells are going off.

"Are you okay?" I sit up straighter against the couch, squeezing my phone tighter as if that'll somehow help.

"I'm at your apartment, or what's left of it. What the hell happened? It looks like a freaking bomb went off in here." Her voice wavers, and I cringe as I picture the mess she's seeing. I haven't been back there since it was broken into, and I can only imagine how bad it must look to her.

"What are you doing at my apartment?" It isn't like her just to show up unannounced like this. "And whose phone are you using, Fi?" Calling me from an unknown number only adds to the weirdness of this whole situation.

Rory sits up ramrod straight and scoots closer to me at the mention of her name. He's hanging onto my every word, and I suddenly feel like I'm in the hot seat.

"It's a long story. The short version is that my dad's a major asshole, and I needed a break. I came here and found your place trashed. Your turn." She never takes a breath from the moment she starts talking.

"Someone broke into my place, so I've been staying at Zane's until we can get it taken care of." I do my best to keep my tone casual and not freak her out. It doesn't escape my attention that she never even bothered to answer my second question.

"What? Why didn't you say anything to me?" Her quick, shallow breathing echoes into the phone.

"I've been trying to call you for days, but you haven't answered." I do my best not to sound like a nagging parent, but I have been worried out of my mind.

"I am so sorry that I've been such a shit friend. I swear I didn't mean to disappear on you. Things have been a little crazy at home, and I took off to have some space to breathe." I hear a loud bang, followed by a familiar bark. "Oh my god! What a cute dog." Fiona claps as I hear a muffled voice in the background.

"Is Mrs. Baker there with you, Fi?" I push my glasses up the bridge of my nose as my gaze travels to the television. Having my brother's scrutinizing stare fixated on me makes this conversation more awkward than it should be.

"She just came over to check on me and brought her cute little guy with her." She coos into the phone as she no doubt lathers Thor with attention, then she sighs. "Shit."

"What's wrong?" I twist at the collar of my T-shirt to keep from losing my sanity with her.

"My phone's about to die, and I forgot the stupid charger at home." I don't miss the hesitancy in her voice as she says that. It's a dead giveaway my friend is lying to me. I'm just not sure why she feels the need to.

"Why don't you go wait with Mrs. Baker, and we'll be there as fast as we can." The sooner we get to her, the sooner I can get my answers.

"We?" she squeaks out loud enough for Rory to hear her through the phone.

"Yeah, just Rory and me." I watch my brother as I answer her. The longer our conversation lasts, the more I can see something working behind his eyes.

"Okay, but nobody else." She hesitates again before adding, "One more thing. Don't tell either of our dads where I am."

"Why not?" My eyes narrow at that. Something is off with her, and I can't wait to get to her and find out what it is.

"Just promise me," she snaps.

"I promise." I hold Rory's stare as I answer, daring him to break it, but he stays quiet.

"Good. See you when you get here." She hangs up, but not before I hear her talking to Thor.

Ten minutes later, I'm dressed in the only outfit that seems to fit me lately, a pair of black leggings and my favorite purple tunic. Other than a quick text to Teegan and a bathroom break for me, it doesn't take long for us to head out and climb inside Rory's truck, but before we can even make it out of the driveway, my brother has his phone up to his ear. "Found something of yours and on my way to go pick her up." He ends the call without waiting for a response and sticks his key into the ignition.

"What the hell are you doing?" I smack him on the shoulder, knocking his phone out of his hand. He's lucky I don't do more damage. "She said not to tell our dads she's here."

"I'm not," he says before turning the ignition and heading out onto the highway.

I'm not buying it, but I'll deal with it once we're back from my apartment. I lean back against my seat and stare out the window the whole drive. Our conversation is on a constant loop in my head as I try to put the pieces together on what the hell is going on with her.

When we pull up to my apartment complex, I take my seat belt off, ready to hop out of the vehicle and rush up there, when my brother grabs me by the shoulder.

"You even think of jumping out of this vehicle while we're still moving, I'm going to have no choice but to hog-tie your ass and let you explain to your husband why."

"Seriously?" My hands clench into fists at his threat, and I fight the urge to smack him again. He's treating me like I'm a little kid.

"If it means keeping you from doing something stupid and risking getting hurt, then take it however you want." He holds my stare and shrugs.

I slump back against the seat and cross my arms over my chest while waiting for him to park. He's right about me not being reckless, but it doesn't mean I have to like him treating me like a child.

Once he pulls into the nearest parking space and shuts off the engine, I growl out, "Can I go now, Dad?"

"Smart-ass." Rory shakes his head and reaches into his back pocket. He pulls out his favorite Bowie knife and holds it out to me. "Take this."

"Why?" My eyebrows pinch together as I stare at the leather-covered blade.

"Just in case." He shrugs. "You never know how shit

can go sideways, and it'll make me feel a feck of a lot better if you have it on you."

"Okay." I shove the knife in the waistband of my leggings before climbing out of the truck. Rory follows on my heels through the lobby and into the elevator.

When we get off on my floor, I notice two things. One, it's too quiet for this time of day. There are usually at least a couple of other neighbors hanging out at the end of the hall. The second thing is that the hallway is much colder than it usually is, even for this time of year.

As we approach Mrs. Baker's door, Rory knocks. "Remember, we need to get in and out. The last thing I want is your pissed-off baby daddy jumping down my shit for taking you out."

"Yes, sir." I roll my eyes at his bossy attitude as we hear the locks open.

Mrs. Baker answers the door in her usual attire of a pink robe and matching slippers. There's a decent-sized bruise on her cheek.

"Are you all right, Mrs. Baker?" My eyes widen as I take in how bad the bruising is.

Her hand comes up to cup her cheek. "I'm fine. Just getting clumsier in my old age." She smiles, but it doesn't reach her eyes. Her hands clutch the collar of her robe tighter as she steps back for us to enter. "Come on in."

"Thanks." I walk over the threshold with Rory following right behind me. "Is my friend here?" My eyes wander around her apartment, but Fiona isn't anywhere to be found.

"Of course. She's in the back bedroom, lying down. The poor thing said she had a headache from traveling. You can go on in and get her. It's the last door on the left." Then she turns her attention to Rory. "Would you mind helping me get a dish down from the kitchen cabinet while you're here, young man? I don't want to end up with another bruise."

"Yes, ma'am." Rory nods and then mouths to me, "Five minutes." Without a backward glance, he moves to follow Mrs. Baker into her kitchen.

I walk down the hall and up to the bedroom door at the end. I knock to make sure Fiona is decent when I hear muffled cries coming from the room. The hair at the back of my scalp prickles. Something is off. My fingers grip the knob and twist, and when I open the door and catch a glimpse inside, my jaw drops.

"Fiona?" I gasp out and run over to my friend sitting on the floor. Some black zip ties tie her wrists and ankles together, and a piece of duct tape covers her mouth. Her brown hair is a matted mess, and there's a small cut on her head. Her hazel eyes are red and puffy as if she's been crying.

I kneel and tug on the zip ties, but they don't give. Time isn't on our side, and it takes everything in me to keep calm. Silently, I thank my brother for being an overbearing ass and slip the knife from the waistband of my leggings.

"I'm going to get you free, and then we'll get the hell out of here." She nods as I suck in a deep breath and slide the knife between her wrists and the zip ties. I tug, but before I can break them, she starts screaming behind her gag and looks behind me. My shoulders tighten, but I force myself to turn around, and that's when pain explodes along the back of my head. The next thing I know, everything goes black.

25
ZANE

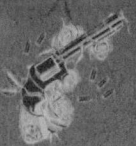

Asher chased after the shooter, but whoever they were disappeared into the crowd before he could find them. It was only a matter of time before someone came and found Admiral Wallace, so I called in a family favor. When Finn's cleaning crew arrived a short time later, we got the hell out of there. If my mind wasn't preoccupied with lots of other shit, then I would have stopped and questioned why it only took them seconds to find us.

The silence in the truck weighs us all down. Wallace didn't tell us shit, and we're still stuck at square one with who the fuck is behind all of this. Our only improvement is that we now have a name to go on. There has to be a bigger piece of the puzzle we're missing, and my gut tells me it's closer to home than we'd like.

More than halfway into our drive, Axel's phone vibrates, cutting into the heavy silence that fills the cab. "I swear to you, Wildcat, I didn't look." The smile on his face drops the longer he listens to Kelsey speak. There's a slight shift in the air of the cab as Asher and I both zone in on that subtle change in his body language. Isaac wouldn't notice because he doesn't know our baby brother or his tells like we do. Then his eyes meet mine, and every one of my muscles tenses up. "I'll handle it. Thanks. I love you."

He ends the call and rubs his thumb along his bottom lip but doesn't say anything. Time seems to slow as I watch and wait for him to say something, anything. Instead, he remains silent until I'm left with no choice but to get it out of him.

"What did she say?" My eyes narrow as I follow the movement of his thumb.

Still no answer. It's like he's stalling on purpose, and it's starting to piss me off. "Axel?"

"Promise me that you won't freak the fuck out, Z." He keeps his voice smooth and even, like he's talking to a wounded animal, and I don't like that one fucking bit.

I twist further in my seat, ready to jump into the back seat and beat his ass if he doesn't start talking. "What. Did. Kelsey. Say?" Each word comes out slow and controlled, but inside, the storm is building. I make no promises on freaking the fuck out because my mind is already racing with possibilities after being shot at again, and none of them are good.

"Ax, if you know something, you need to fucking spill it now," Asher warns from the driver's seat, never taking his eyes off the road.

My little brother sighs and drops his thumb from his mouth. "Kennedy's friend Fiona showed up at her apartment and called her all freaked out, so Rory took her to pick her up."

"That all?" My muscles loosen a fraction. That

doesn't sound too bad, but I'm still on edge because something tells me there's more to it.

"No." A muscle jerks in his cheek as he holds my stare. "That was an hour ago, and nobody can get ahold of them. Both of their phones are going straight to voicemail."

The vein on the side of my neck throbs as what he's saying sinks in. I shift my gaze over to Asher as I clench my fists together. "Ash—"

"On it." My big brother nods, slamming his foot down on the gas and hauling ass to Kennedy's apartment complex.

He gets us there in record time, but my stomach has been in knots since Kelsey's call. The truck pulls right up to the curb by the entrance, and he kills the ignition. He's in a loading zone and will more than likely be towed, but none of us give a shit. The only thing that matters is finding out what the fuck is going on and where my wife is.

The four of us swarm into the elevator and count the floors in silence, with our guns out and ready. Someone may see us when we enter the hall, but it's a risk we're willing to take. After what happened at the club, we're not taking any chances of being caught off guard again tonight.

When we reach Kennedy's apartment, the door is closed. I could take out the key I had made, but it'll waste too much time. I've got a much faster solution in mind. I lift my foot and kick her door down with the heel of my boot. With our guns out in front, we rush inside Kennedy's place. It doesn't take long for us to clear it. It's tiny as fuck. Nothing looks out of place since the last time we were here, but that makes no sense.

Asher and Axel are in the back bedroom and bathroom, but Isaac is heading toward me.

"Anything?" I watch his body language for any sign he's lying to me, but he's rock solid.

"Not a fucking thing." Isaac shakes his head with his gun draped at his side.

Asher and Axel come back into the living room soon after, offering me the same empty answer.

"Fuck!" I fist my hair, doing a piss-poor attempt at reigning in my temper, and glance around the space. Her place is still trashed, but there has to be a clue that we aren't seeing. "And there was no bag or something telling us that they've been here?"

"We looked, brother." Asher shakes his head. "There's nothing."

"It's like they were never even here, Z." Axel grits his teeth, mirroring my frustration at this clusterfuck of a situation.

"There has to be something that we aren't seeing." I tug on the end of my beard and refuse to believe there's not a clue or anything telling us that they made it inside the apartment.

Barking cuts into my thoughts, and I growl. Dealing with that little shit is the last thing I have time for right now, but when I spin around to toss him out the door, where he snuck in, my heart drops into my stomach.

"Fuck." I bend down and pick Thor up as carefully as I can. His white coat is covered in blood, and I'm not sure if it's his or not.

"Is he hurt?" Isaac asks.

I run my hands over his furry body but don't feel any cuts or bumps. "No. He's clean."

"Oh shit. Look, Z." Axel points to the red paw prints

that Thor left behind. A trail of them leads out the door and into the hall.

We follow his bloody path over to Mrs. Baker's apartment. When we get to the front door, it's cracked open just a fraction and not enough to see inside. I hand Thor over to Axel for safekeeping since he still hasn't stopped bitching about Isaac's fish and internally prepare myself for what I might find inside.

"Why the fuck do I have to hold the dog?" Axel whispers to my back, but we ignore him. His bitching becomes background noise as I get my head in the game and focus on what I might find on the other side of that door.

"On three," Asher whispers, holding both my and Isaac's gaze. He counts down with his mouth, and when he gets to one, he kicks the door in with his gun out. Isaac and I follow inside right behind him, keeping our eyes peeled for anything and everything.

There's a trail of bloody paw prints from the door and down into the hallway. Beads of sweat drip down my temple as I follow it to the last door on the left. I reach out to turn the knob but hesitate. My life could change forever when I open it, and I'm not sure if I'm ready for the guilt those consequences will have.

"I'm right behind you, Z." I'm so lost in my head that I never even heard Isaac approach, but his reassurance that he has my back through this is all I need to find my balls and go through with it.

I nod and squeeze the knob with my heart in my fucking throat. The bloody trail continues around to the side of the bed where the far wall is. A sliver of tension leaves me when I reach it, and I let out a breath I didn't realize I was holding. "It's not her."

Mrs. Baker lies on her back, eyes wide open and life-less as they stare up at the ceiling. Her face is beaten and bruised, but it's the slash across her throat that gives away how she died.

Thor comes rushing in, almost knocking me off my feet, and curls up on her chest. The movement causes some of her hair to shift out of the way, and everything inside me goes numb.

"Isaac!" I move the side of Mrs. Baker's neck, exposing the rest of the tattoo.

"Son of a bitch." His eyes narrow as he gets a better view. "Is that what I think it is?"

"Yup." A fucking paw print tattoo is high up on the side of her neck. The collar of her robe always hid it.

"Just how fucking long have they been watching us?" He presses his mouth together in a tight line.

"I don't know." And that thought terrifies the living fuck out of me. They've been out here all this time, right under our fucking noses. The same pricks that are responsible for our night of hell.

"Listen." Isaac cocks his head to the side, concentrat-ing. "You hear that?"

I do the same, and sure enough, there's a thumping sound coming from behind the adjoining bathroom door. "What the hell?"

I creep over to the door, with Isaac following close behind me, and open it. Rory falls out onto the floor at my feet. His hands are tied behind his back with zip ties, and his ankles are bound with the same type of restraint. There's a small gash on the back of his head that has his brown hair soaked with blood, where I'm assuming he was hit over the head with something, and a piece of duct tape covering his mouth, but other than that, he looks to be in one piece.

I kneel and rip the tape off in one quick motion like a Band-Aid because doing it slower just hurts like a bitch. "Where's Ken?"

Rory's blue eyes are dazed and confused as he struggles to gain his bearings. "I don't know. The fecking bastard hit me from behind, and everything went black. Never even saw them coming." His nostrils flare as his mind takes him back to earlier.

I grit my teeth and fight the urge to put my fist through the nearest wall. Tonight keeps going from one dead-end to the next, and I'm getting fucking tired of it.

"Zane! You need to see this," Asher calls from the living room. I hesitate, torn between interrogating Rory for more answers or seeing what my brother found.

Sensing my frustration, Isaac pulls out his knife and bends down to cut away Rory's zip ties. "I got him."

I push up to my feet and walk out into the living room where Asher and Axel are. They're staring at the wall with the only family picture in Mrs. Baker's apartment. There's one word written right above it in blood —Lobo.

It feels like the floor falls out from under me. The son of a bitch was here. While we were trying to find him, he managed to sneak in under the radar.

"Who would hurt an old lady?" Axel takes the picture off the wall and tilts his head to the side.

I don't answer him. I can't. The reasons are fucking with my head.

Isaac and Rory come into the living room and see the present left for us.

"What the feck does that mean?" Rory asks as he stands next to me.

Isaac takes a stand next to Axel but shares a look with me. Neither one of us answers him. The last thing I want to do is tell my hot-headed brother-in-law about my past or that whoever took his sister might be selling her off to the highest bidder.

Isaac peers over Axel's shoulder, and his eyes widen. He rips the photo out of his hand as his nostrils flare. "Motherfucker."

"What the hell, man?" Axel shakes off his annoyance when he catches a glimpse of Isaac's face.

"What is it?" Judging by Isaac's body language, I'm not gonna like his answer.

"See for yourself." Isaac holds the photo out to me, and the second my gaze lands on that bastard's smug face, my gut tightens, but when I see the wolf tattoo on his middle finger, everything inside me goes numb.

I spin on my heels, ready to get the hell out of there when the sound of glass crunches underneath my boots. "What the fuck?" I kneel and pick up the transparent frames. A knot forms in my throat the second I look at them. I'd know these frames anywhere. Kennedy can't see shit without them. The lenses are cracked, but there's a small patch of blood in the upper left corner. My fingers clench around the frames until they're digging into the metal of my wedding ring.

"He's fucking dead." I grind my teeth together as everything inside of me ignites into a storm. He's fucked with what belongs to me. And there will be no mercy when I find him.

26

KENNEDY

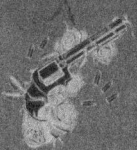

Musty, stale air hits me the moment I wake up. I inhale and realize that it's coming from my shirt, but when I pull it up to my nose, the material is different. It's rough and itchy, nothing like the top I was wearing before I blacked out, and it's much longer. Almost like a hospital gown, but much thinner. Goose bumps form along my legs as the cool temperature brushes against the exposed skin.

My eyes blink open, trying to take in my surroundings, but nothing is coming into focus. It's a void of shadows. It doesn't help that I'm blind as hell without my glasses. The hardness of the concrete digs into the skin of my hip as I push up onto my side. Pain explodes along the back of my head.

"Shit." I grab the side of my head and wince.

"Ken?" Her tiny voice cracks through the darkness, giving me a fraction of hope. Neither of us is dead yet.

"Fiona?" I turn my head toward the sound of her voice. There's a tiny sliver of light coming through the crack underneath the door, but it isn't enough to give away where either of us is. All I can make out are plain walls and her tiny form.

"Oh, thank God. I thought you were dead." She lets out a long breath.

"Are you hurt?" I need to know how bad off we are because we need to come up with a plan on how we're going to get the hell out of here.

"I'm good. A little bruised, but it could be worse." Her voice trembles, and I can hear her body shiver from across the room.

"Yeah, it could." I sit up on my hands and knees and crawl forward toward the sound of her voice. The bottom of my gown covers my knees and acts as a slight buffer from the rough floor until I reach her, and her outline comes into focus. When I'm right in front of her, she reaches out and swallows me up into a giant hug. I wrap my arms around her and let out a small sigh.

"I'm so sorry." She sobs against my shoulder, causing her whole body to shake.

"Shh. It's okay. We're going to be okay." I rub her back, sounding much braver than I feel. The same rough material as I'm wearing is covering her as well.

"It's all my fault." Her voice cracks, causing my eyes to well up with tears and a lump to form in my throat. My pregnancy hormones are no match for her emotions right now.

"No, it's not." I wipe the tears off my cheeks and pull back to face her. All I can make out is her dark silhouette, but for right now, it's enough. "Don't you dare blame yourself for this. Do you hear me?"

"If you hadn't come to get me, we wouldn't be in this

mess." She sniffles, and I see the vague outline of her hand wiping her cheeks.

"Stop. If anyone is to blame, it's the assholes that took us." I want to ask her what happened to make her run away and end up at my front door, but now isn't the time. We have bigger things to worry about.

I scoot closer to her and press back against the wall until we're shoulder to shoulder, and I lean my head down. "Fi?"

"Yeah?" She toys with the ends of my hair like she used to do when we were kids.

"I don't have my glasses. That means I need you to be my eyes for me. Can you do that?" I keep my voice low and controlled. My dad always taught me to keep a clear head. Panicking does nothing but make a situation worse. If we're going to figure a way out of here, we need to be smart.

"I can." Her hands freeze. "But Ken, it's too dark. I'm about as blind as you are right now."

"Since when has that stopped us?" I tease.

"When Connor walked into a wall and cut his forehead." She laughs at the memory, and some of the tension leaves her.

"Yeah, he was pretty pissed about that. I'm surprised he didn't rat us out." It would have served us right since we set up a type of maze in the basement and cut the power to the house.

"Me too." She slumps farther back against the wall. Our conversation drifts off, but I refuse to just sit here.

"Stand up." I tug on her arm and pull her to her feet.

"Now what?" she asks.

"Now we see if we can find a light." I glance around the darkness, hoping for a miracle.

With one hand in hers, I keep my other one out in front of me, and we make our way forward to the light that's coming from under the door. The coldness of the concrete chills me to the bone, but we keep moving. There has to be a lock or something we can pick.

We make it halfway there when the sound of footsteps has us holding our breath. My heart pounds against my chest as we wait to see if they keep going, but we're not that lucky. They stop right in front of the door.

"Shit. Get back," I whisper over my shoulder and shove her back the way we came until we feel the familiar coldness at our backs.

Keys jangle, and a lock turns. Light floods the room, blinding us as the door opens, revealing a blurry figure. All I can make out is that it's a man. He enters the room, and my pulse pounds in my throat as I await our fate. It doesn't escape my attention that he left the door open.

He keeps moving forward until he's standing right in front of us. I can't make out much of his face, but I can tell he has dark hair and tanned skin. The only other feature I can make out is the image of a wolf on his left middle finger. His head tilts to the side, studying us. The silence stretches for what seems like an eternity as he stares like we're cattle he's appraising.

"Stand up," he orders.

Fiona squeezes my hand as we both do as ordered and stand to our feet. My legs tremble, but I brace my back against the wall for support. The last thing I want to do is fall flat on my face and show any sign of weakness.

He crosses his arms over his chest and continues to watch us. "Take off your clothes."

I cringe at his request, but instead of cowering down

and giving in, I press my shoulders back and stare at his blurry face. "No."

He smirks. "Stubborn. I can see why he married you." My back goes ramrod straight at the mention of Zane, but he doesn't give me long to come to terms with that before he's repeating his demand. "Do it now. Or I'll do it for you."

"No." I'm not doing a damn thing this asshole asks of me. It might be stupid, but it'll give me the chance I need for Fiona to escape and get help. I twirl the diamond of my wedding ring around until it's facing my palm and wait. I only have one shot at this.

"Fine." He drops his arms and steps close enough into my space that I can reach him.

With an open palm, I slap him across the face, slicing my diamond into the flesh of his cheek in an upward motion. "Run, Fi!"

She doesn't look back as she runs out the open door with me following right behind her to what I hope is our one shot at freedom. I make it two steps out the door when I'm pulled back by my hair. Pain explodes along my scalp, where they hit me earlier, and I'm slammed back against a rock-hard chest.

Fiona cries out as two blurry figures drag her back into the room, kicking and screaming.

"That was fucking stupid." The one with the wolf tattoo jerks me around by my hair to face him and slaps me across the face with a closed fist. Heat rushes to my cheek, but I'm too hopped up on adrenaline to feel it. "And you're going to pay for that."

"Go to hell, you son of a bitch." I spit in his face and lift my leg to kick out his foot, but he's ready for me and grabs me by the throat.

"You have no idea what hell is, but I'll give you a taste." He lets out a hollow laugh and shoves me backward. "Put her up over in the corner."

"No. Let me go!" Hands grab me from behind and drag me across the room. I kick out and try to twist out of their hold, but their grip is too tight. I'm not going anywhere.

He keeps dragging me until I'm in an area of the room that I didn't pay much attention to before. He grabs both of my wrists and places them into a set of metal shackles hanging from the ceiling. My heart pounds against my chest, but I suck in a breath and do my best to remain calm as the metal clanks close. The tops of my toes barely touch the ground, and the angle stretches my arms up over my head to the point of breaking.

Fiona screams and fights with her attacker, but he strikes her so hard that she gets knocked to the ground and goes limp.

"Not the fucking face."

"Sorry, Lobo." He stops where he's standing. I can't make out his face from this far away without my glasses, but his body language tenses up. Whoever this Lobo is must be running things.

"Fucking *idiota*." The silver of Lobo's ring catches the light as he comes closer. At least now I have a name to put with the bastard.

Heat hits my back, and I know it's him before he speaks. I squeeze my eyes shut, wishing that I were anywhere else but here.

"Remember what happened to the last girl who thought she could outsmart the big bad wolf?" he whispers against my neck. "He ate her."

I swallow down the bile that threatens to come up my throat as my limbs begin to shake. Cold metal touches the skin of my upper back, and I flinch, but I don't cry out as I fight against the shackles on my wrists.

"Don't fucking move." He grips the collar of my gown and brings the knife down the center, slicing the back of it in half.

The cool air hits my bare back, and I dig my toes into the concrete to keep from losing my balance. I swallow down the vomit building in my throat as calloused fingers run along my spine.

"So smooth. Untainted." He leans forward and sinks his teeth into the base of his neck. "And I can't wait to mark you." His lips curve into a smile against my skin. "Fuck, maybe I'll even keep you for myself for a little while." Then his hand slides down my back and across to cup my lower stomach. "Never fucked a pregnant bitch before." He presses his groin into my ass, and I can feel how excited he is at the thought. "There's a first time for everything."

"He will find me. And when he does, he'll kill you." I won't elaborate on who *he* is because we both know. Zane will find us in time. I know it. He has to.

"He's not going to want you when I'm through with you." Lobo presses a kiss to the side of my head. The heat leaves my back as he steps back, and I can hear his ragged breathing behind me, but I keep my eyes forward and on Fiona's lifeless form. The only good that will come out of this is that she's not awake to see what-ever's about to happen to me.

The crack is the only warning I get before fire licks all along my back from the whip in his hand. My whole body tenses as I throw my head back and scream. The pain is unlike anything I've ever felt before. It feels like my skin is being peeled away from my body.

"It always gets my dick hard when you bitches scream for me." He laughs and licks the side of my face. "The louder, the better."

The whip slices through the air, and I brace, ready for what's about to happen this time. He takes his time making sure to hit fresh skin every time. I bite down on my bottom lip to keep from crying out. The metallic taste of blood fills my mouth, but I don't relent. I won't give him the satisfaction of hearing me scream for him again.

Fiona begins to come to on the ground, and when our eyes meet, we both know that things are about to get much worse before they get better. She keeps her gaze on mine as tears stream down our cheeks. The whip continues to tear up my back, but I do my best to tune out the noise.

Each strike is more brutal than the last. All of the muscles in my body are pushed past the point of exhaustion as I struggle to keep myself upright. I don't have the strength to hold my head up much longer. I'm strung up like a marionette, and he's the puppeteer pulling my strings.

The heat of his breath hits my shoulder, and my stomach turns. "He will spend the rest of his life looking for you, but it'll be too late. He won't be able to save you, just like he failed to save her."

My hands clench into fists as I focus on my breathing. It's the only way to get through this. Warm liquid drips down my back, but he keeps going. I've lost count of how many slashes I've been given.

Time stands still as I linger in between the space

where dreams and reality collide. It feels like I'm floating out of my skin. The sounds of him hitting my back become more and more distant until it eventually fades into the background. I shut my eyes one final time, letting it all go silent and letting the nightmare finally end.

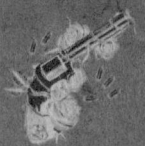

The metal shackles dig into the torn skin of my wrists as blood pools into the back of my throat, but her sobs are the only sound that echoes in the room.

She's naked and on her knees in front of me. The bastard holding her by the throat is hiding among the shadows. He's afraid to show his face, and I want to rip him apart with my bare hands for violating her the way he did.

Her blond hair is covered in dirt, and there's that fucking paw tattoo on the side of her neck. The black ink looks fresh. Then she lifts her head, and all the air is knocked out of me. Blond hair becomes dark.

"Kennedy!" This can't be fucking happening.

Blue eyes glisten with tears behind her glasses. "Help me, Zane. Please?" She struggles to reach me as his fingers clamp down tighter around her throat.

The face won't come into view. All I can make out is the wolf tattoo on his finger. Then he steps out into the light. "Boo!"

I jolt awake in a cold sweat. I'm still in the same jeans and T-shirt I had on earlier.

"Nightmare?" Asher's sitting in the dark in a chair across from me, with a sleeping Lily on his chest.

"I must have dozed off." I grab a hair tie off the coffee table and pull my hair up into a knot on my head. "What time is it?"

"A little after three."

"Any word from Finn yet?"

"No."

I grind my teeth together. After searching for over an hour, we came up empty. The guy is a fucking ghost. It left us with no other choice but to ask my father-in-law for help. The crazy fucker has sources we don't. I'd work with the devil himself if it brought her back to me. Waiting around isn't me. I need to be out there finding the answers myself, but he swore he could find the prick a lot faster than we could. And he better.

Kennedy's naked form flashes in my head, and I have to fight the urge to fuck something up. Those images will haunt me until the day I die. They're etched into my brain, but I'll be damned if history repeats itself. "Why are you down here?"

"Couldn't sleep." He strokes a hand across Lily's back as he watches her. She's wearing one of those flowery pajama things that covers her feet. Her dark hair is sticking up all over the place, and there's a bit of drool coming out of her mouth, soaking Asher's shirt.

I watch the motion, an ache spreading across my chest. In a few months, it will be me in the same position. Until now, it hasn't occurred to me just how much is on the line if we fail. I need a distraction while we wait for Finn to come through or I'm gonna lose my fucking mind. "Charlee will kick your ass when she finds out you held her all night like that."

"Do you know what happens to an ex-cop in prison?" His question throws me for a loop. It's not what I expected him to say, but Asher never does what you expect.

"Ash." Muscles in my jaw clench as he brings up his past. Neither one of us likes to talk about this shit. We prefer our demons to stay dead and buried, so I am not sure why we're even talking about it now.

"It takes a toll on your soul. Every single day I woke up wondering if it would be my last." He runs a tatted finger along Lily's cheek, letting his words linger in the silence before continuing.

"I need to know she's real. That they both are." His eyes meet mine, and for the first time in months, I see it. The fear. The pain. It's like I'm looking in a fucking mirror.

"Axel was right." I sag back against my chair and wait him out. He came to me for a reason, and he has to tell me on his own terms, in his own way.

"What if I—" His voice falls as he struggles to find the words. "I can't fail them too."

"Christ, Ash. Is that what this is about? Charlee knows all about your past, and she's accepted it. I thought you did too. Lauren and your son will always be a part of you. None of us have forgotten them."

He nods, still lost in his own head. "I know."

"Then what's this about?" There's more. There always is when he's in one of his moods.

"We can't protect them from everything." Lily stirs, and he kisses the top of her head, coaxing her back to sleep.

"We sure as fuck can try." My eyes narrow, not liking where his head is at. I need him all in with me when it's time to find Kennedy.

"What if they need protecting from me?" His question takes me by surprise.

"You really believe that you'd hurt your own kid?" I shift in the chair and give him a sideways glance.

"Don't you?" He flips the tables on me, and it all comes full circle.

"I don't know." And that's the truth. "But, I think I'm ready to try."

He lets the conversation drop, but not for long. "She's been gone for five hours now."

"Don't pull your cop bullshit. Not on me, Ash."

"All I'm saying is that the more time goes by, the smaller the window we have." He keeps his voice low and calm, as not to wake Lily, but he might as well have yelled them from the fucking rooftops with how hard they're hitting me.

"Don't project your demons onto me." I give him a warning glare, but my big brother isn't done twisting the knife.

"Kennedy and your kid are out there, and you need to prepare for the fact that we may not get to them in time."

"Fuck you." I push to my feet, doing my best not to scare Lily by raising my voice. "She's coming back." I won't accept any other outcome. "And when she does, I will spend every day letting her know what she means to me. Can you say the same?"

Asher opens his mouth, ready to rip my head off, but Axel barrels into the room like a fucking bomb with

Thor on his heels. He narrows his eyes. "Why the fuck is that thing in my house?"

"Don't tell me you're anti-dog too. What the hell, man? Kids love dogs." Axel throws his hands up but doesn't stop Thor from exploring.

"He shits on my floor, I'm kicking your ass," Asher says.

"Whatever." Axel rolls his eyes and takes the two of us in. "I must have missed the memo for the slumber party."

"What do you want, Ax?" Neither one of us is in the mood for his bullshit right now.

"Oh, nothing. Finn just called, but I can come back and get y'all later."

"Fucking dickhead." I race out of the house like my ass is on fire.

When the five of us make it to Finn's, we find him sitting in his living room wearing another pin-striped suit with a cigar in between his fingers. Nothing out of the ordinary for him, but it's who's sitting next to him that has all the blood rushing to my head. Things are about to go from bad to worse.

"What the fuck are you doing here, Rosenberg?"

Rosenberg stays seated, playing with an imaginary piece of lint, not answering right away.

"I asked you a question, Counselor." Asher puffs out his chest as Axel steps up next to him, ready to do damage control.

"I'm the one keeping your asses out of the fire while you cause a bloodbath." Rosenberg cocks his blond head to the side.

"Bullshit." Asher clenches his fists at his sides.

"Why do you think you haven't been sent back to jail?" Those hazel eyes narrow at my brother.

Finn watches the two of them for a minute, assessing the situation, and when he's satisfied, he decides to chime in with a drink in his other hand. Judging by the darkness of the liquid, I'd be willing to bet it's Jameson. He's a proud Irish fuck who won't drink any other brand. He tilts his head to the side, watching me. And it grates on my last nerve.

"Why do ye think ye weren't sent back to prison?"

"What?" Asher turns his angry stare onto Finn.

"I pulled a few strings after ye helped me niece." Finn shrugs.

"Shit," Axel says what we're all thinking. That's something none of us saw coming, but some things are starting to make sense.

Rosenberg stands and eyes Asher the whole way out the door. My big brother doesn't relax until he's out the door and gone.

"Where's yer head at, lad?" Finn redirects my attention to him and takes a quick sip of whiskey as he watches me out of the corner of his eye.

"What's that supposed to mean?"

"I had to clean up two of yer messes in one night because ye let shit get out of hand. And now me feckin' daughter and her friend are missin'." He remains calm the entire time, and it's almost worse than if he lost his shit. "I need to know just far yer willing to go. How dirty yer willin' to get. And if ye can keep yer head above yer arse long enough to get the job done."

"I'll bathe in the fucker's blood if I have to." I don't like being second-guessed. Not by him. Not by anyone. Especially when it comes to her. "All I need to know is that you'll continue to clean up my messes."

He leans back against the couch and pinches the cigar between his lips. "I have a present for ye." He stands and buttons his suit jacket.

We follow him down into his basement and keep going until we come to a bookshelf. Finn hits a button, and the shelf slides, giving way to a doorway. Block walls over an inch thick surround the wooden stairs as we descend farther underground. It's his very own playground, and nobody knows it exists.

The last time we were here, he disposed of Kelsey's dad. When you're a man like Finnegan Donnelly, it isn't hard to make even the governor of Georgia disappear. Last I heard, his missing person's case was still open, but nobody looked into it. That's what happens when you're a piece of shit.

Finn stops at a big metal door on the right and takes out a ring of keys. He flips through them until he finds the right one and slips it into the lock. It unlatches, and the door opens, revealing my present inside.

In the middle of the room is the man in the photograph. Directly underneath him is a decent-size floor drain. There's nothing else inside except for a rusty table with various tools of the trade on top.

His wrists are tied to the arms of the metal chair with zip ties, and his ankles are done up the same way against the legs of the chair. Blood drips down his face, and I narrow my eyes at Finn.

He shrugs it off. "Ye have ten minutes. He doesn't talk, I send Rory in. I'm sure he'd like to take a crack at the fecker." The door closes, leaving me, my brothers, and Isaac alone with the only one who holds the answers we need.

Asher and Isaac stay back, leaning against the wall by the door, watching. They both know exactly what is going through my head right now.

"Miguel Hernandez?" I use his name, letting him in on how fucked he is. We already know who he is and what he's done.

His dark hair is covered in blood as he lifts his head to look up at me but remains silent. It seems like he's gonna need some motivation.

I grab a pair of pliers off the rusty table on the side of the room. His black eyes follow my every move, and I can only imagine what must be going through his head. The last thing I want to do is disappoint him.

"Keep him still." I slam my hand against his wrist and feel his muscles tense up underneath my grip.

Axel grips him by his hair and forces his chin to stay up. "You aren't gonna want to miss this."

I place the tip of the pliers on the edge of his pointer fingernail and wait him out. Sometimes it's what you don't do or say that scares people more. And I'll fuck with his head any way I can until he gives me what I want.

"Who is Lobo?"

"*Chingàte tu madre, puto.*" He spits blood in my face and laughs.

"What did he say?" Axel asks.

"Fuck your mother, bitch," Isaac answers from next to the doorway.

Axel slaps him upside the head. "Let's leave our mama out of this, asshole."

"Hold him still, Ax." I clamp down on the handles until I feel the teeth grip onto his fingernail and pull back toward me, ripping it clean off in one go.

The smug look drops off his face as he screams like a little bitch and fights against the chair, but he can't move. The legs are bolted to the floor. It really is the perfect playground.

"Nine more to go." I hold up the pliers, showing off my handiwork. "We run out of nails, we'll start with your fingers next and work our way down to the rest."

I keep at him for the next five minutes, pulling out each fingernail one by one. Pretty soon, he's almost out of fingernails, and I'm running out of patience. The fucker is persistent. I'll give him that.

Sweat drips down his neck as his head hangs limp against his chest. He's close to passing out, but I will revive him and do this all over again if I have to.

"Feel like chatting yet?" I give him one last chance to tell me what I want to know. "I guess not."

"This little pinky went to the market," Axel taunts as I latch the teeth of the pliers just below the knuckle of his index finger. It's meatier, and he'll have nothing but a fucking nub left.

I watch him for any sign he'll break and strike out. My hand clamps down onto his finger and squeezes until his blood coats my hands.

Miguel's head falls back, and he screams once more as I work the pliers from side to side, cutting through flesh and eventually bone. "Farmhouse. He's got them out at the abandoned farmhouse on Pickett's Mill Dive."

Just because he gave up the information doesn't

mean he's off the hook. I finish severing the finger and step back to admire my handiwork. He's seconds from passing out as I tap him across the face. "Was that so hard?"

"Shit," Asher grinds out.

"What?"

Asher's frowning at his phone. "That's just over an hour away."

Axel shows me the time on his phone, and everything inside me stills.

"You're too late. Pickup's at six." Miguel starts laughing and choking on his own blood. "You'll never make it in time. I made sure of that."

"I will. Can't say the same for you." I pull out my gun and unload the entire clip into his chest.

I'll get to her in time. I have to. Failure isn't an option.

28

KENNEDY

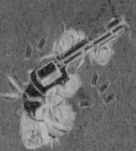

My back is on fire, and the rest of my body is too weak to move. After the bastard finished whipping, he threw us two water bottles and a bucket for a makeshift toilet. That was several hours ago, and he hasn't been back since.

I've been lying down on my side with my head in Fiona's lap, picturing myself anywhere but here. My body's gone numb from the cold, but I can imagine the sun's warmth beating down on my face like I'm at the beach. I can even smell the saltwater in the air.

Fiona strokes the back of my head, running her fingers through my hair. It's the same thing my mother used to do to me as a child.

"Ken?" Her voice cracks as she whispers my name.

"Yeah?" I keep my gaze fixed on the darkness in front of me. If I can't make out where we are, I can still pretend that we're back at my house having a sleepover like we've done numerous times.

"Can you promise something?" She sniffles.

"What's that?"

"If something happens and we get separated." She pauses, and I can hear her swallow back her tears. "Or if I don't make it out of this alive, will you tell my mother that I'm sorry for being such a pain in the ass?"

A lump forms in my throat as I squeeze the side of her leg, fighting back tears of my own. "Don't say stuff like that. We're going to be fine." We have to be. We have too many people looking for us to fail.

"Let's face it, Ken. Our chances of making it out of this alive aren't looking so good. Nobody even knows where we are. They removed our clothes and took our phones. Our families have no way of tracking us." Her voice hitches on the last of her words.

"I refuse to lose hope. We do that, they win." This gilded cage might be our prison, but it won't kill my spirit.

"I guess," she agrees, but I can tell she isn't buying into it. Fiona has always been more practical than I am.

The lock turns, and the door swings open. Nausea hits me as two sets of footsteps come closer. I sit up and grip Fiona's hand as we watch them step right up to where we're sitting on the floor. They both tower over us like a hunter about to devour his prey. They're still too far away for me to make out their faces without my damn glasses, but there's no missing that wolf. The eyes glare back at me, taunting me.

When we don't move, Lobo kicks at my feet. "Get the fuck up. Both of you, now."

Fiona and I slowly climb to our feet, bracing against the wall for balance.

"Where are we going?" I stand on shaky legs and try to keep the rag I'm wearing from sliding off. It's pointless since he cut it down the back.

"Road trip." His smile sends chills racing through me. "Give me your hands." I hesitate, and his voice hardens. "Now. Or I can always punish you again."

My whole body shivers at the thought of the whip coming anywhere near my broken skin. It's enough to make me do something I loathe—comply.

"Good girl." He clucks his tongue in approval.

My hands ball into fists to avoid punching that smirk off his face. Something tells me that would make things much worse for us right now.

He wraps a zip tie around my wrists and cinches it tight enough that the inside of them rubs together. The guy that came in with him does the same to Fiona's wrists, and I can make out a scar on his chin.

"Make sure she can't get loose like the last cunt, Javi," Lobo orders.

"That wasn't my fault. The bitch tricked me," Javi snaps back.

"Did I fucking ask for excuses?" Lobo's voice hardens, putting an end to their conversation.

Fiona and I share a look at their topic of conversation. This is more serious than we thought. We need to figure out something fast because if they move us, the chances of being found are slim to none.

Lobo drops his hands, but before he moves away from me, he slides my wedding ring off and slips it into his back pocket. "You won't be needing that where you're going."

He grabs me by the upper arm and spins me around to face the open doorway. His grip tightens as he drags me out the door. The air changes the second we step foot out of the tiny room, and it feels as if we're walking out toward the guillotine for our final resting place. My heart pounds against my chest so hard that I'm surprised I don't break a rib.

Fiona whimpers behind me as she's forced to follow out after us and into a small hallway that leads up to a set of wooden stairs. Splinters dig into my bare feet, but I keep quiet and study every detail.

We keep going through another door that opens up to a moderately sized kitchen. It's neglected and in need of some serious repairs. Half of the cabinets are missing off the walls, and there's a massive crack in the porcelain sink. Wherever we are, it's off the radar, which means no one will even think to look for us here. My stomach sinks at that letdown.

There's an old wooden table in the middle of the kitchen, and two men are sitting at it playing some kind of card game. When they hear our steps, they give Fiona and me a quick once-over before dismissing us and returning to their game.

Fresh air hits me as we make our way out of the kitchen and into the fresh morning air. We've been stuck in the dark for so long that the sunshine feels like heaven on my numb limbs.

The floor beneath me changes from dingy linoleum to grass. It scrapes at the bottoms of my feet, but I ignore it and glance around. There's not a lot I can make out without my glasses, but there are the blurry outlines of Georgia Pines as far as the eye can see. The green is so thick that I can't even make out a glimpse of the sun. Wherever we are, the property is a good size. It's a minor setback, but it will give us enough cover to hide in until we can find our way to the road and get help.

I can make out the vague outline of a yellow box truck sitting in the driveway with the engine running, and my heart jumps into my throat. If they enclose us inside, we're as good as dead.

Everything Connor and Rory taught me about self-defense comes rushing back as I run through different scenarios in my head. They never covered what to do when zip ties bound my hands together, but I'll just have to think on my feet. The quicker I come up with a plan, the better. One they won't suspect. I just hope it's enough.

I tangle up my feet and pretend to lose my balance. It's a tactic that's worked on winning fights with my brothers in the past. Most of my body weight shifts forward, causing Lobo to lose his balance. We teeter forward, but he pulls me back upright before either one of us can hit the ground.

"Watch where you're going, you stupid fucking bitch!" His hand clamps down on my arm so hard that I wince at the pain. I can already feel the burn of the bruise forming, but it gives me the opportunity I need. I let the momentum of his body force me back and work in my favor. I slam my head back until I hear the crunching of bone.

"Goddammit!" He drops his hold on me to cover his nose, and I don't wait around to find out how bad the damage is.

Fiona did something similar because Javi shouts out in pain as well. It's our one shot, and we're going to take it.

"Run!" I grab Fiona's bound hands with my own, and we rush toward the cover of the forest like our lives depend on it because they do.

"Lobo!" another voice shouts from the truck, but I don't look back to see who it belongs to.

"Get the cunt!" Lobo's nasally voice shouts. From the sounds of it, I got him good.

A smile spreads across my face. It doesn't make up for the way he slashed up my back, but I still managed to inflict some type of damage, and I'm damn proud of myself.

Dirt and sticks dig into the soles of our bare feet the farther away we get. Gunshots ring out and hit the ground next to us, but we keep going. We're almost there. A few more feet, and we'll be safe.

Freedom is within reach, but just as we're about to disappear into safety, I'm grabbed from behind. I lose my hold on Fiona as I'm lifted off the ground. "No! Let me go, you asshole." I kick and scream, ignoring the fire crawling all along my back.

"Did you think you could escape me?" he growls in my ear. "I've hunted down and killed more skilled targets than you." He spins me around and forces me back the way we came. "Walk."

We make it only two steps when an explosion hits, knocking us back off our feet. The wind is knocked out of me as my ass hits the dirt.

"Kennedy!" A sudden lightness fills me at the sound of that familiar voice.

I open my mouth to let him know where I am when Lobo points the barrel of his gun at my forehead. "Don't you fucking open that mouth."

"What are we going to do, Lobo?" Javi asks, out of breath.

"She's the one he came for, so let's leave him a bread crumb." He jerks his chin in Fiona's direction, and chills rush through me.

Javi takes out a knife and slams it straight into her stomach. She hunches over and falls to the ground.

"Fiona!" Tears fall down my cheeks as I watch my friend lie there with her hand covering the wound. Blood leaks out over the dingy gown they gave us to wear.

Lobo slaps his palm over my mouth, cutting off the rest of my words. "Shut up. Or I'll carve you up next and send you back to him in pieces." He forces me up against his chest and walks backward. The house becomes farther and farther away until we disappear into the covering of the forest.

Javi follows after us, wiping Fiona's blood off on the front of his T-shirt. They leave her on the ground like she's nothing more than the trash they dumped off.

"Head that way toward the back of the property, and we'll meet up on the other side." Lobo jerks his head to the left, keeping his hand around my mouth.

"You sure we should split up?" Javi's forehead wrinkles.

"I'm sure. They can't follow us both." Lobo spins us around and continues to walk deeper into the forest.

I dig my heels into the ground to slow us down, but it doesn't work. My ankle twists as I'm shoved forward.

"Do that again. I fucking dare you." He digs the barrel of the gun deeper into my temple, and I shiver. "Keep moving. You try any more shit, and it won't end well. I promise you that."

The birds chirp as he forces me to walk through the dense forest. Pine needles scrape across my skin as I struggle to breathe. His grip is so tight that I can't get much air. We walk a few more steps when we're tackled from the side. I tuck and roll to avoid my weight landing on my stomach. It isn't easy with the zip ties around my wrists, but I somehow manage. The impact causes Lobo to lose his grip on me for a fraction of a second, and then he's on his feet a short time later. I stay on the ground, trying to catch my bearings.

"That's far enough, Grady." Zane's gun is out and aimed at who I know now is Grady's head.

My body sags deeper against the ground at the sound of his voice. He's here. He found me.

"Been a long time, Z." Grady chuckles, looking every bit the wolf he calls himself. The deep sound sends shivers down my spine. "How'd you find me?"

"Your cousin squeals like a bitch." Zane's face is a blank mask as I squint to try and see him clearer. It doesn't work. They're both blurry outlines. "He never would have made it through basic."

"I'm surprised it took you this long to figure it out." Grady cranes his head to the side, keeping his gaze planted on Zane and ignoring the remark about his cousin. "What gave me away?"

"Your tattoo." Zane scowls.

"Always did have a thing for theatrics." Grady's grin widens.

"Nelson's dead because of you." A vein bulges out on the side of Zane's neck as his face reddens.

"It was business." Grady's face hardens. "It wouldn't have happened if Wallace did what he was told. He thought he could just quit, and the bosses didn't like that."

"So you took his daughter to keep him in line." Every muscle in Zane's body is tight.

"It worked, didn't it? We've made millions." He

slams a hand into the center of his chest. "And we've lived like kings."

"Off the blood of the innocent." Zane's hand squeezes the handle of his gun, keeping it aimed at Grady.

"No one is truly innocent." Grady's mouth pinches together. "Ever."

"Tell that to Isaac. He trusted you to have his back out there." Zane steps closer, encroaching on the space between them. "You killed his woman. She had nothing to do with any of this."

"He stuck his nose where it didn't belong. Sacrifices had to be made. You both were a liability. I don't expect you to understand that. You've always been blinded by your moral compass. You never did have the balls to do what needs to be done." Spit flies out of the corner of his mouth as his temper flares.

"Never knew you were such a pussy that you off old ladies."

"That old cunt had it coming. Thought she could try to save your bitch and her friend." Grady curls up the corner of his lip, and my heart drops at the thought of what happened to Mrs. Baker.

Zane does a quick once-over of my body, and when he lands on my face, his nostrils flare. Then he turns his attention back to Grady. "I'm gonna skin you alive for touching her."

Grady's body goes rigid. "It's your fault. All you had to do was fucking die." He squeezes the trigger, but Zane manages to duck out of the way before the bullet can hit him. He kicks out, slamming his foot into Grady's shin. The bone snaps, and Grady groans as he goes down, grabbing Zane by the shirt and pulling him down with him.

"Fuck you, Z."

"No. Fuck you." Zane slams his fist into Grady's chin, knocking his head back and making his teeth rattle together, but it doesn't loosen Grady's grip on his shirt.

"You hit like a bitch." Grady chuckles.

The two of them roll around on the ground kicking up rocks and bits of Georgia clay as they throw punches. Some land on their intended target, while others hit the dirt.

I crawl backward to keep out of their way, but I don't move too far. Otherwise, I won't be able to make out who is who.

Zane punches Grady one last time, and his body goes limp. He releases his grip and stands to his feet, making his way over to me when Grady moves.

"Zane, behind you." I bite at my fingernails, helpless to watch with my hands bound together.

"Catch." Grady throws a snake at his face, but Zane manages to dodge out of the way in time before it can get him and uses his booted foot to toss it farther out of the way.

"You're done, Grady."

"The fuck you say." Grady sits up and wipes at the cut on his lip. He bends down to pick up his gun, and I hold my breath.

"Remember me, asshole? You killed my woman." Isaac strolls out from under cover of the trees and steps on Grady's hand until I hear it crack.

"Get out of here, Ken." Zane spares me a glance as he and Isaac close in on Grady.

"No! I'm not leaving you." My pulse pounds in my

throat as a million different scenarios race through my mind. None of them are any good.

"I've got her." Rory comes up next to me and kneels onto the ground to slide his hands underneath me.

"No. I can't. Don't ask me to." Tears spill down my dirty cheeks as I plead with my brother to leave me where I am.

"He'll be fine. We need to get you out of here." Rory scoops me up in his arms and tucks me against his chest. I wince when he bumps the cuts on my back. "Feck. I'm sorry, *deirfiúr*."

"Fiona?" I grip the collar of his shirt and hold my breath. My back throbs, and the adrenaline crash is starting to hit, but my friend's well-being takes priority.

"Connor's got her." Rory sighs but won't look at me.

"Is she okay?" I swallow the lump forming in my throat and hold my brother's gaze.

"Ken—"

"Don't patronize me, Ror. Is she going to make it?" I cut him off because I know he's about to spew me a line of bullshit, and that's the last thing I need right now. My fingers dig into the cotton of his shirt, trying to keep from passing out. I'm not distracted by staying alive, and my body is starting to come down off the adrenaline high.

"It didn't look good." A muscle jerks in his cheek, and my heart plummets into my stomach.

I cry into my brother's chest until there's nothing left in me. Everything inside me throbs and aches, but I'm numb to it all. Zane better come back to me because I can't do this without him.

29

ZANE

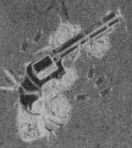

I slam the door of Axel's truck and haul ass toward Finn's house. The only thing on my mind is getting to Kennedy. Grady's being taken down to Finn's playroom by Isaac until we're ready to dispose of him, and he can wait. She's the only thing that matters to me right now. I can't slow the pounding of my heart against my chest as the images of her bloody back hit me. A million different thoughts are racing through my mind, but nothing will settle the ache in my gut until I see Kennedy for myself and see that she's okay.

Asher and Axel flank my sides, but before any of us can make it to the first step, her brothers are blocking our path. Connor, Rory, and Keegan have their legs planted wide and arms crossed over their chests.

My jaw sets as I glance around at the three of them. I'm in no mood for their bullshit right now. "Where is she?"

"Not so fast, Savage. We need to talk." Connor broadens his shoulders, doing his best to appear much larger than me. Too bad we're evenly matched in that department, and his intimidation tactics won't work on me.

"Get the fuck out of my way. I'm not in the mood for your bullshit." The words leave me in a low growl, but there's no missing the intention behind them.

"That's too fecking bad." Connor steps closer into my space until we're standing toe-to-toe. Rory and Keegan remain silent next to him, but there's no missing the way they're watching, ready to jump in. "She could have been killed, and it's all your fecking fault."

Asher and Axel stand stock-still, waiting on a sign from me. They're both pissed on my behalf and willing to cross the line. The Donnellys may be a tight-knit family, but we're just as close. We're Savages. We hunt together. We die together. End of the motherfucking story.

I glare at the Irish prick standing between me and my woman, doing my damndest to suck in slow, even breaths. An ache pierces my jaw as I grind my teeth until they crack. I'm not waiting another second after the hell I've been through for the last several hours. "Move."

Connor stays planted where he is. "None of our shit is supposed to fall back to our women, and you brought it right to our motherfecking doorstep." A vein throbs on the side of his temple.

"Last warning. Step aside, *brother*." I clench my fists tighter until my knuckles protest from the pressure. Things will get out of hand and fast if he doesn't get the hell out of my way.

"Make me." He shoves my shoulder, knocking me back a step. That's all it takes for me to snap, and all hell breaks loose. My fist flies out, swinging into his cheek, twisting his head to the side. The metal of my wedding ring digs into my skin, but I don't feel it. Adrenaline is flooding my veins.

Asher and Rory go at it, swinging at each other. At the same time, I see Axel put Keegan into a headlock out of the corner of my eye. It seems all hell has broken loose in the Donnellys' driveway.

Connor takes advantage of my distraction and nails me in the cheek with his right hook. It throws me off balance, but only for a moment. I shake it off and lunge at him with a jab, but he bobs out of the way and hits me in the temple. It looks like my brother-in-law can give as good as he gets. My face burns with each punch he lands. He bobs and weaves a few times, but I've figured out his pattern and slam my fist into his gut, knocking the wind out of him. He folds like a house of cards against the concrete driveway.

I step around him, but he grabs me by the ankles and drags me to the ground.

"Kennedy!" My head jerks back, hitting Connor in the forehead, but the fucker won't budge.

"It's all your fecking fault. She was never supposed to be there." Connor wraps his arms around my throat in a chokehold. "She never would have gotten stabbed if it weren't for you."

"What the fuck are you talking about? Ken wasn't stabbed." I grunt out as I punch my elbow into his side and flip over onto my back. There's no fucking way. I wouldn't have noticed that when I checked her over, and I never would have let Rory take her if that was the case.

He grips me by the collar of my shirt and gets up in my face. "Not her, you fecking gobshite. Fiona!" The veins on his temple strain against his skin as his face reddens.

"That had nothing to do with me, and you know it." Things are becoming clearer on what this is really about. It's nothing to do with me at all. That's an issue he will need to deal with on his own.

"Feck you." His grip shakes, but eventually, he releases his hold and sits back on his heels.

"What the hell are you idiots doing?" All tension leaves my body at the sound of her voice.

"Ken!" I push up to my knees, not giving a shit about the roughness of the concrete digging into my jeans, and find her bruised face watching me. She's changed out of that scrap of clothes they had her in and into a clean blue dress. Her glasses are still missing, but if it weren't for the swelling and cuts.

I crawl closer and wrap my arms around her waist, burying my head into her growing stomach. "I'm sorry. I'm so fucking sorry."

Her fingers tangle through my hair as she holds me tighter against her. "I'm okay." She pulls me to my feet and gasps when she sees the mess her brother made of my face. "Oh my god. I'm going to kill Connor." Her hands ball into fists as she turns to go after her brother, but I'm done being away from her.

"Not today, Hummingbird." I grab ahold of her ass and lift her, wrapping her legs around my waist. She crosses her feet at the ankles, hooks her arms around my neck, and buries her head into the side of my neck. A calmness settles over me the second I have her in my arms. Like everything has been made right. My hands keep a firm grip around her thighs as I walk up the front steps with her clinging to me.

When I make it through the front door, Finn is standing in the middle of the living room with his hands in the front pockets of his suit, watching my every move. We lock gazes, sizing the other up, and I prepare for another fight, but he nods and steps to the side, to my surprise. No words are needed. The torch has been passed. She's no longer his little girl but my wife. Mine to keep. And mine to protect.

I carry Kennedy up the set of stairs, down the hall, through her bedroom, and into the connecting bathroom, leaving our families behind to deal with the aftermath. They can handle themselves—everything that matters to me at this moment I hold in my hands.

When we reach the shower, I turn it on and step inside, clothes and all. Kennedy lets out a small squeal, and her thighs clench against my waist, but I keep moving back until her back is braced against the wall and press my mouth to hers. The taste of her lemon scent explodes on my tongue as I devour her. She's tart and sweet all in one. And I'll happily eat her up all fucking day long.

Water seeps into our clothes, as everything around us is drowned out and turned into a sea of white noise. Nothing exists in this little bubble I've created but the two of us. Right here. Right now. The world could burn down, but I know we'll survive the flames as long as she's here with me.

I pull back and press my forehead against hers, letting out a deep sigh. "Hey."

"Hey." She smiles as dark, wet strands of hair stick to the side of her face.

"Are you sure you're all right?" My throat constricts

at the thought of anything happening to either one of them.

"I am." The tip of her index finger runs along the cuts on my temple, and I soak up the connection. "My dad had Dr. Rourke come by to check on the baby and me."

"And?"

"And everything looks fine." She tugs on my beard at the same time, her eyes soften.

"Thank fuck." My body relaxes deeper into hers. "You mad at me?"

"A part of me is because you made me leave without you." Her fingers interlock around my neck as she pulls me in closer, and one hand tugs on the end of my beard. "Don't ever do that again. We're a team. Remember?"

"I know." I don't tell her that if it's in her best interest, I will do whatever the fuck is necessary to protect her and our baby. We can argue about that later. Instead, I reach into my back pocket and pull out my gift for her. "Give me your hand."

"Why?" She pulls back as her nose wrinkles.

"Ken." I lean forward and nip at her bottom lip with my teeth.

"Fine." She sighs but gives in, dropping her hold on my beard and giving me her right one. "Here."

"Not that one." I switch it out for her left one. Holding her ring finger, I keep my eyes fixed on hers. "Forgive me for staying behind, but I had to get this back for you." I slip her wedding ring back onto her finger, where it will stay for the foreseeable future.

"Thank you." Her eyes gloss over, and she sniffles, but I know my hummingbird, and those are happy tears.

"Anytime." I glance down and find her hardened nipples poking against the wet material of her blue dress. "Cold?"

"No." Her face flushes as her thoughts begin to mirror my own.

"Good." I slide my hands up her sides, taking the sides of the dress with me, and whip it up over her head. Her bare breasts greet my hungry eyes, and like the starving man I am, my mouth waters to taste them.

"You're fucking perfect." My fingers pinch around her left nipple, teasing and toying with it until she's grinding up and down against the seam of my jeans. I arch her back and lean down, wrapping my lips around her hardened flesh. She lets out a laugh as the tips of my beard tickle her belly. The sound is soft and sweet, just like her, and has all the blood flowing straight to my dick, and I'm not gonna last at this rate. Too much has happened, and I'm on edge, ready to explode before we even get started.

"I'm gonna come in my fucking pants because of you, stop that." I fight back a growl as she rolls her hips once more. "Ken," I warn, but she has her own agenda.

"Off." She leans back and tugs on the ends of my shirt.

I press my groin deeper into hers, pinning her against the wall and reminding her of who's in charge. "Don't move."

She rolls her eyes but does as she's told.

"Good girl." I reach my right hand back to lift off my shirt one-handed. I throw it on the shower floor and run my hands along the smooth skin of her thighs, anxious to feel them tighten around me, just like her pussy does when I make her come. I hook my thumb into the sides of my underwear and rip them off, tossing them over my shoulder. They land somewhere on the shower floor behind me, but it doesn't distract me from the view in front of me.

She undoes my jeans, and together we shove them down my legs. The rough, wet material sticks to my skin, but between the two of us, we manage to remove them.

"That for me?" Her pupils dilate as her gaze drops down straight to my dick, more accurately my piercings.

"It's always for you." I stroke myself a few times, tugging on the metal barbell. The slight sting of pain igniting an ache deep within my balls.

She tugs on my nipple piercings and sinks her teeth into her bottom lip. "I want it."

"And you'll get it, but not until I get what I want first." I drop my dick and slide my hand between the lips of her pussy. My wrists move back and forth, working her clit with my fingers over and over until I see her body convulse and the signs of her orgasm coming.

"Oh fuck. I'm going to come." Her head drops back against the marble shower wall, exposing the column of her neck.

"I fucking love your pregnancy hormones." They make her come from the faintest touch. I lean down to kiss that creamy skin but stop when I see it. Blood pounds in my ears at the bite mark marring her perfect body. It's still red and fresh, which means it was done recently, and I know exactly by whom.

"Hey." Her hands cup my face and force me to meet her gaze. "Come back to me."

"I'm gonna kill him." I slam my hand against the

marble, relishing in the pain ricocheting up my arm. The motherfucker is gonna pay.

"Yes, you will." She kisses the corner of my mouth, bringing me back down to the present. "But first, you're going to fuck your wife." Her hands wrap around my length and guide me into her core.

I stay still, letting her sink down on me, watching her mouth drop open as my piercing slides along her inner walls.

"I forgot how fucking big you are." I smile at that as she takes a minute to become adjusted to me. It isn't long before her hips start to wiggle, and I take the hint.

My hips pull back until I'm all the way out and slam back inside her in one quick thrust.

A moan leaves her as I increase my rhythm. Her body slides up along the marble, and that's when I glimpse down at her face because I love watching my woman come, but what I see has my heart freezing in my chest. Her face is tilted back, and she's flinching with each thrust.

"Fuck. I forgot about your back. Why didn't you say anything?" I start to pull back when she grabs me by the ass and forces me to stay put.

"Because then you'd be treating me like broken glass, and that's not what I need. I want to feel the pain too." I'm shaking my head when she stops me. "Please?"

A tightness spreads in my gut because I know what it feels like to need the pain. It dulls out all the other bullshit in my head. But I'd rather cut off my dick than ever hurt her. Then I see it. The need to find another way to heal, and I sigh, knowing that I'll never be able to deny this woman a fucking thing. She owns me, body and soul. "Hold on to me." I keep a firm grip on her waist and thrust in and out of her. Pushing and pulling until I don't know where she ends and I begin.

Steam thickens the air, heating our oversensitive skin, but I don't stop. I can't. "Never again, Ken." When she doesn't answer me, I swivel my hips and piston into her harder, making sure she understands what I'm saying. "Do you hear me?"

"I hear you." Her fingers dig into my shoulders as my hips twist and grind against her clit, hitting where I know she needs it most.

"Good." I pick up my punishing pace. Fucking her until I feel the walls of her pussy tighten and clamp down on my dick. I don't stop until my balls tighten and I explode inside of her.

My heart pounds in my throat as our heavy breathing fills the room. We stay where we are, with me still buried deep inside her because I'm not ready to sever our connection just yet.

She rests her head on my shoulder and rubs her hands along the marks on my back. "We're going to have matching scars now." Her breath hitches, and it takes everything in me to fight the urge of leaving right now to go beat the fuck out of Grady for putting that sadness in her voice.

"Look at me." I hook my finger under her chin and force her head up to look at me. "We all have scars. Each of us is a little bit tarnished, but sometimes a short fiery brunette comes along to remind us that those marks show that we've lived. It's our story, and I don't regret a fucking second of it if it brought me to you."

"You came for me." She sniffles, changing the subject on me.

"I'll always come for you, Hummingbird. I love you."

"I love you too."

"Good. Because I can't do this anymore without you." I press my hand to the small bump that's growing our child. "Either one of you."

"You going to kill a man every time I lose this?" She holds her hand up, the diamond of her wedding ring glistening under the shower light. Seeing the smile appear on her face has a lightness filling my limbs.

"Maybe." I rub my thumb along the apple of her cheek, doing my best to avoid the bruises. Even if I have to tattoo my initials on her somewhere, they will always know she belongs to me. "And I haven't killed him yet."

"Such a charmer." She rolls her eyes.

"You married me."

"That I did. And I'd do it all over again." She leans forward and claims my mouth with hers. Her tongue reaches out and licks along the seam of my lips, but a gasp leaves her when she feels my dick hardening inside of her.

"Again?" She pulls back and cocks an eyebrow at me.

"Always. Like you said before. You danced with my demons when no one else would."

And I spend the rest of the day showing my wife why she's the most important thing in the world to me.

When I walk into Finn's playroom, Isaac sits on a stool in the corner smoking a cigarette. Blood splatters decorate his shirt and face. Asher and Axel are leaning back against the table with their feet crossed at the ankles, watching Grady wheeze.

Speaking of the fucker, he's a mess. He's strapped to a giant cross, bloody and naked. Nails are impaled into the tops of his feet and the palms of his hands. His left eye is swelling shut, and there's a decent-sized cut on his bottom lip.

Finn's enjoyment of theatrics and irony isn't lost on me. In fact, I think I have a newfound respect for my crazy-ass father-in-law.

"Start without me?" I swing my gaze back to Isaac and cock an eyebrow at him.

"Got bored." Isaac's dark eyes are glazed over as he exhales a cloud of smoke.

Axel waves his hands in Grady's direction. "Do y'all have an aversion to doing this shit with their clothes on? I've seen enough of other guys' dicks to last me a lifetime."

"Turnabout is fair play. He stripped them of their dignity and took from them without asking." I tilt my head from side to side, toying with several ideas on how to make Grady squirm. They all end with him the same way. Dead.

"That's cold, Z." Axel laughs as he lights up a cigarette. "I like it."

I pick up the cat-o'-nine-tails whip from the table and run my fingers through the strands. Finn's had this piece modified. Metal beads are tied to the ends of each piece. The leather creaks as I let them fall between my fingers. The amount of care he puts into this is a work of art.

"You killed an old lady. You took my wife." I close

the distance between us until I'm standing right in front of him. "And you marked her."

I strike out so fast he never even sees it coming. The metal beads dig into his flesh, tearing off some skin. Welts appear across his chest as I repeat the move a few more times.

"That looks like it hurts." Axel whistles as he opens a bag of Doritos and makes himself comfortable for the show.

"The old bitch had it coming. She tried to stop us. And as for your woman, I should have fucked her when I had the chance. I bet her pussy's tight as fuck." Grady laughs, but the joke's on him. He's only feeding the monster.

"Pliers, Ax."

"Here ya go." Axel can't hand them to me fast enough.

My fingers clasp around the metal, letting the weight settle in my hand as Grady's eyes widen.

Asher steps up next to me and switches out the pliers for a rusty machete without me even having to ask. That just proves how in sync my big brother and I are. He knew what I wanted before I did. "Ax."

"On it." He licks the cheese dust off his fingers and steps up to Grady. "Open up, you piece of shit." He shoves his fingers inside Grady's mouth and pries it open.

Asher grabs his tongue and clamps down on it with the pliers. "You fucked with the wrong family, asshole." He gives me a nod, and that's all the okay I need.

I bring the blade down on his tongue. Grady screams and fights against us, but it's pointless. He's nailed and not going anywhere. "You don't deserve to even say her name."

Axel shakes out the pliers and drops the organ onto the floor. We step back, watching blood pool out of his mouth. A sense of pride washes over me at our family project.

"Go to hell," Grady spits a mouthful of it at my feet. Or at least he tries to. It's hard to talk without a fucking tongue.

"That's exactly where you're going." I slice into his throat with the blunt end of the rusty machete. Blood drips down the column of his throat, and it's like watching art come to life as images of what he did to Kennedy fill my head. The blade is dull, so it takes much longer to cut through all the layers of muscle and tissue. I have to put more strength behind it when I get to the bone, but I don't stop until his head rolls onto the floor at my feet. "For Nelson, you son of a bitch."

"Savages for life." Asher and Axel put a hand on my shoulder and squeeze as the four of us watch Grady bleed out onto the floor.

It's done, but it's not over. It will never be over. There will always be those who think they can come after us. Jobs will come and go, but with my brothers and my friend by my side, I will always let my demons out to play in the only way I know how. The only way I will be when it comes to protecting my family.

Ruthless.

EPILOGUE

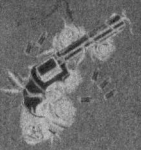

"What's with the all-black look?" Axel asks as he holds Lily in his lap. She's wearing a dark green dress that brings out the same color in her eyes. Bits of frosting from the cake she's currently eating decorate all down the front. Her dark hair is pinned up with a crown of flowers like a halo.

"Easier to blend in." I sip on my whiskey, letting the burn wash away that I'm in a damn tux. Something I never thought in a million years I would do again, but here we are. Although, with the way Kennedy keeps checking me out, I might suffer through it more than once if I get a repeat performance of the storage closet we were in earlier.

"We're in an Irish pub, and you look like the grim reaper." Axel's still bitching about my color choice.

"Better than looking like a fucking leprechaun," I toss back as the tiny bundle in my arm awakens, and I change position, laying her up against my chest. Her dark hair is the same shade as her mother's, but she's got those Savage dimples. Seven months ago, Aislyn

Marie Savage entered this world kicking and screaming at just over six pounds, and she's been the best gift my wife has ever given me.

"Green happens to be the color of their wedding, and an Irish one at that. Face it, I'm more of a chameleon and blend in much better than your lame ass ever could." He waves the hand not holding on to Lily in my direction.

"I think you're just whining like a little bitch because I stood next to Asher." I can't resist throwing that dig in there. The truth is, we were both his best men, but Axel is still sore that he couldn't walk down the aisle with Kelsey since she was Charlee's maid of honor.

"Eat shit, asshole." His eyes widen, and I know I've struck a nerve.

"Ax," Kelsey sighs. She and Kennedy are both dressed in form-hugging bridesmaids' dresses that are the same shade as Lily's. Her red hair is down, letting her natural curls run wild. "You are so embarrassing." She scoots down lower in her chair, and I laugh at how she just chastised him.

His lips press together, but he doesn't argue with her. Instead, he goes back to watching Lily feed herself. She lifts a piece that's too big for her tiny mouth, but half the cake falls off the fork and into her lap.

"Uh-oh, Unc As." Her small mouth widens as she stares up at my little brother. She's fourteen months old now and just started talking words here and there. They aren't always clear, but we manage to make them out. I'm proud to admit I may have had something to do with my brother's new nickname.

"It's all good, Wildflower." He takes a napkin and

wipes it up, smearing some of the frosting into the material.

"Charlee is going to hurt you when she sees the mess you made of her. They still have more pictures to take," Kelsey hums out.

"Nothing could make my Wildflower look bad." He bends down to steal the new piece of cake Lily just scooped up. She throws her head back and laughs at the dipshit with crumbs on her chubby cheeks.

The DJ announces the first dance as "Scars" by James Bay starts to play through the pub's speakers, and everyone grows silent. All eyes go to the dance floor.

Asher leads Charlee into the middle of the room and wraps her up in his arms. He's wearing an all-black tux similar to mine. Axel's the only one that's an attention whore in the family and wants to wear the same colors as a fucking leprechaun.

Charlee's long hair is down in curls, touching the top of her white strapless dress that flows as she walks. I think Kennedy called it a ballgown or some shit like that. Her mouth is curved into a wide grin as they get lost in each other.

"They look so happy." Kennedy smiles at them and then looks up at me, those blue eyes sparkling behind the lens of her glasses. Her dark hair is down in loose waves, and I can't wait to fist it in my hands as I fuck her from behind later tonight. The quickie we had earlier isn't enough.

"That they do, Hummingbird." I gently pat Aislyn's back as she starts to stir.

"You know you can't hold her all the time, right?" She tilts her head and watches me dote on our daughter.

My mind flashes back to Asher holding Lily all those nights ago when I thought I lost them both, and I finally understood what he meant. They become your everything. "Watch me." I press a kiss to Kennedy's temple.

"It's like a fairy tale." Kelsey leans back in her chair and sighs as she rests her hand over her rounded stomach. She's due any day, and I can't wait for that kid to give Axel a run for his money.

"Thank fuck he got his head out of his ass and finally got her to the altar." Axel pulls out a cigarette and pinches it between his lips.

"Ax, you can't smoke that in here." Kelsey yanks the cigarette out of his mouth and tosses it onto the table. It lands in one of the untouched glasses of water with a small splash.

"Juicy Fruit?" I arch an eyebrow at him, dangling the yellow pack out to him.

He stares at it for a beat before he jerks it out of my hand, bitching the whole time as he rips it open and shoves a wad into his mouth.

I scratch the side of my face, giving him the finger where the girls can't see, and he kicks my shin from underneath the table. I'll pay the little fucker back for that later when we're sparring in the basement.

"What are you feckers doing over here?" Rory comes to our table and leans down to kiss his sister on the cheek. He then runs a finger over Aislyn's silky dark hair. "*Neacht*," he uses the Gaelic word for niece. Being around them more, I'm starting to pick up words here and there. Since he was the first one of Kennedy's brothers to hold her—a fact he likes to remind everyone of—he tries to hold her any chance he can, which means he's over all the fucking time.

Rory jerks his chin at our glasses. "How does real whiskey taste, Country?"

"It's okay." Axel shrugs. "It's no Jack Daniels, but it's not bad, Irish."

"Oh, feck off with that." Rory frowns as he tosses back his glass. "It's Jameson. There's nothing better than Irish whiskey." With that parting line, he walks off to join Teegan and Keegan in the back corner with Isaac. The twins have been taking turns between hitting on anything in a dress and keeping Isaac busy since the reception started. It's good to see my old friend getting out there and socializing again. He bounces back and forth between here and Florida, but I'm pretty sure that a certain blue-haired devil is the reason why.

"You look beautiful, *a stóirín.*" Finn comes up behind us in a black pinstripe suit, kisses Kennedy on the top of her head, and turns his attention to Aislyn. He runs his finger along her soft cheek and smiles. "*Aingeal.*"

It's fitting that the man they often call the devil refers to his granddaughter as an angel. All of us dote on Aislyn, but he outright spoils the shit out of her. Who knew the psycho Finnegan Donnelly would be brought to his knees by a baby?

"She looks an awful lot like yer mum, *a stóirín.*" A flicker of emotion flashes through his eyes, but it's gone in an instant. "Drink up, lads." He lifts his glass in a toast and walks off to join the rest of the guests. We were skeptical when he offered to foot the bill for this and hold it inside his pub, Donnelly's, but he said Asher and Charlee are as good as his family.

Axel leans down and whispers out the side of his mouth at me. "How much do you want to bet that he's got someone being slaughtered in the back room right now?"

I open my mouth to take him up on that bet when a small voice carries across the room.

"Fuck you, Connor Donnelly."

Our heads snap over to the exit to see Kennedy's pint-sized friend Fiona ball her hand into a fist and slug Connor in the gut. She storms off without a backward glance.

"Wonder what that was all about?" Kennedy wrinkles her eyebrows as she watches her friend disappear from view.

Axel and I share a look. "Nothing," we answer at the same time.

None of us are saying shit until they figure it out for themselves. Whatever Fiona chooses to share is on her. I'm not getting in the middle of whatever that is.

"I can't believe the first two new generations of Savages are girls." Axel's eyes land on my daughter as he says that, but just like Lily, Aislyn has had him wrapped around her finger from the time she was born. "Thank fuck I'll be having all boys to even shit out."

"You do realize that's not how that works?" I don't call him a dickhead out loud since Lily is still within hearing distance.

"Not gonna happen. There are winners and losers, and the universe wouldn't do that to me." Axel sinks back in his chair and rests his arm on the back of Kelsey's.

"Um, Ax?" Kelsey clears her throat and sits up straighter in her chair.

"Yeah, Wildcat." He cranes his head to the side to look at her.

She mumbles something none of us can make out.

"What?" He leans in to hear her better.

"We are having a girl." She points to her belly with a wide grin and says it loud enough for us all to hear.

"Are you fucking with me right now, Wildcat?" He covers Lily's ears and yells so loud that half the wedding party stops what they're doing to stare at our table.

"Feck," Lily's tiny voice repeats. Earmuffs aren't enough to save us from our little parrot. And I'm sure Asher will love that she's picking up on the Irish lilt from the Donnellys.

"No. I'm not fucking with you, Axel Shaun Savage." Kelsey's face reddens, almost matching her hair, and I brace for impact. That's why she used his full name. It's her way of calling him an ass without actually calling him an ass. "I know I said I wanted it to be a surprise, but I couldn't wait."

"Shit." Axel runs a hand over his face. He's digging himself deeper into the doghouse, and I have no intention of helping him out.

"Shit," Lily repeats him once more.

"Shh. Stop that, Wildflower." Axel tries to quiet her, but she's a Savage and will never be told what to do.

"Yeah, we don't want Daddy to break Unc As's nose again." I would feel bad about that, but he had it coming when he let Thor shit all over Asher's shoes. Damn dog is as spoiled as the kids.

Axel stabs his fork into his cake and slides half of it onto her plate. "Here." Asher is gonna kick his ass for that sugar overload later, and again, I'm not helping him.

Lily claps and uses her hands to dig in. Then she wipes the frosting on Axel's face, getting it all over him.

"Wildflower." Axel wrinkles his nose and wipes at the sticky shit that's dripping onto that ugly fucking green tux he's wearing.

Kennedy laughs next to me, and my heart feels complete. The light from the ceiling shines down on her like a halo, and she looks like a fucking angel. My angel. The one who brought me out of the dark and into her light. My demons will never disappear, but she's enough to silence them. She and our daughter will always be enough.

A LOOK AT:
DESTINED TRINITY

A dark, slow-burn reverse harem fantasy romance full of forbidden desire, ancient curses, and deadly enemies fated to become lovers. Perfect for fans of *Crescent Kingdom* and *the Cursed Legacies series*.

Three cursed immortals.

One destined mate.

A war that will decide the fate of the Nephilim and the Lycans.

Cast out by the heavens and damned to eternal night, the Nephilim have lived for centuries as monsters—feared, hated, and forgotten. But behind the walls of their Budapest castle, two ancient beings search for the one who can break their curse: the final piece of their *destined trinity*.

She was born with power in her blood and danger at her back. Raised in a coven that never truly accepted her, she's always been taught to fear the Nephilim—creatures bred for destruction and vengeance.

Now they've found her.

Pulled into a world of shadows, lies, and passion, she begins to question everything she thought she knew about her past, her power, and the men she was sworn to hate.

Is she their salvation or their undoing? And when destiny demands her choice... will she destroy the world, or remake it?

AVAILABLE NOW

ACKNOWLEDGMENTS

Thank you so much for reading this entire series and falling in love with these brothers and all of their imperfections. This wasn't a journey I set out on taking when Asher first started speaking to me. He was simply a way for me to express myself when I was having one of my darkest days and ended up showing me the light.

Finishing this book was both a bittersweet and emotional experience for me. These characters have become a part of me, and I think it took me longer to finish this series because I wasn't ready to let them go just yet. They will forever have a special place in my heart.

There are so many people I need to thank for helping me make it to the finish line with this book. Some days it was really a struggle to get the words out and without the support of my crazy crew, I wouldn't have been able to get past that first page.

First up, I have to thank my Z. Without you I'd be lost. You support me and my writing, whether it's by being my sounding board or attending signings and becoming one of the girls for the weekend. Thank you for putting up with all of my chaos and loving me through it all. I love you so much!

Thank you so much to my girls, Lisa and Christy. You put up with listening to me bitch and moan about my self-doubt and writer's block like the badass friends you are. You two are my rocks as I do my best not to drown some days and I love your faces so much for it. My betas—Evelyn and Rebecca—thank you so much for all of your feedback. I'd be lost without you. To all of the bloggers who took the time to share and read my words, y'all are loved and appreciated more than you know. To my editor, Ellie, thank you for always going above and beyond in making sure my grammar is spot on and holding nothing back. (Obviously, she hasn't seen this page.)

I'm going to take a deep breath before diving back into the spin-off series of the Donnellys. Next up is Connor and Fiona's story, so please subscribe to my newsletter for any updates on release info for that.

Christine Besze is a writer, reader, mother, wife, and lover of all things wine. She lives in her own world of crazy most days, because the voices inside her head hold some great conversation. When she does have to come back to reality and act like an actual grown-up, she spends her time with her handsome hubby Z, their two gorgeous gingers and their mini-herd of German Shepherds. Born in sunny Southern California, she now lives with her family on the East Coast and couldn't be happier. You'll still find her in flip-flops—with a full glass of wine—all year round.

www.christinebesze.net